Sou

...Howell...

You (Macmillan), a ...

Vow is her first book ...

KT-215-943

You can follow @debbie__howells on Twitter.

C334546643

THE
VOW

DEBBIE HOWELLS

avon.

Published by AVON
A division of HarperCollins*Publishers* Ltd
1 London Bridge Street
London SE1 9GF

www.harpercollins.co.uk

A Paperback Original 2020
1

First published in Great Britain by HarperCollins*Publishers* 2020

Copyright © Debbie Howells 2020

Debbie Howells asserts the moral right
to be identified as the author of this work.

A catalogue copy of this book is available from the British Library.

ISBN: 978-0-00-840016-3

This novel is entirely a work of fiction. The names, characters and incidents
portrayed in it are the work of the author's imagination. Any resemblance
to actual persons, living or dead, events or localities is entirely coincidental.

Typeset in Bembo by Palimpsest Book Production Limited,
Falkirk, Stirlingshire

Printed and bound in UK by CPI Group (UK) Ltd,
Croydon CR0 4YY

All rights reserved. No part of this text may be
reproduced, transmitted, down-loaded, decompiled, reverse engineered,
or stored in or introduced into any information storage and retrieval system,
in any form or by any means, whether electronic or mechanical,
without the express written permission of the publishers.

MIX
Paper from
responsible sources
FSC
www.fsc.org   FSC™ C007454

This book is produced from independently certified FSC™ paper
to ensure responsible forest management.

For more information visit: www.harpercollins.co.uk/green

For Clare

You didn't know about the alchemist's curse.
About the significance that lay, not just in essence but in intent.

PART ONE

1996

A summer of cornflower skies and bleached stubble fields; of friendship forged amongst wild strawberries and banks of thyme, whispered secrets known only to you, as you sat in the shade of the woods.

It was a summer that seemed brighter, hotter, the weeks somehow stretched endlessly ahead. A summer of giddy heights; of first love, as you pulled apart the delicate pink dog roses that grew on arching stems amongst the hedgerows, one gossamer petal after another until you found what you wanted.

He loves me. He loves me not. He loves me.

You glanced towards him, as you fed your obsession; punishing yourself, as you took in his hand holding hers, his eyes unable to look away from her, wanting them for your own, unable to hide what was in your heart.

And as the petals wilted, you tried so hard to hide what was in your eyes: not just the hunger or the jealousy that devoured you, but the bittersweet pain of unrequited love.

Amy

Chapter One

Two weeks before our wedding, after Matt leaves for work, I find a piece of paper in the kitchen. As soon as I start reading, I put it down. When we decided to write our own wedding vows, we agreed that we wouldn't share them until our wedding day. I imagine him printing them off, wanting to commit them to memory; the piece of paper left out unintentionally. I know I should put it away, out of sight, but unable to resist, I pick it up.

I promise to hold your hand, to steer you through life's sorrow and darkness, on a path towards justice and hope. I will endeavour to know what's best for you, to protect you from your past, help you build the future you deserve. Then when I can no longer be with you, a part of me will always be there, watching over you. In the shadows of your heart, on the soft curves of your skin, in the long-forgotten corners of your mind.

Frowning, I read it again. While my own vows overflow with love and romance, this isn't quite what I was expecting, until I remind myself it's what Matt's always done. He looks out for me. After so many years alone, I'm lucky.

But as I drive to Brighton, a feeling of foreboding hangs over me. The days before a wedding *should* be the happiest of times. In the distance, the shimmering sea looks ice-blue. Then the city comes into view, cast in soft light as the sun rises. It's a familiar sight, one I love, and yet a shadow follows me while I deliver my herbal remedies to two of my regular clients, before walking through the Lanes back to my car. Lost in my thoughts, at first, I don't notice the footsteps behind me.

'Excuse me . . .'

The voice is unfamiliar. I hesitate, unsure if it's directed at me, then as the footsteps come closer, I turn around to find myself staring at a stranger.

'I need to talk to you.' As the woman speaks, I feel myself freeze. She looks older than her voice sounds, her grey hair wispy, her face strangely unlined. But it's the colour of her eyes, a transparent ice-blue, that is hypnotic. For a moment, I'm mesmerised, then as a van speeds past, her hand grips my arm, pulling me away from the road. 'I have to talk to you.' There's an unmistakable urgency in her voice. 'Someone's watching you. They know where you go, everything you do.'

As she speaks, my blood runs cold. 'Who are you?'

Without telling me, she goes on. 'You think you're meant to be together.' Each word both softly spoken and crystal clear, her eyes fixed on mine so that I can't look away. 'You think he's the love of your life.' She pauses for a moment. 'He isn't who you think he is.' Then a strange look crosses her face. 'You're in danger.'

For a few moments, it's as though I'm in a trance. Then I pull my eyes away from hers, confused, then suddenly angry. Matt and I are getting married, every detail of our wedding thoughtfully planned, from the country house venue down to the smallest flower. We're happily settled in our house in Steyning, with its chalk grey walls, the floorboards we've sanded and waxed, the garden with far-reaching views of the Sussex landscape that lies beyond. No-one, least of all a stranger, is taking that away from me. I notice her hand still clutching at my arm.

'Let go of me!' Wrenching it away, I step back and start hurrying towards my car, fighting my irritation, telling myself she's probably harmless. A harmless, mad old woman.

But she's spooked me. Hearing footsteps following me, I break into a jog, my feet crunching on fallen leaves, as she seems to read my mind.

'I'm not mad,' she calls after me. 'Watch your back. Don't trust him . . .'

Later, I tell the police, that was when it all started. With a sinister warning from a woman I'd never met before; if I had, I'd have remembered her eyes; with the cries of seagulls from the rooftops, the whisper of deception in the salt air. But I didn't know it began much longer ago, with all that went before. With events that belong in the past. With beginnings that can't be traced, that are infinite.

★

As I drive home, I'm on edge. It's mild for November, the stark outline of the trees softened only by the last autumn leaves that have yet to fall. Turning into my lane, I park outside the house, still shaken as I get out, the woman's words replaying in my head, while I tell myself she knows nothing about me. Or about Matt. Unable to ignore the voice that whispers in my mind: *or does she?*

In the kitchen, I drop my bag onto the faded sofa. It's a large room, with pale curtains lining the windows, the floor tiled with slate. Neutral and uncluttered, the perfect foil for the garden that lies beyond.

Clearing the plates and mugs left from breakfast, I switch on the kettle, before going over to the sliding doors. Opening them, I step outside, drawn as I always am by the movement of the air, the crescendo of birdsong, the onset of winter showing in the paper-thin hydrangea flowers and dried seed heads. Gravel paths wander amongst the herbs and flowers I've planted, moss softening the stone wall along one side, a hedge marking the far end. The peacefulness is broken only by the sound of my mobile buzzing. I know instantly from the ringtone that it's Matt.

'I'm going to be late, Amy. There's a client over from the States. David wants me to take him to dinner. I tried to get out of it, but you know what David's like.'

He sounds distracted, irritated, though later, when the police ask me what he said, in my memory, I remember him as flustered. My heart sinks slightly. There are last-minute wedding details to finalise, but I know Matt wouldn't be doing this unless he had to.

'Hey, don't worry. It's fine. Really. If you're not back, I'll have another look at the seating plan without you. Oh – and your cousin emailed to say that . . .'

He interrupts me. 'I have to go, Amy. Dave's about to come in.' But then his voice is low as he adds, 'I need to talk to you later.'

Something in his tone makes me uneasy. 'Is everything OK?'

There's a split-second hesitation, then in the background, I hear someone call out to him before in a louder, brighter voice, he says to me, 'Take care, babe.'

Then he's gone, leaving me standing there, staring at my phone. Three words that leave me totally wrong-footed, because

Matt's never called me babe. And it's a throwaway phrase, but he never says *take care*, not like that. Trying to rationalise it, I tell myself he's preoccupied with work or conscious of his boss standing there, pushing my unease from my mind as I head across the garden towards my workshop.

Surrounded by trees, it's permeated by a sense of calm, but today as I walk inside, that calmness somehow eludes me. Standing there, I look at the old oak table that dominates the space, the wall beyond it given over to shelves of books about herbalism and carefully labelled jars of herbs. Most are harvested from my garden and on the table are fragrant bay, rosemary and sage stems, cut earlier before I went out. The richness of their scents intensifies as I start to strip the leaves, but I'm distracted again, thinking of the woman in Brighton, then of Matt's call.

While I work methodically, the wedding is never far from my mind. I think of my fairytale dress, hidden in the spare room, imagining the warmth of the country house hotel with log fires and candlelight. My daughter Jess beside me, our friends gathered. Then my mind wanders further back, to when I first moved here. Stripping wallpaper and ripping up old carpets, I'd started putting my own stamp on each of the rooms, before beginning on the garden.

Distracted by the ping of my work email, I scan a couple of repeat orders I'm expecting, before opening one from a new customer. It's an urgent request from a Namita Gill for a remedy to soothe her three-year-old daughter's skin condition. I check the address, before replying. *I can deliver tomorrow morning between 9 and 9.30. Will you be in?*

While I put her order together, her reply comes back. *Is there any way you could deliver tonight? I can pay extra but I'm at my wit's end. My daughter is so distressed and I've tried everything else. I don't know who else to turn to. I can pay you cash when you arrive.*

My heart sinks slightly. I'd envisaged a quiet evening, the curtains closed and the wood burner lit, while I go through last minute wedding details so that I can run them by Matt when he gets home. But I remember the childhood eczema that used to drive Jess to distraction. The delivery won't take me long. Emailing her back, I make a note of her address: Flat 5, 13 Brunswick Square, BN3 1EH. Then picking up the order, I switch off the light before closing the workshop door behind me.

As I make my way back to the house, the temperature has dropped sharply, so that in the hedge, desiccated stems of old man's beard are painted in relief by a hint of frost. Inside, logs are piled by the wood burning stove waiting to be lit, the bleached wooden worktops empty. Hunting around for my silver jacket, when I don't find it, I settle for an old one of Jess's, before finding my car keys and heading back outside.

Already, a thin layer of frost covers my car. Climbing in, I start the engine and turn the heater on, before entering the delivery address into my satnav. As I set off, a fine layer of mist is visible in the beam from my headlights. The roads are quiet and it doesn't take long to reach the outskirts of Brighton. I've always loved how the seafront looks at night, where what traffic there is flows steadily, the promenade sparkling with street lights. As I turn into Brunswick Square, I find a parking space almost immediately. Picking up the order, I get out, already scrutinising the house numbers on the elegant façades. As I walk, I pass only a few people, reaching the top of the Square and following it around, as No 13 comes into view. Walking up the steps, I pause, looking at the doorbell, searching for Flat 5, a frown crossing my face as I check the house number again. Reaching for my phone, I check Namita's email. It's definitely the right address, but instead of residential, this building is a heritage centre and museum. Flat number 5 doesn't exist.

As I walk back to my car, I imagine that under the pressure of caring for her sick daughter, Namita must have given me the wrong address. Getting into my car, I email her, asking her to confirm where she lives, waiting for her to reply. But she doesn't. By the time I arrive back at home, she still hasn't. As I walk inside, apart from the slow tick of the clock on the wall, the house is silent. For a moment, I ache for Jess's presence and the inevitable chaos it brings, nostalgic for the days it was just the two of us. Now in her second year at Falmouth uni, her absence bestows the house with an emptiness that's unfamiliar.

Ten years have passed since we moved here. The house was more remote than I'd been looking for, but still reeling from the breakup of my marriage, as well as the potential the house offered, I'd felt an unmistakable sense of sanctuary. With over an acre of garden and the outbuilding that's become my workshop, there's sheltered chalk soil and clean air; beyond a thick hedge of hawthorn and wild rose, unobstructed views of the Downs.

I'd started learning about herbalism before we came here, before studying it at college, wanting to heal the eczema that for years had plagued Jess, leaving her arms and legs scarred. But it's here I've learned about alchemy, subtlety, the effect of scent.

The garden is beautiful, bordering on mystical. There is a potency in plants – when you know – and it's here where the elements of my tinctures are nurtured. When Matt first came here and saw me at work, he laughingly called me a witch. I

11

let him laugh, mildly irritated that he found it amusing. Witchcraft and herbal folklore are not so far apart.

Like any garden, mine is constantly evolving, my plans sketched out in the large notebook I keep – a kind of scrapbook of inspiring images, words, quotes, scribbled notes. Glancing at the book, lying where it's always left next to the sofa, I lock the doors and pull the curtains closed. As my unease comes back, I remember the woman in Brighton this morning. It occurs to me to report her – but for what, exactly? She didn't harm me, but it was the way she spoke. Not just her warning, but the conviction in her voice, that she knew something about my life that I didn't.

Telling myself it isn't possible, I try to push the thought from my head, but then I think of Namita and of the address that doesn't exist. Checking my emails, I find a reply from her. *I'm so sorry, Amy, but I have to cancel my order. My husband got really mad. He doesn't like alternative remedies.* There's no reference to her address.

I write her off as erratic, but as I go upstairs, I can't shake the uneasiness that hangs over me. Then halfway up, my skin prickles. No floorboard creaks – the house is silent, yet it's as if there's an echo of something. Later, I wonder if I detected the faintest trace of scent – the olfactory sense is closely linked to memory. But if I did, it wasn't Matt's. If it was, I would have known.

At the top of the stairs, still unsettled, I go to each bedroom in turn, checking that they're empty. Aware my behaviour is ridiculous, verging on paranoid, I'm unable to shake the sense that I'm not alone. Changing into a loose-fitting sweatshirt and yoga pants, I scrunch my hair into a topknot, pausing to study my reflection. Fair hair, pale skin; clear eyes that give nothing away. Not even the smallest hint of fear.

After what's been the strangest day, all I want is for Matt to come home, so that we can add the final touches to our wedding plans, then go to bed. But I'm still in the dark at this point. As I turn to go downstairs, I have no way of knowing what lies ahead.

Chapter Two

The kitchen is lit by the dim glow from a corner lamp, the sense of unease still with me as I pile dry kindling into the wood burner before lighting it, then add seasoned wood. In no time it's throwing out heat, the crackle of flames welcome, breaking the silence. After making a cup of tea, I switch on my laptop, bringing up the file that contains our wedding plans. From food and wine to flowers and music, each detail has been carefully chosen – by both of us.

After Matt proposed, I'd wanted to get married on a faraway beach, imagining Jess and I barefoot in dusky dresses, our hair windswept by a tropical breeze. I'd provisionally booked a place in the Caribbean, a small bougainvillea–clad hotel, looking onto white sand shaded by palm trees, beyond which clear turquoise water stretched. But in the end, we decided on an intimate wedding at home, Jess my only bridesmaid, trading the Caribbean sun for candlelight, winter flowers and wood smoke.

It would be no less the fairy tale. And it was the wedding itself that mattered. When Matt reminded me of the obvious impracticalities of having our wedding so far away, I had to concede he had a point. Both of us wanted our closest friends and family to be there. I've tried to explain to Jess how relationships are about compromise. That not all battles are worth fighting, because it's what I believe. Over the years, I've learned to trust my instincts, listen to my inner voice. Ninety-nine per cent of the time, it serves me well. But when I think about the stranger in Brighton this morning, it's oddly absent.

I have no reason to believe anyone wishes me harm. No reason not to trust Matt. But it's the way he sounded earlier when he called me – not just what he said, but the way he said it. *I need to talk to you later.* Then, *take care, babe* . . .

None of it was in any way normal, I tell the police much later on. It was the way his voice changed, as though he knew someone would overhear him. I know the way Matt thinks, how he speaks. When he called me earlier today, something was wrong.

The silence is broken by the ping of an email into my inbox, from our wedding planner, Lara. An old friend of Matt's, when she heard we were getting married, she offered to help us, saving us the hours it would take to find suppliers. Her email's about finalising the seating plan that Matt and I had planned to look at tonight. Reading through the document she's attached, making one or two changes, I keep it to run past him before replying. Then I click on my vows, re-reading the words I know so well for the hundredth time.

I promise to always be there for you. To be the moon in your darkness, your wildflowers in the shade of the forest, your brightest star lighting the night sky. My heart is yours, Matt; my love a forever love. I am yours for the rest of my life. Words I've deliberated over for hours, that are mine and no-one else's; that on our wedding day will be my gift to Matt.

Seeing the piece of paper with Matt's vows, I fold it and put it out of sight, already regretting reading them this morning.

When we'd agreed not to share them until our wedding day, it feels like a betrayal of trust.

It's nearly ten by the time I finish going through my emails, replying to a WhatsApp from Jess about when she's next coming back from Falmouth. Switching on another light, I pour myself a glass of wine before calling Cath, my closest friend.

'Hey! How's it going?'

In need of a fresh start, she's packing up her flat. She moves next week – to Bristol.

'Since you ask, horrible. I've had to throw so much out, but at least it's a distraction. To be honest, I'm trying not to think about it.'

'This move is what you need,' I tell her. 'A change of scene, your new job . . . Who knows what might happen – in time.'

'As long as it doesn't involve men,' she says shortly. 'Honestly, I'm relishing being single again.'

I'm silent for a moment. Cath's suffered.

'How are you?' Her voice rallies. 'I keep meaning to call round.'

'So come tomorrow. We'll have lunch. I need to tell you about something weird that happened today – when I was in Brighton.'

'I'm intrigued.' She sounds curious. 'Can't you tell me now?'

Hearing a car outside, I'm guessing it's Matt. 'I think Matt's just come back. It'll wait.'

'OK.' Cath hesitates. 'How is Matt?'

'He's good. We're just putting the final touches together for the big day. You wouldn't believe how long everything takes.'

'I'm happy never to find out.' Cath's voice is cynical, then she sounds apologetic. 'Look, I didn't mean that. I'm sure it will be a great day.'

After her abusive ex-boyfriend, Oliver, reduced her emotionally to the shadow of the woman I know so well, she's trying to rebuild her life – alone. If I hadn't seen it happen, I wouldn't have believed it possible, because I've always thought of her as strong, but Oliver's manipulation was masterful.

'Don't worry about it,' I tell her. 'I'm just glad you've got away from Oliver. I know it's hard right now, but it will get easier.'

'I hope so.' She's quiet for a moment. 'But you're happy? You and Matt?'

There's no hesitation as I answer. 'Blissfully.'

★

But the car I hear isn't Matt's. By eleven, when he still isn't home, I'm only mildly surprised, but it's happened before, a business dinner morphing into a late session in a bar. I frown, wondering what it is he wanted to talk to me about, but it will have to wait. With an early start ahead of me, I text him briefly as I go to bed. When he doesn't reply, I imagine him deep in conversation over yet another scotch. I've no reason to worry. Not yet.

When I stir in the night and realise the bed is empty beside me, it vaguely registers as odd. Thinking of our wedding, imagining us side by side as we become husband and wife, I drift back to sleep. But it isn't until I awake the next morning, and find he still hasn't come home that alarm bells start to ring. Nor has he replied to any of my texts, and when I call him, like last night, it goes to voicemail.

★

An air of unreality hangs over me as I shower and dress, stopping now and then to try him again. When my phone eventually buzzes with a text, my heart leaps, but instead of Matt, it's a client wanting to check on a delivery. The order is prepared, but I'm worried about Matt and it's slipped my mind that I'd promised it for this morning.

Pulling on a jacket and boots, I hurry outside. The grass is crisp with last night's frost, glistening where the sun reaches it, my hands pink with cold as I open my workshop. Inside, the temperature is higher but only marginally, as after picking up the order, I take it out to my car.

Normally I love early mornings, the way the low light casts shadows, how the world is slowly stirring into life. But today, as I drive, I don't see any of it. Instead, uncertainty fills the air as I call Matt, leaving him another message. My mind in a whirl. Five minutes later, I try again. Then, because she's been keeping in touch with both of us about the wedding, I pull over at the side of the road and call Lara.

By the time I remember how early it still is, she's already answered. 'Hi, Amy.' Her voice is sleepy, as though I've just woken her. 'What's up?'

'I'm sorry to call like this.' I feel a rush of guilt for disturbing her. 'Have you by any chance heard from Matt?'

'No. Should I have?' She pauses. 'Is something wrong?' Her voice is suddenly wide awake.

I hesitate. 'He didn't come home last night. I'm really worried about him. I've called him several times, but it goes to voicemail. I just wondered when you last spoke to him.'

There's a brief hesitation before she speaks. 'A couple of days ago. Sunday — it was to do with the orders of service.' She's quiet for a moment. 'I'm sure he's fine, Amy. He probably had too much to drink and crashed out somewhere.'

'You're probably right.' I'm nodding as I speak, but he would have been in touch. And in all the time I've known him, Matt's always made it home after a night out.

Her voice cuts into my thoughts. 'Have you thought about calling the police?'

At the mention of the police, my heart quickens. I've been

19

putting off thinking about it, not wanting Matt to be a missing person, hoping he'll reappear with a credible excuse that will make everything OK. *I crashed out at the hotel . . . I lost my phone.* 'I thought it was too soon. They won't do anything, will they? Not for at least twenty-four hours.' My voice is husky, the note of panic one I can't hide. 'The chances are you're right. He's got held up somewhere. It's probably nothing.' I say it as much for my benefit as Lara's. 'He might have lost his phone – or broken it. Ended up spending the night in a hotel . . . there could be any number of possibilities.' But it isn't what my instincts are telling me. No longer silent, they're screaming at me that something's happened to him.

'Sure.' Lara doesn't sound convinced.

Glancing at the clock on the dashboard, I remember the delivery. 'I should go. I have a delivery to make. Can you let me know if you hear from him?'

'Of course.' She sounds uncertain. 'Can you do the same?'

Chapter Three

I drive towards Brighton on autopilot, barely noticing as the sea, then the town come into view. Reaching the outskirts, I hit the early morning traffic, slowed by roadworks that weren't there yesterday, unable to stop worrying about Matt. When at last I turn off the main road and head for the quiet tree-lined street of Regency houses where my client lives, I'm running late. Managing to park outside her house, I'm flustered as I take her order from the back of my car and ring the bell. Davina opens the door straight away.

'Amy. I was about to call you. I was getting worried.' There's a look of concern in her clear brown eyes as an air of strong perfume and calm wafts over me. A client for five years, Davina's always the same, unflustered – her dark hair sleek, her make-up minimal. As she looks at me, she frowns. 'Is everything OK?'

'I'm so sorry.' My nerves are on edge. 'I should have been here ages ago. I hit the traffic.' Trying to compose myself, I pass her the order. 'You should find everything's there.'

'Thank you. Is the invoice inside?'

I flounder for a moment, realising my error, then shake my head. 'I completely forgot. Can I email it to you?'

As I walk back to my car, I'm cursing myself. I'm meticulous about finances and I've never forgotten an invoice. But Matt has never gone missing before. With hindsight, I wished I'd told her what had happened. I've no way of knowing that when the police talk to her, she'll tell them I was agitated, flustered, as though my mind was elsewhere. I didn't tell her that my head was spinning, how worried about Matt I was.

Before I head home, I call him again. When it goes to voicemail, I call his office. A management consultant for a company called Orbital, Matt can work anywhere their clients are based, but at the moment I happen to know he's working in Brighton.

'Good morning. Can I speak to Matthew Roche?'

'One moment please.' I don't recognise the clipped, professional voice of the receptionist, unlike her predecessor, Sophie, who would have known instantly who I was. 'I'll put you through. Who's calling, please?'

I forget that he hasn't called me in nearly twenty-four hours, just feel a layer of normality return, relief flooding through me that he's there. 'Amy – his fiancée.'

As she connects me and the line starts to ring, I feel a weight start to lift. Then the ringing stops, but instead of Matt's voice, it's the receptionist again. 'I'm sorry. Mr Roche doesn't appear to be in his office. Would you like to leave a message?'

Any sense of relief instantly vanishes. Instead my voice is shaking, as my fear comes flooding back. 'Yes. Please ask him to call Amy. As soon as he gets in. It's important.'

Ending the call, I sit there for a moment, oblivious to the rush hour traffic flashing past, trying to think of who else I can call. Pete, his best man, is the obvious place to start. Then, even though I've never met them, his parents. Knowing their contact details should be in our wedding file, I pull out onto the road again.

In a hurry to get home, I drive too fast, unable to concentrate. Then as I turn into our lane, I catch sight of the stooped figure of Mrs Guthrie, our closest neighbour, who lives in one of the three cottages further up the lane. She may look fragile, but she ferociously maintains her independence. Recognising my car, she raises a hand in greeting, as hope rises in me that she may have seen Matt. Pulling into my driveway, I get out and hurry to meet her. 'Morning . . . How are you?'

Wearing a padded coat that hides her diminutive frame, her face breaks into a smile. Then as I get closer, she peers into my face. 'Amy, dear. I was going to come and see you. My Japanese anemones are still flowering and I thought you might like some for your wedding.' Her garden has always been her passion, as mine is to me.

'I'd love some – thank you.' It's by some quirk of her garden's microclimate that her flowers bloom slightly later in the year than mine. But right now, I can't think about flowers. 'I don't suppose you've seen anything of Matt?'

'Now why would you be asking me about Matt?' She starts to chuckle, then realising I'm serious, stops. 'Is something wrong?' A frown wrinkles her brow as she studies me.

'It's probably nothing.' Even now, I try to play it down. 'It's just that he went out with a client last night and didn't come home. He hasn't called me, either.'

She doesn't hesitate. 'Then you should call the police, dear, don't you think?'

★

23

As I walk back home and go inside, my fear is building, that something terrible has happened. But when I think about what Mrs Guthrie said, I'm convinced it's still too soon for the police to be interested. Knowing I need to make some calls, I open my laptop and bring up our wedding file. Sure enough, Pete's mobile number is there. With shaking hands, I call it.

'Pete? It's Amy.'

'Hey. How's it going?' His voice is characteristically cheerful. 'Not long till the big day, is it! How can I help?'

'It's Matt.' My voice is husky as I grip my phone. 'I don't know where he is. Have you spoken to him?'

'Is something wrong?' Suddenly he's sharp. 'When did you last see him?'

'Yesterday. Before he left for work,' I whisper. 'Then he called me during the morning, to tell me he'd be late home – he had to take a client out. I've been calling him ever since. Countless times, but he isn't answering his phone.' There's a note of panic in my voice. 'I've called his office, too. But he wasn't there.'

'Jeez, Amy. I last spoke to him the day before that, but not since. You must be worried sick.'

My eyes fill with tears. 'I am.'

'There has to be an explanation.' Pete's silent for a moment. 'Have you spoken to his parents?'

'Not yet. I was going to call them next, after speaking to you.'

'I'll make some calls. Check out the bars he goes to. Let me know when you've spoken to his parents. But if there's still no sign of him . . .'

'I know.' I'm biting my lip. 'I'll call the police.'

Putting down my mobile, I turn back to my laptop, scrolling down the list of wedding guests until I find Matt's parents. Punching the number into my phone, I pause for a moment, knowing whatever I say, I'm going to worry them. But I make the call anyway, steeling myself to explain to them why I'm phoning, but instead of someone answering, the line goes dead.

Frowning, I check the number, but when I try it again, the same thing happens. Staring at my phone, there's only one explanation, that Matt must have made a mistake when he typed the number next to their names on the wedding list. Uncomfortable, I call Pete again, swearing under my breath when my call goes to voicemail, before texting him instead. *The number I have for Matt's parents isn't connected.* Sitting there, I wait for his response, but when I remember the list of orders I need to prepare I head outside towards my workshop.

Even in my sanctuary, it's impossible to focus. My unease, no longer a shadow, is palpable. Trying to distract myself, I think about our wedding, holding on to the image of us in my mind. Matt tall, his suit and white shirt showing off the tan he'll have after his stag do in Malaga; me spray-tanned, because it's all I have time for, setting off the dusky pink dress that's hanging in the spare room. The flowers I'm growing from which to make the simplest, most delicate of bouquets; Jess beside me in pale grey, her long hair loosely pinned up. The hotel cosy, decorated with flowers and candles, the wood fires lit, on the most perfect of winter days where the air is crisp, the sky blue, the sun shining. In the dream, the sun always shines.

A text from Pete jolts me out of my thoughts. *He must have made a mistake. I've been asking around but no-one's seen him. I'd call the police, Amy. And keep in touch.*

Still holding on to hope that Matt will call me, that there's an innocent explanation, I put it off a little longer, turning my attention to the orders coming in, until by mid-morning, fear gets the better of me. Filled with trepidation, as I walk back to the house, I dial 999. Half expecting to be told to give it

25

twenty-four hours, I'm surprised when the woman who takes my call efficiently records my details, before putting me through to a PC Page.

'When did you last see your fiancé?' From her voice, I know she's taking me seriously. It's what I'd dreaded most before I called – not being taken seriously.

'Yesterday.' Then I question myself, because it's been a day in which so much has changed. But it's the difference between the known and unknown that makes it feel more like a lifetime ago. 'Yesterday morning. Just before he went to work.'

'And you last heard from him when?'

'He called me later that morning from his office, to say he was going to be late.' Aware of my voice shaking, I pause. 'It was a last minute change to his plans. He had a client over from the States. His boss had asked Matt to take him out to dinner.'

'And that was usual?'

'It doesn't happen that often, but I suppose often enough that it didn't seem strange.' I'm gabbling, needing her to understand the feeling I have, deep in my bones, that something's happened to Matt. 'He sounded odd. I mean, he said something he wouldn't normally say. It was as though he was irritated about something. Then he said he'd talk to me later. Just before he hung up, he said, *take care, babe*.' I break off, knowing that to anyone who doesn't know Matt, it sounds trivial. 'I know it doesn't sound like much. But it was out of character. It's not the kind of thing he ever says.'

PC Page is quiet for a moment. 'Do you know who the client was?'

'I've no idea.' For the first time, I'm berating myself that I never ask him, but Matt's clients are people I never meet. He rarely tells me their names.

'Did he give you any indication where he was going last night?'

'He didn't say.' Suddenly I remember something. 'His boss might know. David. It was David who wanted him to take the client out.' I can't believe I haven't thought of this before. As I speak, my sense of urgency grows. 'I'll call him. He's bound to know something.'

'If you give me his details, we'll speak to him. We need your fiancé's contact details, too.' She sounds in control, but her business-like manner does nothing to reassure me.

'His name is David Avery. They work for a company called Orbital.' I give her Matt's mobile number and David's work number. 'Matt drove to work yesterday morning. He has a red Audi.' Sharing the car's registration, I wonder what else she needs to know.

'Do you have a recent photograph you can email to us?'

'Of course. Where shall I send it?'

'I'll give you an email address. Do you have a pen?'

After I write it down, she goes on. 'If you hear anything from him or think of anything else that might be useful, could you let us know? We'll start making enquiries straight away. Have you been in touch with any local surgeries and hospitals?'

Her words set off alarm bells. 'I haven't.' Oh God. It hadn't even occurred to me that he might have been taken ill or involved in an accident.

'It's unlikely there's been an accident, or we'd have heard about it . . .' She hesitates for a moment. 'Are there any family members nearby? Siblings – or close friends?'

'No. His parents are in Scotland. He's an only child.'

'Have you spoken to them?'

'I tried calling them, but the line was dead. Matt must have accidentally written down the wrong number.'

'Do you have their address?'

Frowning, I try to think. 'Only their email address. It's how we sent out our wedding invitations.' I pause, remembering querying Matt about whether his parents would prefer a printed invitation and his amusement when he told me about how his dad was more tech-savvy than even he was.

'Perhaps you could email them? See when they last heard from him?' She's silent for a moment. 'I'm sorry, but I have to ask this. It may sound far-fetched, but do you think there's any possibility he's keeping anything from you? Financial worries or anything like that?'

'No.' Indignant at what she's suggesting, my face grows hot. 'Matt wouldn't get involved in anything irresponsible. We're getting married in two weeks. We don't keep secrets from each other.'

'Of course.' Her voice is crisp. 'Well, we have what we need for now. Perhaps we can talk again later on.'

I clutch my phone tightly. 'Do you think you'll find him? I mean, what usually happens?' Futile questions, impossible for her to answer, as I seek a reassurance that doesn't exist.

'In most cases, missing persons turn up; a day, sometimes a week later, sometimes longer than that.' Her voice is matter of fact. 'It's early days, Ms Reid. There's no point worrying too much. Not just yet.'

Her words do little to set my mind at rest. After ending the call, I sit there, my mind a million miles away as I consider every possible scenario. Then I imagine her thinking I'm naïve, that no-one ever thinks their partner would deceive them – until it happens.

Firing up my laptop, I open our wedding file, copying Matt's parents' email address, staring at the screen while I work out what to write.

I'm sure it's nothing to worry about, but I wondered when you last spoke to Matt? I haven't been able to contact him for a couple of days. Actually, to be honest, I'm really worried . . .

Deleting the last line, I add something about how much I'm looking forward to meeting them at the wedding, then press send. While I wait for a response, I email the photo of Matt to PC Page. Then suddenly needing to hear Jess's voice, I send her a WhatsApp. *How are you Jess? Can you give me a quick call when you have time? Xxx*

Ten minutes later, she calls me. 'Mum? Is everything OK?'

'Not really.' Then I take a deep breath. 'I don't know where Matt is, Jess. I haven't been able to contact him.'

'What d'you mean?' She sounds alarmed. 'Since when?'

My voice wobbles. 'Yesterday morning. I had this really odd call from him saying he would be late because his boss had asked him to take a client out, and that was the last I heard from him.'

'Why didn't you tell me?' Her voice is sharp.

'I didn't want to worry you. I was hoping he'd just reappear with an explanation. I've been in touch with the police. They may want to talk to you at some point – if he doesn't turn up. At the moment, I'm still hoping he will . . .' Breaking off, I swallow the lump in my throat.

'Mum, people don't just disappear . . . Something must have happened to him. The police will find him, won't they? But are you OK?' Her voice is suddenly anxious. 'I can come home. I'll get a train. I can leave later – or first thing tomorrow . . .'

'Please don't, Jess. There's nothing you can do – and you're coming back in just over a week for our wedding, anyway.'

'But if he doesn't . . .'

Knowing what she's about to say, about the wedding, I interrupt. 'I'm taking each day at a time.' I try to keep my voice level, because right now, I can't think that far ahead. 'It's the only way.' Though I want her here more than anything, she has to think of her coursework. And the moment she comes home, in my mind at least, everything escalates.

After forcing a promise from me to keep her updated, she reluctantly agrees to stay where she is – at least for now. But her unspoken words hang in the air. Less than a fortnight away, ever since we decided on a date, our wedding has filled my head. For a moment, I allow my mind to linger: on my beautiful dress, my vows, everyone important to me in one place. But instead of Matt beside me, I imagine an empty space, as I feel myself shiver. I never thought the day would come I'd have to think about cancelling it.

As I sit there, a knock on the door makes me jump. Getting up, I go to answer it, but when I see Cath's face pressed against the glass, my heart sinks.

'I brought lunch!' As I open the door, she holds up a brown paper carrier bag from the farm shop she would have driven past on her way here. 'This too.' She holds up a bottle of champagne. 'I thought we'd celebrate – your up and coming nuptials and my escape from Oliver. If you're not too busy?' She hesitates, frowning as she stares at me. 'What's going on?'

I shake my head. 'Sorry, I'd completely forgotten you were coming. Can we do this some other time?' It isn't that I don't want to see her, but today, I don't have the capacity to listen to her problems or buoy her up. Until I find out where Matt is, there isn't space in my mind for anything else.

'What's happened? Is Jess OK?' Cath stands there. 'Amy, you're worrying me.'

I hesitate, in my state of denial not wanting to tell anyone, still hoping that at any minute Matt will turn up. But she's one of my oldest friends. 'You better come in.'

Closing the door behind us, she follows me through to the kitchen, where she pulls off her jacket then stands there, her eyes fixed on mine, as I perch on the edge of the sofa.

'Matt's gone missing.' I say it quietly, reticent, because the more I talk about it, the more real it becomes; the more my fear grows. Not because I don't care, as the police later suggested. Even with their specialist training, their expertise in psychological profiling, they couldn't understand how I was so calm.

A look of incredulity on her face, Cath doesn't miss a beat. 'Since when?' Her voice is sharp.

'Last night.' Feeling tears fill my eyes, I wipe them away. 'He didn't come home. I thought he was out late with a business client. I didn't think any more of it, until this morning.'

A frown wrinkles her forehead. 'He isn't answering his phone?'

I shake my head. 'I've been trying all day. I've called his office, too. Left messages, but no-one's heard from him. Just now, I called the police.'

'Jesus.' White as a sheet, Cath sits down next to me. A hint of her scent reaches me. Citrus notes – and basil. 'I mean, that's so not like Matt.'

'I know.' I've never known her lost for words before. Then I tell her about the old woman and what she said to me.

A look of shock crosses her face. 'You were right when you said it was weird. It's too much of a coincidence, surely.' Cath stares at me. 'What happens now?'

'So now, I wait for the police to get back to me. Unless he turns up – in which case I call them.'

'Jesus, Amy.' Cath sits there, then she gets up again. 'There's an explanation. There has to be. You're getting married. You're love's dream, for fuck's sake. Don't I know better than anyone.'

Hearing the bitterness in her voice, I look up. I hadn't realised she felt that way.

31

'Don't mind me.' She shakes her head. 'I'm cynical and twisted because of Oliver, but I'll get over it.'

I stare at her, not knowing what to say. Then something makes me look at her more closely, as I notice how much weight she's lost, how she's cut her hair shorter, so that it falls in soft waves that frame her face. I've always thought of her as large-framed, heavy, but she isn't. Her broken heart has left her slender.

Cath gazes out of the window. 'It's OK. It really is. It was a bit galling for a while, if I'm honest. There's nothing like looking at other people and wishing you had even a fraction of their happiness. But Oliver's gone and I'm moving to Bristol. It's fine – honestly. I'm happy for you.' But the tightness of her voice belies her words.

Later, when the police asked about our friends, their lives, how well we knew them, I told them what Cath said, watching them write it down, word for word, only then remembering the hardness in her eyes, the bitterness in her voice, as the first waves of suspicion crept over me, that there was something she wasn't telling me. Jealousy was toxic enough, but unrequited love could be just as destructive; could drive the most unlikely person over the edge.

*

After a lunch that neither Cath nor I have an appetite for, our mood is subdued and she doesn't stay long. Checking my emails, there's no reply yet from Matt's parents and as I head across the garden towards my workshop, I'm unsettled. Ignoring the list of orders waiting for me, I wander over to the bench under the oak tree, placed there for the most far-reaching views of the Downs. Sitting down, I gaze out across the outline of the hills, my mind flitting all over the place as I breathe deeply, trying to slow it down, still jittery as the buzz of my mobile startles me.

'Ms Reid? It's PC Page.'

As she speaks, fear courses through me. 'Have you heard anything?'

'Not as yet.' She hesitates. 'I wanted to clarify one or two things about the conversation you had with your fiancé yesterday morning. Earlier, you told me his boss had asked him to take an American client out to dinner – that's correct isn't it?'

I frown, wondering why she's asking. 'Yes. Why?'

As she goes on, she sounds puzzled. 'The thing is, we spoke to David Avery – Matthew's boss. He says he doesn't know anything about an American client.'

'That's ridiculous.' My heart misses a beat. It doesn't make sense that Matt would have lied to me. 'David must have that wrong. There's no other explanation. Why else would Matt have told me that?'

'I'm only repeating what he told us. According to Mr Avery, Matthew left work at the normal time, but to the best of his knowledge, there are no clients from the States – at least, not at this present time. Currently their work is here and in Dubai.'

'He must have made a mistake . . .' I'm searching wildly for answers. 'There could be someone David doesn't know about. A new client . . . Matt wouldn't lie about something like that.' Mystified, my voice fades to a whisper.

'I take it you still haven't heard from him?' PC Page speaks quietly.

'Not yet.' I'm trying to take in what she's said. 'He'll call me, though. I'm sure he will – if he can.' But it's myself I'm trying to convince, rather than her.

'Did you email his parents?'

'I did. They haven't replied yet.'

'I'm sorry, but I have to ask this.' PC Page sounds reluctant. 'Can you think of any reason why Matt would just take off? Were there any problems between you? Had you argued, for example?'

'No.' I'm outraged that she's even asking. 'We're getting married in two weeks. Like I said to you before, everything is fine between us.'

It's what I want to believe. But I'm running out of logical explanations. Matt wouldn't take off – not unless he'd inadvertently got caught up in something and had no choice. It's either that, or something's happened to him.

After PC Page's call, uncertainty hangs over me as my restlessness builds. Not knowing what to do with myself, I pull on a coat and trainers, needing to breathe in cold air to clear my head. Closing the door behind me, instead of heading for the road that winds downhill towards Steyning, I walk up the lane, past Mrs Guthrie's house. Walking further on, I pass the pair of semi-detached flint cottages, then where the road ends, I climb the stile onto the footpath.

Snaking beneath tall beech trees, the path is covered in autumn leaves and I follow it until it eventually opens out onto sloping grassland. Wanting to push my body, to reach the top and feel the force of the wind around me, I take the steeper of the two paths. Narrow and chalky, it's slippery underfoot. Oblivious to the water soaking through my trainers, I constantly check my phone, racking my brain for the smallest detail that might make sense of everything, tears filling my eyes as I think about the future I'd believed lay ahead of us. A future that's been disrupted, unexpectedly, without warning or explanation, leaving me in unknown territory, where I no longer know what tomorrow holds.

At the top, I keep walking as my emotions overwhelm me;

walking faster, racked with sobs, until physically and emotion-ally, I'm exhausted. Losing track of time, I berate myself when I realise how late it's got. What if Matt's come back and he's at home, wondering where I am? But I know he isn't. If he was, he would have called me.

As the light fades, I turn to make my way back, dusk descending into darkness by the time I reach my lane. But it's not too dark to know that while I was out, someone's been here. As the house comes into view, I see that there are flowers on the doorstep.

Chapter Four

When I pick it up, the bouquet is heavy enough that it takes both hands to carry it inside, as it occurs to me fleetingly that Matt might have sent it. Pushing the front door closed with one foot, I carry it along the hallway to the kitchen.

Switching on the light, I place the bouquet on one of the worktops, taking in the densely packed white lilies and tulips, intermingled with deep red velvet roses – expensive, hot house varieties, with lavish layers of elaborate wrapping concealing the bag of water encasing the stems. Peeling off the envelope that's been attached, I imagine an apology – or an explanation, then my mind races. Maybe it's a surprise and Matt's already here waiting for me. Filled with hope, I call out. 'Matt? Honey? Are you there?'

The silence adds to my already fraying nerves, the scent from the lilies cloying, the significance of red and white flowers not lost on me. Silence has a weight, I wanted to explain to the police later. If I could have felt what it contained, listened to its secrets, maybe it would have told me where Matt was.

Through the kitchen window, a sudden movement catches

my eye. 'Matt?' Spinning round, I knock the bouquet, watching as it sways for a moment before falling sideways, then slipping slow motion to the floor.

As water leaks out onto the dark slate, I curse my clumsiness. Crouching down, as I go to pick it up, an alien scent reaches my nostrils, growing stronger, more abhorrent, as simultaneously I notice splatters of red on the white tulips. Recoiling, shock hits me as I realise. It isn't water on the floor. The stems of the bouquet have been wrapped in blood.

★

'I went for a walk. They were on my doorstep when I got home.' My voice echoes in the silence of the kitchen. 'I assumed they were from Matt — an apology or something.'

'You've no idea who might have sent them?' As she stares at the flowers, PC Page is smaller, younger than I'd imagined from talking to her on the phone. Slightly built, her straight fair hair doesn't quite touch her shoulders.

'No.' Shivering, I stare at the blood still splattered across the floor. 'This was with them.' I pass her the card I'd found in the envelope. 'There was no name on it.'

'Do you recognise the handwriting?' She picks up the card, frowning as she reads it. It has *with sympathy for your loss* printed in one corner and a message written across the centre.

Kill one man and you are a murderer.

'No.' I shake my head, then as the pungent odour of rust fills my nostrils again, fold my arms around myself. I'd started to clear up the blood before leaving it, realising the police should see it. Now that they have, I need to get rid of it. Going over to the sliding doors, I open them, letting the cold air flow in, trying to imagine the kind of sick bastard who sends flowers with their stems encased in a bag of blood.

'This happened when?' PC Page glances at my clothes.

'About an hour ago. I had to change.' I hesitate. 'It was on my clothes.' But it was the smell that was worst, filling my lungs, leaching through my clothes onto my skin. After calling the police, I'd rushed upstairs, ripping off my clothes and standing under the shower, scrubbing myself frenziedly, unable to get rid of it. 'I've left my clothes soaking upstairs.'

'We need to take a sample and run some tests.' She nods towards the young PC accompanying her. As I watch him, he bends down to collect a sample of the blood.

I look at her, uncertain. 'What kind of tests?'

'We need to ascertain if it's human or animal.' As she speaks, I'm light-headed, not wanting to think about the origin of it. Then she looks at the flowers. 'It used to be symbolic, didn't it? Mixing red and white flowers? They mean blood and tears.' She pauses. 'Can you think of anyone who'd want to upset you? Or harm you, even?'

Unable to speak, I stare at her, horrified.

She goes on. 'It doesn't matter how long ago. Sometimes people store away grudges and let them fester. It could be a friend, work colleague, even a family member – and it can happen years later, but sometimes, all it takes is a single unrelated event to take the lid off and bring the whole lot to the surface.'

Her brown eyes appear thoughtful. When I got to know her better, it was what I liked about PC Page. The way she thinks. But in this instance, she's wrong. I lead a peaceful life. As a herbalist, I work in synergy with nature; extract the magic contained in petals, bark, leaves, roots, seeds, with artistry, subtlety, alchemy. Working according to a healer's code, my intention is only to do good, a philosophy that extends into my personal life. I shake my head. 'I don't have any close family. And I work alone. I'm a herbalist. My workshop is in my garden. I really can't think of anyone who'd want to hurt me.' I watch her face to see if she believes me.

She hesitates. 'It's also possible someone's using you to get at Matt. There could be something in his life you don't know about. Even the most unlikely people can be pushed by extreme circumstances to behave completely out of character – I don't mean Matt, necessarily, but maybe someone he knows. Or maybe someone from his past that he hasn't told you about.'

'If there was anyone like that, I'm sure I'd know.' Shaking my head, I speak firmly, because she doesn't know him like I do. 'You have to trust me on this one.'

She glances around, her eyes lingering on a framed photo of Jess and me. 'Is that your daughter?'

I nod. 'Jess – she's at uni – in Falmouth. It was taken when I was interviewed for a magazine a couple of years ago. They were writing a series of pieces about women running their own businesses and they wanted to feature a herbalist.'

She studies it for a moment. 'Is Matt her father?'

I shake my head. 'Her father and I divorced when she was five.'

Frowning slightly, she goes on. 'Is there any chance your ex might have something against you and Matt being together? Or about Matt being a father figure in Jess's life?'

'That's hardly likely. Dominic – my ex-husband – left me for someone else. Ever since, he's had little time for Jess. He's still in her life, but only sparingly.' There's bitterness in my voice, but there's no point in hiding the truth. Everything is on Dominic's terms, his daughter's needs have always come second to his own.

She looks thoughtful. 'Do Matt and your daughter get on?'

Her question takes me by surprise. 'They've always got on

fine – when she's here. At the moment, she's away at uni. Matt's more significant in her life than her father is. She's excited about our wedding – all Jess wants is for me to be happy.'

'And there's no ex on Matt's side who might be jealous?'

I shake my head. 'He hasn't been married before. His last relationship became difficult, but it ended a long time ago. Mandy, his ex, has moved on now. He was on his own for quite a while, until he met me.'

'How long have you two known each other?'

'Getting on for a couple of years.'

Surprise flickers across her face. 'So fairly recent.'

'When you meet the right person, you know, don't you?'

But she doesn't respond. 'It's still possible that there's an innocent explanation and he'll turn up. It could be a case of cold feet. However unlikely that might seem, you'd be surprised how often it happens. Taking time out before the biggest decision of your life isn't so implausible.'

'What about the flowers?' As my gaze shifts towards the bloodstained floor, my shiver is involuntary. 'There's nothing innocent about the blood.'

'No.' Pausing, a frown crosses her face. 'I don't suppose there was anything to identify where they came from, was there?'

I shake my head. 'But there wouldn't be, would there? Not if you were delivering flowers with a message like that.'

'Most likely not.'

I look at her. 'You think the threat was directed at me, don't you? Not Matt?'

'It was obviously directed at one of you.' She pauses. 'Do you or your neighbours have CCTV?'

I shake my head. 'Not as far as I know.' In a quiet lane that doesn't go anywhere, you don't expect to need it.

'We'll ask your neighbours in case anyone saw them being

dropped off. Someone may have noticed. In the meantime . . .' Her eyes flicker away briefly. 'Be careful. Keep your doors locked, that sort of thing. And if you see anyone hanging around, don't hesitate to call us.'

Her words do little to allay my fear. Whoever left the flowers is still out there. Closing the door behind her, I lock it, then slide the bolt across, wishing the police would arrange for someone to watch the house – or at least call back later. What if the person who left the flowers decides to come back?

Chapter Five

By the end of the day, the ground has shifted beneath my feet. I've always trusted Matt implicitly, would have trusted him with my life, but I no longer know what to think. As darkness falls, all I can rely on are the facts. Matt lied when he told me he was taking a client from the States for dinner; a client his boss knows nothing about. How many other lies are there I don't know about? But I'm holding on to hope, that there might be a reason; any explanation other than the most obvious one, *that he lied*. Matt could have been on his way home, after dinner, when someone attacked him and took his phone. Or worse, but I can't bring myself to go there.

But he still lied. The brightness of the moon casts the garden in a dim glow and I shiver, despite what's happened, suddenly missing him desperately. Missing Jess too, craving the comfort and reassurance her presence brings. I've always felt safe here, but now, I'm imagining eyes watching me from the shadows, my every move known, Matt's too. Was that how it started? Were we watched?

I try to imagine Matt in a hotel somewhere, working through

a personal crisis of some kind, except somehow I know he isn't. He would have sent a message to tell me where he was, which can only mean that wherever he is, he can't. Had it been a warning yesterday, when he called me? Was he trying to tell me something? The most innocuous of phrases his only way of alerting me to the fact that something was wrong? Knowing I'd be able to check with David about the client dinner, that it wouldn't take much for me to work out he was lying. Knowing that when he and I never lie to each other, it would be reason enough for me to ask *why*?

Turning on my laptop, I bring up my Facebook page, then switch to Matt's, scrutinising his photos and posts, checking to see who's liked them. He isn't a great user of social media, though he comments and shares posts from time to time. But there's nothing recent. The last time was several days ago.

Getting up, I go through to the sitting room. It's a room we rarely use, with a single window that looks onto the lane. Two velvet sofas are arranged in an 'L' shape facing the fireplace, above which there's an abstract painting of Matt's, with a simple neutral rug on the wooden floor. Glancing around, I don't know what I'm looking for, but there has to be a clue, somewhere in this house, as to what's happened. Searching through the small pile of magazines on the coffee table, nothing is out of place. From there, I open the antique pine cupboard, filled as I knew it would be with photos and Jess's old school books.

Rifling through everything, I grow increasingly more frantic, apart from the painting, finding no trace of anything that belongs to Matt. It's the same everywhere I look, the only clues in the room that Matt lives here at all are the new sofas, the sanded floors, the muted shades of Farrow and Ball on the walls.

Normally, I wouldn't dream of going through Matt's things, but nothing is normal any more. Going upstairs, I open the wardrobe, beginning with his jackets, then moving to his jeans and trousers. All of them neatly folded; I pull them out, checking each pocket. Finding them empty, I go through drawers, removing t-shirts and underwear, my frustration growing, until the last drawer is empty. I slump onto the floor. Surrounded by his clothes, I pick up one of his sweaters, burying my face in it, inhaling his familiar scent, as despair fills me.

When at last I get up, I cast my eyes around the room, looking for the backpack he takes to work. But then I remember that when he left here yesterday, he was carrying it. Making a mental note to ask David if he's noticed it in Matt's office, I keep searching the remaining cupboards, moving to the desk in our tiny study, the spare bedroom, even taking a quick glance around Jess's room and the bathroom, looking for anything out of the ordinary, but it's the same everywhere I look. Nothing is out of place. All I have is his unfamiliar words and the memory of a scent.

★

I've always believed our closeness is tangible; that if anything happened to one of us, the other would somehow know. But that night, as I lie in bed, I'm numb. Troubled not just by the uncertainty. It's the knowledge that Matt and I aren't what I thought we were.

I cling on to the hope that there could still be a reasonable explanation for all of this. But there's no way to normalise the bouquet of flowers. As I think of them, the stench of the blood comes back to me, my head filling with the worst scenarios as I imagine where it might have come from. After that, sleep is impossible. Instead, fear looms from every direction, a cloak of darkness suffocating me.

★

Another night passes when I hear nothing, until the next morning, when I get a call from PC Page. As she speaks, I'm forced to confront a far more sinister reality.

'We ran some tests on the sample of blood from the bouquet. It was human. Type B positive.' She hesitates. 'I'm sorry to ask you this, but do you happen to know Matt's blood type?'

For a moment I can't speak. Nausea rises in my throat, unthinkable images filling my head.

'Ms Reid? Are you alright? We really need to know.'

'I don't know.' Sickened at the thought that someone had somehow got hold of Matt's blood, I try to pull myself together, remind myself that as yet, we don't know.

'Is he registered with a doctor's practice locally?'

'Yes . . . we both are – with the one in Steyning. Why?' But as she speaks, I realise the police must try to rule out the likelihood that it's Matt's blood, before they can consider the shocking possibility that it might be.

'They should be able to tell us. Don't worry – we'll find the number. I take it you've still heard nothing from him?'

'No. I've kept trying to call and left messages for him. I've even looked on Facebook to see if he's posted anything, but he hasn't.'

PC Page is quiet for a moment. 'Can you send me a link to his profile? And in the meantime, can you contact any friends he's likely to have been in touch with? See if anyone's heard from him or noticed anything out of character. Might he have been in touch with your daughter?'

I shake my head. 'He hasn't. And I spoke to his best man. Pete. And our wedding planner. Neither of them have heard from him, either.' Feeling nauseous again as I ask. 'Will you let me know when you find out – about the blood type?' But I'm already reasoning that even if it turns out to be the same as Matt's, it still won't prove it was his.

'Of course. Do you have Matt's best man's contact details? And the wedding planner?'

'They're on my phone. Can you hold on?' Finding Pete's number, then Lara's, I write them down, then repeat them back to PC Page.

'Thank you. In the meantime, as I said before, you need to be careful. There's someone out there who got hold of a pint of human blood.' PC Page's voice is grim. 'Unless we can rule it out as some kind of sick joke, we can't take any risks. If you see anything even remotely out of place, please call us.'

Her words remind me of the woman in Brighton. *You're not safe. Someone's watching you. You're in danger.* Then I realise that I haven't even told her.

'There's something else I should have mentioned, but at the time, it seemed too unbelievable. It happened the day that Matt disappeared. I was walking through the Lanes, when a woman stopped me. She told me I was being watched. Then she told me Matt wasn't who I thought he was and that I was in danger. It was strange. I'd never met her before but she was most insistent.'

There's a brief silence. 'You've no idea who she was?'

'I'd never seen her before.' I hesitate, then blurt it out. 'But now, I can't help thinking, what if she's right?'

★

With Matt missing, nowhere feels safe. Even as I walk down my garden, I imagine someone hidden, watching me. I try to work, but it's impossible to concentrate. Both Cath and Lara call me, brief conversations which end abruptly because I have no news, nor can I think about anything else. Eventually, when I call Matt's boss, David, he sounds flustered.

'I wish I could help you, Amy. To be honest, he's taken quite a few days off recently and it's left me in rather an awkward position.'

As he speaks, a chill runs through me. He took some time off to look at wedding venues, but that was months ago. 'But that was a while ago – when we were booking our wedding. The only days he hasn't been in, he's had client meetings.'

David's silent for a moment. 'I think you'll find it's been more than that. Maybe I'm exaggerating – I'll have to check.' He sighs. 'The point is, I need him in the office. The project he's been overseeing is with one of our biggest clients. So far, I've fobbed them off, but I can't for much longer. If he doesn't turn up soon, I need someone to take over from him.'

Far from reassuring me, the conversation leaves me floundering. Matt has always been meticulous, reliable. It's only been a couple of days – David's being unreasonable. 'I'm sure there's a good reason. There has to be. Matt's good at his job.' Clutching my phone, I remember what PC Page said to me. 'How has he seemed to you? Has he said anything that's out of character? It's just that the police were asking.'

'They've already asked me the same questions. Over the last month, we haven't seen much of each other. I was in Dubai last week, and Matt's either been here in the office or occasionally in London, managing this project. He's seemed the same as usual, Amy. He's mentioned your wedding once or twice – he said nothing to indicate he wasn't looking forward to it. I certainly wasn't aware of anything wrong.'

My hands grip my phone. 'Have you told the police all of this? They asked me if he might be having second thoughts.'

'I can't imagine that's the case.' David's voice is softer.

Hot tears are pouring down my cheeks. 'Can you please tell the police that? I need them to know how out of character this is.'

'I will.' David pauses. 'Try not to worry, Amy. I'm sure there's an explanation. Let's hope he turns up soon – for both our sakes.'

'Yes.' Wiping my face, I remember Matt's backpack. 'Have you checked inside his office? I wondered if he might have left his backpack there.'

'I looked after speaking to the police. It isn't here, I'm afraid.'

'What about his car?' I'm desperate for any clues that might shed light on what's happened. 'Have you noticed if it's still parked outside?'

'It isn't. He must have picked it up that evening at some point. When I came in yesterday, it had gone.' He sounds regretful. 'Look, I'm sorry, Amy – I have to go. I'm already running late for a meeting. Let's hope he turns up very soon.'

After the call, the rest of the morning passes interminably slowly. In an attempt to distract myself, I go to my polytunnel to begin planting seeds. It's a task I usually love, imagining the soft colours of California poppies, bright sunflowers, the nasturtiums that always remind me of the south of France, all of which I'll cut during summer months. But as I walk in, I see the wedding flowers I've been growing, large terracotta pots of white narcissi and hyacinths, their planting timed so that they'll flower just before our wedding. Then I picture the bouquet I'm planning to make – simple, delicate, scented; another smaller one for Jess, as a lump lodges in my throat.

Turning away, I start to fill seed trays and carefully label them, but my heart isn't in it. Instead, I discover how agonisingly slowly time can pass; how when you're waiting for news, a call, or anything to happen, every second feels ten times longer.

As the stress catches up with me, my heart starts to race. Suddenly shaky, my grip on life seems to be loosening, a

49

full-blown sense of panic consuming me as I remember the last time it happened. I'd been at my lowest ebb after my marriage to Dominic ended. On the verge of a breakdown, even.

Back then, I hadn't known what was happening to me, but this time I recognise the symptoms. Terrified it's happening again, I think about calling the therapist I used to see back then. Sonia Richardson. But I can't bring myself to make the call. She'd be another person to whom I'd have to explain Matt's lies.

*

The thought of cancelling the wedding dominates my mind. But at least work forces me out of the house for a couple of hours. As I drive to Shoreham, in my fragile state I'm easily distracted, almost pulling out in front of a van, only narrowly avoiding hitting it. It shocks me into concentrating long enough to make my deliveries, before heading straight home when I call Lara.

'Have you heard anything?' It's the first thing she says to me, without so much as a hello.

'No. Lara . . .' I hesitate, but I can't go on putting it off. 'I think I should cancel the wedding.'

'Oh God, Amy.' She sounds shocked. 'Why not leave it a few more days?'

'People need to know. Some are travelling quite a distance.' Trying to keep my voice level, I'm thinking of people like Matt's parents. Then I remember – they still haven't replied to my email. I make a mental note to try them again. 'And if I do it now,' I continue, 'maybe I can get some of the money back.'

'Amy . . .' She sounds confused. 'Matt told me . . . I thought you knew . . .'

My ears prick up. 'Knew what?'

'He took out insurance. I assumed he would have told you. He asked me to organise it a couple of months ago – not for any particular reason. I think he saw the costs adding up and wanted to protect what you were paying out.'

It's another secret. I feel my skin crawl at the thought that he's kept this from me. Silent for a moment, I try to imagine why he would have done such a thing. 'There's been so much going on. It's possible he did tell me and I forgot.'

As she speaks, she sounds hesitant. 'I would have thought you'd have remembered something like that. And I can't imagine why he'd hide it from you?'

But he *had* hidden it – why, I can't imagine. Stunned into silence, a conversation we had comes back to me. At the beginning, it had been me who suggested it, when we were booking the venue, after hearing horror stories of last minute double bookings and cancellations. I remember Matt's words. *It's a waste of money. It's hardly as though either of us will change our minds.*

'Maybe he forgot to tell you.' Lara tries to sound reassuring, but there's an edge of uncertainty in her voice. 'But basically, if the wedding's cancelled at the last minute, everything's covered.'

Any relief I might feel that the costs are covered is outweighed by the fact that Matt didn't tell me. It's impossible to ignore the glimmer of suspicion that creeps into my head. He must have done it, because something had changed. Had he already decided our wedding wasn't going ahead? I can't think of any other reason why he wouldn't have told me.

After speaking to Lara, I remember I haven't told her the police asked for her mobile number. But needing to clear my head, I pull on my coat, close the front door behind me, and instead of heading for the Downs, walk the other way, towards Steyning. The air is still, pale streaks of light filtering through the clouds, lifting the gloom. Either side of me, banks of russet-coloured bracken edge the lane, behind them trees, their stark branches meeting overhead. It's the kind of evening that I would normally breathe in, savouring the scent of damp earth, the turn of autumn to winter, listening to the dusk song of the blackbird perched nearby. But tonight, I barely notice.

As I walk, denial holds me in its grip. Even after what Lara told me about insuring the wedding, I don't want to believe that Matt's been deceiving me. Closer to the village, the lane slopes more steeply and I turn back, not wanting to run the risk of seeing anyone I know, asking questions I can't answer. Easier, for now, to be alone.

By the time I get back to the house, through the dusk, I make out a shadowy figure near the door. Fleetingly imagining it's Matt, my heart instinctively leaps. But if it was him, he wouldn't be standing there – he'd be inside. Only then do I see the police car, recognise PC Page waiting for me.

'Sorry to drop in like this.' In the dim glow of the outside light, her face is clouded. 'Do you mind if I come in? There are one or two things I'd like to talk to you about.'

I nod, my fingers clumsy as I fumble with my key. 'Of course.' But I know the police don't turn up unannounced with good news. Inside, my stomach churns as I anticipate the worst.

Jess

Matt came into our lives on a day of burnished copper leaves and an autumn breeze scented with wood smoke; in one of those before and after moments life is filled with. My mother and I walking up the village High Street, past the characterful shopfronts and the pub where people were spilling out onto the pavement, our lives as they'd been for as long as I could remember. My mother in skinny jeans and a silky black top, me in boots and a short red dress.

We were on our way to my friend Sasha's parents' annual party, with live music and a barbecue in the grounds of their house. Up a narrow lane in the village, a wooden door in a flint wall opened into their front garden. I remember the roses growing up the house that were still in flower, their scent mingling with that of the smoke; the neatly mown lawn, its single apple tree heavy with fruit, the front door open, so that sounds from the party drifted outside.

All of those moments belonged to before. As we went inside, making our way through to the big kitchen, a throng of people milled. I watched a man glance towards my mother, a curious expression crossing his face, almost as if he was waiting for her. Then I saw their eyes meet. Felt that moment in my bones when before became after.

I couldn't have known, but after that, nothing would ever be the same. From the start, he unnerved me. It was the way his eyes cruised restlessly, hovering on other women, until they came to rest on my mother.

He was too contrived, too watchful. I was sure he was playing a game. When he made his way over to her, I watched her body language, defensive at first, slightly awkward; his persistence, her defences slowly being eroded; her face growing more animated as he leaned in closer. There was an expression in her eyes I hadn't seen before. A look in his, as he turned round and his eyes locked with mine, hostile, challenging me; holding my gaze for several seconds, before deliberately smiling. There was no question he knew who I was, that this man was playing a game with both of us.

'Who's that?' I whispered to Sasha, as soon as I had the chance.

'How should I know? Why?'

'He's flirting with my mother.'

Sasha looked at me as though I was missing something. 'That's good, isn't it? I mean, you're going to uni soon. Wouldn't it be good if she met someone?'

'Yes.' I wanted my mother to find someone. But he reminded me of a cat prowling, toying with its prey, reeling it in, before pouncing.

Amy

Chapter Six

I'm on edge as PC Page follows me through to the kitchen, where I take off my coat and hang it over the back of one of the chairs, before going to close the curtains. 'I'll put the kettle on. Would you like tea? Have a seat.' Putting off the moment I know is coming, I nod towards the table.

'No – thanks.' Pulling out one of the chairs and sitting down, she looks at me. 'Amy . . . why don't you sit down?'

I tense, as fear gets the better of me. It's the tone of her voice, her deliberate hesitation, preparing me. Pulling out a chair, my stomach churns as I sit down. *Oh God. Has the worst happened?* 'What is it? Have you found Matt?'

'Not yet.' Pausing, she shakes her head. 'But there's something I have to tell you.' She hesitates again, her eyes steady as she looks at me. 'There's no easy way to say this. But yesterday, we had another report of a missing person. Another man. The call came from a woman in Brighton, reporting her partner as missing. She couldn't be sure for how long, exactly. They don't live together. It sounds as though they lead quite independent lives. Anyway . . .' Her eyes look directly at me. 'We took his details, including a physical description. Then she gave us his name.' She pauses. 'Matthew Roche. I'm sorry Amy, but we've every reason to believe it's your fiancé.'

I stare at her in disbelief. Then I shake my head and get up, walking across the room, standing with my back to her, trying to take in what she's saying, before turning back to look at her. 'That's impossible. It couldn't be him.' What she's suggesting is outrageous.

'I agree it doesn't sound plausible.' PC Page is silent for a moment. 'It's exactly what I thought, at first. But one of our officers went over there with the photo you gave us. This woman had photos, too – not just of him, but of them together. She described his job as a management consultant at Orbital. She knows about you, too.' She breaks off, watching me. When she goes on, her voice is more sympathetic. 'There's no question it's him. Your Matt. It very much looks as though he's leading a double life.'

There's a moment of silence as I stare at her, reeling, before the shock hits me. Then common sense kicks in. 'There's no way.' I shake my head, adamant. 'He can't be. Matt lives here. With me. He wouldn't live a lie. We're getting married. We've written our vows. His are here – somewhere. I saw them, only a couple of days ago.' I'm clutching at straws as I frantically search for the piece of paper. 'He goes to work, then he comes home. To me,' I add, desperately, unable to find it, sitting down again. 'There aren't enough hours in the day for anyone else.' But as I speak, I'm remembering what David said about all the time Matt had been taking off, of how convinced I'd been that he'd made a mistake. But if what she's saying is right, maybe he hasn't. Maybe instead of being at work, Matt's been with *her*.

'I know this must come as a terrible shock to you.' Her voice is gentle and I know as she speaks, there's more.

'Please, just tell me.' I'm dreading what else she's going to say, but however unpalatable the truth might be, limbo is worse.

PC Page hesitates, then speaks slowly. 'The woman told us that Matt, her boyfriend, was with her the evening he disappeared. She even knew he'd called you about the non-existent American client. She also told us he was about to leave his fiancée for her. Their wedding was coming up. He knew he had to tell her, but he was waiting to find the right moment. I'm so sorry, Amy. He isn't even hiding behind an alias.'

It has to be a mistake. But as I stare at her, I can't think straight. Instead, my mind is all over the place, thinking about what the woman in Brighton said, about Matt insuring our wedding without telling me. And now this.

She goes on. 'Allegedly he was at her flat that evening. He left there just before eleven. He was planning to come back here and talk to you – that same night. But no-one's seen him since.'

As the weight of his duplicity catches up with me, I feel my world collapse into ruins. Our wedding's just days away. It was supposed to have been the happiest of days – the start of the rest of our lives. I thought he loved me. He wouldn't leave me. Not when we'd planned a future together. As my mind takes me back to when Dominic left me, the same sense of betrayal fills me. I need Matt. Staring at the table, I feel desperate.

'Who is she? You have to tell me who she is.'

But PC Page shakes her head. 'I'm sorry, I can't give out personal information.'

'Why not?' My voice brittle, my eyes fill with tears. 'It's my life that's been devastated. I deserve to be told everything you know.'

'Amy, it's the law.' Her voice is understanding, but firm.

'There is another explanation.' Still unable to take it in, I search wildly for anything to disprove what she's telling me. 'Whoever this woman is, she's lying. Maybe she has a thing for Matt – an obsession – and she's jealous of me. It could have been her who left the flowers here, to freak me out. We have a joint bank account.' Getting out my phone, I open the app, checking it for withdrawals. 'Matt hasn't touched our money. And his passport is upstairs. I'm going to get it.' Racing upstairs, I pull open the drawers in the desk in our tiny study, where I find his passport with mine. Hurrying back downstairs, I place it on the table in front of PC Page. 'He'd hardly have left this if he was leaving me.' Thoughts race into my head, thoughts that at last make more sense than anything else I've heard so far as I confront a terrifying possibility. 'Don't you see? She's behind all this. Have you searched where she lives? Maybe she's hurt him or locked him up somewhere. If he was about to call off our wedding, he would have been honest with me. Matt loves me.' Panic in my voice, I stare at PC Page, desperate for her to understand.

'But that's the point.' Her eyes are unflinching. 'The fact is he hasn't been honest with you, surely you can see that. He told you he was meeting an American client the evening he disappeared. A client his boss told us didn't exist.' She pauses. 'I suppose he hadn't taken his passport because he was planning to come back here.'

To tell me he was leaving. In the silence, I feel reality shift further as her words sink in. I think back to Matt's last call and what he said to me, to what David said, shaking my head again, confused. The woman's story conflicts with mine, yet for reasons beyond my grasp, it is somehow more credible to the police.

'Amy . . .' PC Page hesitates. 'The night he went missing,

58

we've every reason to think he was meeting this woman. We've been going over CCTV footage – one section in particular, in which two men are seen entering a bar in the middle of Brighton. We're fairly sure one of them is Matt.'

As she speaks, my stomach churns. 'Do you know who the other one is?' I hesitate, going on before she can answer. 'I might know him. You should show me the image.'

'We're not a hundred per cent sure it is Matt, but for now, we're working on the assumption that it is. The other man . . .'

'He must be the American client Matt told me about,' I interrupt. David must have been wrong. 'This is proof, isn't it?'

But when she pauses, I know there's more. 'I have another theory. According to the woman who contacted us, Matt had gone for a quick drink with one of his work colleagues, before coming out half an hour later and getting in a cab. We managed to get the vehicle registration and we've tracked down the driver, who dimly remembers taking a man to another part of Brighton – apparently he hadn't any cash on him. I guess that would register with a taxi driver.' She frowns at me. 'A woman came out to meet him – it was she who paid the fare. The same woman who later told us he'd gone missing.' She pauses. 'I'm going to level with you. We both know that Matt's been keeping things from you. From the evidence we have, I don't think there's any doubt he's having a relationship with her.'

I stare at her, not wanting to believe her, as she goes on, more kindly. 'Is there someone who could come and be with you? Family, or maybe a friend?'

'There's Jess, but I don't want her to worry about me.' Shaking my head, again I think of calling Sonia, devastated, hating how I have no privacy, that everyone knows the details of Matt's betrayal – if that's what this is, because even with the CCTV footage, the other woman's photos, everything that David's said, I'm in denial; unable to measure the implausible evidence of a stranger against the believable words of the man I love.

Chapter Seven

While PC Page appears convinced that she's right, I'm filled with worry, the unfailing belief I had in Matt tinged with uncertainty, its stain slowly spreading, turning to disbelief shot with moments of hope that are all too fleeting. Her parting words haunt me. *Matt's been leading a double life.*

Even with the evidence the police *think* they have, it's impossible to know who to believe. Since that last time Matt and I spoke, I've held an image of him, walking back in, his eyes full of regret, with an explanation that will make everything OK again – until now. But then the words of the woman in Brighton come back to me. *He isn't who you think he is.*

In bed, I send another email from my iPad to Matt's parents. *Please can you get in touch, here's my mobile number. I need to speak to you, urgently.* Unable to sleep, I'm haunted by images of Matt with a nameless, faceless woman, until eventually when I drift off, I dream I'm in a church. Sitting alone at the back, the darkness is broken only by flickering candlelight. Then as two ghostly figures glide past, somehow I'm watching our wedding take place. Recognising Matt, I feel my heart leap. Handsome in the suit we chose together, the woman beside him is me, wearing my beautiful, dusky dress, except as I look more closely, a sense of foreboding fills me, because everything's wrong. The dress that I coveted has become blackened, the hem ripped, while my hair is tangled, my bare feet engrained with dirt. Then panic sets in, because my daughter is absent. *Where's Jess,* I try to cry out. *Jess has to be here . . .* As I search the shadows for her, the church door bursts open, letting in a swirling wind that one by one extinguishes the candles, while Matt pushes back my tangled hair and lowers his lips to his bride's. Seeing her face for the first time, a silent scream comes from me.

Sitting up in bed, my heart is pounding, my skin damp with sweat, the vision of my dream still horribly vivid, of the woman wearing my dress, of Matt kissing her, saying his vows to her, the scent of incense and mustiness from the church. Desperately trying to calm myself. *It's a dream, Amy. It isn't real.* But as my heart rate slows, the memory of PC Page's visit comes back, and the reality of Matt's betrayal hits me again, knocking the breath out of me.

While I watch the earliest light break the darkness, I think about how my life has become so far removed from what I thought it was. My future with Matt, our plans, all of them meaningless, our relationship a charade, while a churning desire to find this other woman fills me. I need to know her name, the colour of her hair, what she does, where she lives. But most of all, I need her to know what she's done to me.

*

After a string of cold, clear days, the weather changes suddenly, dense fog suspending the landscape in a half-light. Not bothering with a shower or make-up, I pull on yesterday's jeans and an oversized jumper, slipping on my boots before going outside.

The air is clammy, claustrophobic, my vision restricted to a few feet in front of me. There are orders I need to begin prepping, work that each day I'm getting more behind with, but I can't face it. Nor do I want to talk to anyone, replying to Jess's WhatsApp with the briefest of messages, letting even Cath's calls go to voicemail. In the end, I give up, making my way back to the house through the same fog that doesn't seem to have lifted even slightly.

I haven't been inside long when there's a knock on the front door. When I open it, PC Page is there. 'May I come in?'

Nervous all of a sudden, I nod. Coming in, she closes the door behind her. 'What is it?' I ask, staring at her.

She stands there. 'Could we sit down for a minute?'

'Of course.' My face flaming hot, I lead her through to the kitchen, clearing part of the kitchen table as I gesture to her to sit down.

'I won't keep you long. I just have one or two questions.' She hesitates. 'The night Matt disappeared, where were you?'

'Here.' I frown. 'Why?'

'We have a witness who recalls seeing you in Brighton. Not far from where this woman Matt was seeing lives. Near Brunswick Square.'

With everything that's happened, I've forgotten. 'Yes. Of course. I'm sorry. It completely slipped my mind. I was there. I had an order from a desperate mother – her child had skin problems. I went to deliver it, then came straight home.' Frowning, I shake my head. I never did get to the bottom of the wrong address.

'I see.' PC Page writes it down. 'Do you have details of the order?'

'Yes, of course.' But as she speaks, I feel myself frown. It's almost as though she doesn't believe me. 'There was an email.'

I pick up my phone. Scrolling through my inbox, I show it to her.

★

After she leaves, I slump on the sofa. For a couple of hours I don't move. Going over what the police have told me, then PC Page's questions, the level of Matt's deception has devastated me. Staring blankly ahead at the large clock on the kitchen wall, with each slow tick of the second hand I think about cancelling the wedding. The dress I'll never wear, the bouquet I'll never make. The vows that will remain unspoken. The guests I'll have to tell, wondering if any of them have an inkling of what Matt's capable of.

Lower than I've ever felt, it would be so easy, right now, to just give up. There are sleeping pills, upstairs, in the bathroom. It would be the end of all my problems, to drift quietly away and never wake up. But as I contemplate it, my eyes lock onto the photo of Jess and me together, taking in her long hair, the laughter in her eyes, and in that moment, I know I couldn't do this to her.

Shaken by how close I've come, suddenly I'm desperate to talk to Sonia, my therapist. Picking up my phone, I find her number. But as I start to call her, I hesitate. Facing up to how I'm feeling will take a strength that right now, I don't have. *But I can't go on like this*. Thinking of Jess again, I make the call.

Sonia sounds slightly surprised as she answers straight away. 'Amy, how are you?'

My hands are clammy as I grip my phone. I'd assumed she'd be seeing a client. That I'd be leaving a voicemail – but instead, I have to explain. 'Not good.' Hesitant, I break off. 'Something's happened. I'm not coping.' My voice is shaky.

'Let me get my diary.' But the familiar sound of her voice

64

isn't as reassuring as I'd hoped it would be. After making an appointment to see her tomorrow, I lie back on my sofa, darkness settling over me, my consciousness starting to drift. Unaware of time passing, I've no idea how long I've been there, only that the kitchen is dark when I register a knock on the front door, before a voice calls out.

'Amy? Are you in there?'

Confused, I get up. There's no mistaking Sonia's voice. When I thought I was seeing her tomorrow, why is she here? Getting up, I go to open the door. In a green velvet coat, her fair hair is tucked into the upturned collar, her eyes concerned as she looks at me. 'I hope this isn't a bad time? After your call, I was worried about you. Then one of my clients cancelled, so I thought I'd call you, but you didn't pick up. Can I come in?'

I hadn't heard my phone ring. Standing back, I let her in, watching as she closes the door, taking in the knitted dress under her coat, mushroom-coloured boots; the sheen of moisture on her skin left by the fog.

Her face is still anxious as she follows me through to the kitchen, where I go to put the kettle on, aware of Sonia watching me. 'I knew you wouldn't have called me without good reason.' She pauses. 'Why don't you come and sit down? Then you can tell me what's been going on.'

Pulling out a chair, then sitting heavily at the table, I stare at my hands, trying to stop them shaking, working out where to start. 'I was supposed to be getting married.' My voice is flat. 'But two days ago, he disappeared. I found out last night from the police that he's been seeing another woman. She told the police he was going to leave me for her.' As my voice breaks, I'm aware of tears pouring down my face.

'You had no idea?' She sounds shocked. 'Are the police sure about this other woman?'

'That's the thing.' As I look at her, Sonia's face is blurred, my words sticking in my throat. 'For some reason, they believe her over me. They won't even tell me who she is. And it was me he was going to marry.'

'Oh Amy . . .' Her voice is full of sympathy. 'You must be reeling with so many emotions – shock, grief, sadness . . .' She pauses for a moment. 'But right now, whatever else is going on, whatever he has or hasn't done, your first priority is to look after you.'

Hunched, I shake my head. 'I should have known. Aren't women supposed to have a sixth sense about these things? I feel so stupid, Sonia. I hadn't a clue.'

She looks outraged. 'It isn't you who's stupid. Of course you're hurting. And however badly he's behaved, you're grieving. You've not only lost him, you've lost the future you were planning.' She pauses. 'It must be triggering old memories of when Dominic left, too. Do you have any idea where your fiancé might be?'

'I don't.' My words echo in the silence. 'No-one does. The police are investigating. Our wedding was supposed to be next week. My dress is upstairs. We'd even written our own vows.' There's desperation in my voice. 'All that planning . . . and now I have to cancel it.' As I say the words out loud, my body starts to shake.

Sonia's silent for a moment. 'Have you had anything to eat?'

I shake my head. 'I'm not hungry.'

She speaks gently. 'Why don't I make us a pot of tea?'

I think about explaining how I'd rather be on my own, then because her voice is kind and I feel so desperately alone, more tears stream down my face. Embarrassed, I try to wipe them away, apologising. 'I'm sorry.'

'You really have nothing to be sorry about.' As her hand touches my arm, I know she understands.

*

Sitting at the kitchen table, I watch while she makes two mugs of tea, then puts together a sandwich I have no appetite for, before she sits down across the table from me.

'You're dealing with a lot, Amy. And right now, you're feeling the added shock of finding out that Matt has not only lied, he's betrayed you.'

'That's the worst of it.' I stare at my mug. 'I don't understand how he could do that to me . . . And I hate that everyone knows.'

'It's possible he hadn't told you because he couldn't bring himself to hurt you. However it started with this other woman, maybe it got out of control. Obviously, I don't know him but plenty of men cheat because they can.' She speaks carefully. 'I mean, imagine what it does to your ego to know that you have two women in your life. Two women who both want to be with you.' She pauses for a moment. 'I hope you don't mind me asking, but can I ask you about your relationship? Did you honestly believe everything was right between you?'

'On the whole, we were good.' My voice is quiet. 'We seemed to fit together, somehow. Before we met, we'd both been on our own for some time. You reach an age where you don't expect to meet anyone. It makes you see things differently. There was the occasional argument . . . but they were rare. And . . .' I hesitate. 'I know sometimes I did things that annoyed him. But before we were together, I suppose I'd got set in my ways. Jess and I had lived on our own for years.'

Sonia frowns slightly. 'Did you disagree about anything in particular?'

67

For reasons I can't explain, I don't want to tell her the truth – that he could be intolerant of Jess sometimes, that when I intervened he didn't like it. He would often remind me that it wasn't easy being the newcomer when Jess and I were so close.

I shake my head at Sonia.

'The biggest thing was the house. When we were first together, he wanted to sell it and move to Brighton. I didn't want to. The garden is the basis of my work. It takes years to establish herbs.' I turn my gaze towards the window. 'I didn't want to give it up and start again.'

'So you came to an agreement?' Sonia sounds curious.

I sigh. 'Kind of. I thought he'd grow to like living here. He gave up trying to persuade me in the end.' Hunched over the table, I shrug. 'At least, I thought he had. There was another row about it, not that long ago, but that time, he didn't push it. Now, I don't know what to think.' As I speak, I'm twisting my engagement ring around my finger, wondering if he'll want it back. 'This was Matt's grandmother's.' My voice is toneless as I move my hand to show her. After the most romantic dinner, in the most old-fashioned of gestures, Matt had ordered champagne before going down on one knee and giving me the ring. It had been quite early on in our relationship and I'd been ridiculously flattered at being the recipient of a family heirloom. More so, when the ring fitted perfectly. Now, sliding it off my finger, I place it in the middle of the table, then look at her. 'Have you ever been married?'

'No.' Sonia pauses. 'There was someone. Let's just say he wasn't who I thought he was.'

'My best friend's ex-boyfriend wasn't who she thought he was either.' I'm thinking of Cath. 'He seemed so charming, but it wasn't long before he wanted control over every aspect of her life. She couldn't see it, but everyone else could.'

'It's often the way, isn't it?' As she looks at me, Sonia sighs. 'It may not seem like it right now, but for all the people like your friend's ex-partner, and maybe Matt, too, there really are an equal number of good people in the world.'

Shaking my head, I stare at my hands. 'Nothing makes any sense. I was so sure about Matt. I can't believe I didn't see this coming.'

'No. He obviously knew exactly how to fool you.' Sonia's voice is quiet. Then as she goes on, she tries to sound more positive. 'Hopefully the police will find him. And when they do, you'll get the answers you need and he can take his possessions and get out of your life for good. Then, you'll need time to let the dust settle. Going forward, it isn't going to be the life you imagined. But think about it this way. If your wedding had gone ahead, it would have been far more painful if you'd found out further down the line what he's capable of.' Then she sees the flowers on the table. 'Are those from your garden?'

I nod, looking at the vase of parrot tulips, their soft petals shades of pale green tinged with terracotta, their stems uneven lengths, their heads snaking in different directions. Then my gaze drifts back towards the window. 'I've been growing our wedding flowers. They're still out there. White narcissi and hyacinths.' I'd planned to mix them with rosemary, eucalyptus, silver pine. Thinking of the day that's never going to happen, my eyes fill with more tears, while as if in a trance, I get up and go over to the doors, sliding them open and stepping outside.

'Amy, you're not wearing anything on your feet.'

Sonia's voice goes over my head as I start walking, anger rising in me, at Matt, at this other woman, whoever she is. Oblivious to the damp soaking through my socks, to the fog that envelops me, soaking into my clothes, clinging to my hair, her cries float past me as my emotions reach tipping point. Reaching the polytunnel, I go to the flower pots where stems of narcissi are in bud, one by one ripping them out, emptying the pots onto the floor, before starting on the hyacinths. Slowly at first, my anger builds as I move faster, more brutally, my hands cold, covered in damp earth as I hurl the broken stems onto the ground around me, followed by the flower pots, hearing them shatter; ignoring Sonia until I feel her hand on my arm. 'Amy, you should stop . . . You'll regret this.'

But I wrench my arm away, keeping going until every last flower has been torn up. Turning around, I glance at the mess of snapped stems and broken terracotta; at my socks covered in soil, then I look at Sonia. 'This is how it feels,' I whisper fiercely, as at last my anger starts to abate. 'Like this.' I gesture towards the dead flowers. 'This is what Matt has done to me.'

Chapter Eight

Eventually, after picking up the smashed flower pots, I collect up the rest and leave it to rot on the compost heap. But I leave the broken flowers where they are until the following morning. As I walk back towards the house, a flashing blue light reflects through the mist. A feeling of foreboding fills me. The police, again. It must be Matt.

But when I go through the gate to the front of the house, I'm shocked to see an ambulance parked further up the road outside Mrs Guthrie's house. Guiltily, I realise I haven't seen her for a few days. Too wrapped up in my own problems, I haven't given her more than a passing thought. Hoping she hasn't had a fall, I start walking towards the ambulance, but then her daughter's car speeds past, before pulling in and parking just behind it.

As the paramedics disappear through the garden gate, knowing her daughter is there, I turn back, steeling myself to call Lara, the wedding organiser. There's no way the wedding can go ahead.

'Would you like me to contact everyone?' Lara has all the guests' details.

'Would you?' Relief fills me. I'd dreaded having to send emails and field responses.

'I needn't say too much. Just that for unforeseen reasons, the wedding isn't going to go ahead.' Her voice is quiet, but matter of fact.

'OK.'

'I'll call the venue and let them know, if you like. Unless you want to?'

It feels unfair to put it all on her, but she genuinely sounds as though she doesn't mind. 'Not really. I never imagined doing any of this.'

★

Embarrassed about my behaviour while Sonia was here, I text her, putting off the appointment she'd persuaded me to keep till later in the week. Shortly after, Pete texts me, asking if there's news. I text him back. *If the police are right, it sounds as though Matt's been fooling all of us.* He calls me back immediately.

'What's going on? Are you OK?'

'Not really. Matt . . .' I break off, but then because he was going to be Matt's best man, I tell him. 'Apparently Matt's been having an affair. When the woman he was seeing reported him missing, she told the police he was about to leave me for her.'

There's silence. 'You're kidding.' Pete sounds stunned. 'You're sure about this? Of course, you must be. I mean . . . How did I not know?'

'I've asked myself the same question. But the police seem to think they have proof.'

He sounds shocked. 'Oh, Amy . . .'

I pause, knowing I need to ask him. 'You really didn't know anything was wrong?'

'Apart from the times he changed plans at the last minute,

72

no. We'd arranged to meet to talk about the speeches etc. But he's a busy guy. It's only the fact that the wedding was so close that I thought anything of it, because we were running out of time. But apart from that, there really was nothing.'

Then I remember. 'The police asked for your mobile number.'

'They haven't called me yet. And I'm not sure I can tell them anything.'

'Can you let them know how surprised you are, too? They don't seem to believe that I couldn't have known.'

★

After a couple of hours, when I next glance outside, the ambulance has gone. It isn't until PC Page calls me the following day that I find out more.

'I'm not sure if you know, but your neighbour was found dead yesterday. It came as a complete shock to her daughter. Had you seen much of her recently?'

I'm horrified. 'I can't believe it. She seemed OK the last time I saw her – frail, but determined as ever. Do you know how she died?'

'We're not sure. Possibly her heart, but apparently, her house stank of smoke. Her daughter said she was meticulous about getting the chimney swept. Given the circumstances, there'll be a post-mortem, after which we should know more.' PC Page hesitates for a moment. 'Her daughter said you and her mother were quite friendly.'

'We were. I used to see her much more when we first moved here but recently, I've seen her less frequently. Now and then, she'd give me flowers from her garden. She loved her garden – we had that in common, I suppose. She loved my daughter Jess, too.' I break off for a moment. 'I'm so sorry. I can't believe she's gone.'

'Can you remember when you last saw her?'

I remember clearly. 'It was the morning after Matt went missing. I'd just come back after delivering some orders, when I saw her walking down the lane. She had some Japanese anemones in her garden which she said I could use for our wedding.' Frowning, I can't believe I haven't asked. 'Do you know if she saw anyone leave the bouquet outside my door?'

'I did speak to her.' PC Page sounds thoughtful. 'She said she saw a van pull up outside the day it happened.'

I tighten my grip on my phone. 'No-one's told me this.'

'Probably because there isn't much to tell. It was too dark and the van was too far away for her to identify the make or colour. Because of how it parked, she didn't see anyone get in or out of it, either.'

My heart starts to race. 'It must have been whoever left the flowers. Who else could it have been?'

'That's anyone's guess.' There's a pause before she speaks. 'Either way, it doesn't exactly help. But we're doing everything we can to find out.'

★

None of us are immortal, but I'd imagined Mrs Guthrie obstinately refusing to let her age get the better of her, one of those old women who'd struggle on into her nineties, battling her frailty. It crosses my mind that her death is connected to whoever delivered the flowers – the timing seems too much of a coincidence. But whether it is or not, it weaves another layer of uncertainty around me. With Matt gone, Jess away and Mrs Guthrie no longer across the road, my sense of isolation grows. If anything were to happen, I'm alone.

Chapter Nine

Each time Jess says she's coming back, I persuade her not to. I don't want her to see me broken. Nor do I want her here until this day – the day Matt and I were going to be married, a day I've dreaded – is over. Two weeks have passed, and there is too much to forgive. Even if he did come back, I wouldn't want him here.

On the morning of what should have been the happiest day of my life, the early morning mist lifts, leaving a cold, sunlit day as I'd always known it would be. I step outside onto a light covering of frost that sparkles as the first rays of sun catch it. Instead of resounding with joy and love, with the heartfelt best wishes of our friends, it's a day that leaves me ice cold; filled with uncertainty and emptiness. In place of celebratory cards and the scent of flowers filling the house, the wooden floors polished, the windows crystal clear, dust has settled, thick enough that I can trace Matt's name with my finger. *Liar.*

When Cath calls, I let it go to voicemail, before texting her. *I'm OK, I just want to be alone today.*

Not long after, Lara texts me. *I'm here if you need company.*

Only when Jess calls do I pick up.

'Are you OK, Mum? I'm worried about you.' Her voice is anxious.

'Please don't, Jess. I'm fine, really I am. It will be good to have this day behind me.' I try to inject brightness into my voice, hoping she won't pick up on how I'm really feeling.

'If you feel horrible, promise you'll call me?'

'Of course I will. Thank you, Jess, but really. I'm going to be OK.'

Turning off my phone, I think of the bouquet I'd planned to make – amongst stems of winter foliage, the beauty of the flowers speaking for themselves. The same flowers I destroyed when Sonia was here. Going over to the fridge, I take out the bottle of Taittinger that we'd put aside especially for today.

Even though it's early, I open it, pouring some into one of our crystal champagne flutes. Drinking quickly on an empty stomach, I feel the rush as the alcohol goes to my head, as I pour another. On this hateful day, I deserve this, I remind myself. Matt isn't the man I thought he was. There was another woman in his life. He lied.

The champagne works, dulling my pain, fuelling my anger. Halfway through the bottle, I get out my laptop, printing off the vows I've written, folding the piece of paper and pocketing it, before deleting the folder. Then I go upstairs to fetch my wedding dress, unwrapping its embroidered bodice and dusky pink layers – the dress of my dreams, in which I'd naïvely imagined marrying the man of my dreams. Taking it downstairs, I go through to the kitchen, tormenting myself with thoughts of this other woman and how she's stolen Matt, ruined my life. How could she?

Collecting the champagne bottle and an old newspaper, I open the doors and go outside. As I walk down to the far end of the garden, I stop now and then to swig champagne from the bottle. When I reach the bonfire heap, I hesitate only briefly before throwing my dress onto it, screwing up some of the newspaper, pushing it underneath. Striking a match, I light the paper, before watching it smoulder. Then as the fire takes hold, I gaze through the smoke, dead inside, remembering the nightmare I had, while my beautiful dress scorches, wisps of it floating away as it melts into the flames. Reaching into my pocket for the vows I printed off, I crumple up that piece of paper, too, throwing it onto the bonfire. Then as the heat builds, I step back, finishing the champagne while I watch the flames, before dropping the empty bottle to the ground.

As the fire starts to die down, I notice a piece of fabric that's fallen away. Kicking it back into the embers, it flares briefly. Staring at the smouldering flames, I watch the last of the smoke curl into the air, before turning back towards the house. Maintaining my composure until I'm inside, as I close the door behind me, my control vanishes. Pain turns to grief, anger to rage, as I grab the champagne flute from earlier, then hurl it at the wall. Then going to the cupboard, I fetch the rest of the glasses, shattering each of them, my sobbing growing louder.

But it doesn't end there. Plates follow – part of the dinner service we'd chosen together, each pointless plate in turn. There is no place for anything in my life that Matt's had a part in. Only when I'm spent do I survey the wreckage on the floor, realising I have to find his other woman, wherever she is. She deserves to know what she's done to me.

1996

That hot blue skies summer, they didn't need anyone else. They were two halves of the same whole; emboldening each other, invincible; soulmates.

Even their names seemed to fit together. Charlie and Kimberley. Free spirits, roaming across fields, then when the heat got too much, seeking shade in the woods. Their limbs brown, their hair bleached by the sun, as they lay in the long grass together, side by side. Lost in the depths of the sky, watching the swallows soar, he felt her hand reach for his.

He didn't know when he realised they'd always be together, just that somehow he knew he couldn't live without her laughter, her touch, her love. Reading his thoughts, she rolled over, her eyes gazing into his, and in that moment he knew she felt the same.

It was a moment nothing moved, as they seemed to merge into the grass, the sun, the rolling hills, the acres of sky. Caught someplace where time was infinite – but then it caught up with them. Suddenly she got up, pulling him to his feet as she started running back towards her gran's house.

Her gran had stories to tell, about the witches in the elder trees and the spirits in the woods; how nature had a power that could be tapped into, if you learned how. Her own grandmother had taught her, as a child.

It was about the connectedness, she told him. The magic contained in petals, bark, leaves, roots, seeds. In the most delicate flowers, herbs, berries, trees; in artistry, subtlety, alchemy. They could heal, balance, uplift, calm. But what most people didn't know was that your intention had to be pure, your knowledge vital, because in the wrong hands, they could also kill.

Amy

Chapter Ten

For the betrayed there can be no sorrow or fond memories. For us, there are only questions, our grief sharp-edged, cutting deep. More than two weeks have passed since I last saw Matt, but unable to face talking, I haven't seen Sonia again – putting off my scheduled appointments until I reach another low point. Desperate to find a way out of my grief, this time I go.

'I'm sorry I've kept cancelling.' Sonia's counselling room is small, the windowsill crammed with plants, the air calm, as I sit in a small armchair.

'Don't worry about it.' She sounds unfussed. 'How have you been?'

Even before I speak, I'm defensive. Resenting the reasons that have brought me here, I'm hunched, my hands tightly clasped. 'Up and down. The day our wedding should have happened was a low point. But at least that's over now.'

Sonia's silent for a moment. 'Do you think it would help you to tell me more about you and Matt?'

My sigh is shaky. 'Maybe.' I've gone over and over the past, looking for any sign things weren't right. Every time, I've drawn a blank. 'Before I met him, I'd been alone – since Dominic. I'd given up on the idea of meeting anyone. I really wanted it to work. I honestly thought we were good together.'

'The breakup of your marriage was traumatic, wasn't it?' Sonia's voice is quiet. 'And now this happens. How does that make you feel?'

'Stupid?' I offer, tears filling my eyes. 'Let down, powerless, unworthy . . .'

'It's brought it back, hasn't it?' She speaks gently. 'But like last time, you will come through this. And you will be fine.' A frown crosses her face. 'Tell me – what kind of person is Matt? I mean, is he kind? Considerate? Is he thoughtful towards you – and other people?'

I'm silent, because it's obvious what the answer is. Why else would I have been with him? I shrug. 'I always thought he was.'

'How did you meet?' She sounds curious.

'At a party in the village. It was at a friend's house.' Frowning, I break off. Since we've been together, I've lost touch with so many of my friends. 'I haven't seen her for some time. But things have changed since I met Matt. I mean, when you first meet someone, you want to spend time alone, don't you?'

Frowning, Sonia picks up on it straight away. 'Don't you see your friends any more?'

'Not that often.' I hesitate. 'I suppose life has been busy – with work, planning the wedding. I'm sure things would have got back to normal after.' But it isn't Sonia I'm trying to convince. Matt's reticence when it came to seeing my friends has always needled me. I've seen it as a compromise, prioritising his needs before mine. 'Relationships are full of compromises.' Was that so wrong of me?

'It depends on the compromise.' Sonia looks at me. 'Did Matt think the same way? Would you say he compromised?'

Had he? I think of the times I went along with what he wanted, not wanting to rock the boat. Had he done the same for me?

Sonia doesn't push it further. 'Have you thought about maybe seeing your GP? They might be able to prescribe something – even in the short term – that might help you through this.'

★

I decide to take her advice and after a visit to my GP, anti-depressants draw a veil over my emotions, while milestones become a measure of the passing of time. The next comes a week to the day after our wedding should have taken place. Today, at this time, we should have been on our way to Rome airport, our taxi weaving through the streets to catch our return flight, heading home to Christmas together, our hearts filled with joy and regret at leaving a beautiful city. *But we could always come back*, I'd have whispered to Matt, imagining him nodding his agreement, taking my hand. Us: the foolish woman and the liar.

We should have been flying home to the rest of our lives. Gazing out through the kitchen window, I wonder if in a parallel universe, we are there together. Another Matt and Amy, laughing, happy. *Honest*. Waiting for a plane somewhere in Italy; neither of us able to imagine that in another place and another time, he has disappeared and I'm alone.

Then I remind myself what he's done to me, my broken heart raging, warped, illogical, savage with its intent – the Matt who's hurt me so deeply and who I'm incensed with, as I oscillate between tarnished love and noxious hate.

Jess comes home for Christmas earlier than I'm expecting. So far, I've told her as little as I can get away with, but as I recount what the police have told me about Matt's double life, her shock is written on her face.

'I can't believe it. He's vile, Mum. You're well shot of him.' A frown crosses her face. 'I never liked him.'

Her words shock me, then I'm filled with guilt. How had I never noticed? Or had I been so wrapped up in myself, I hadn't seen what was right in front of me? 'Why?'

She shakes her head. 'He was awful to you – so many times. He really was. I don't think you saw it.' She pauses. 'I'm not sure why, but to start with, I'm not sure I did, either. But I didn't say anything, because I thought you were happy.'

For a moment I don't reply. 'You know we had ups and downs, but everyone has them and they were rare. We were OK, Jess.'

'Really? He was always putting you down,' she says softly. 'Sometimes . . .' A cloud crosses her face as she breaks off. 'Never mind.'

'What were you going to say?' I frown at her.

Her eyes are serious as she looks at me. 'I was going to say, I didn't trust him.'

'I had no idea.' Yet again, her words shock me. How hadn't I known how Jess felt? I'd always trusted him – until I had every reason not to. 'I honestly can't believe you felt like that. You should have told me.'

'I couldn't. I thought you wanted to be with him.' She shakes her head. 'But it was the way he used to look at me. Even at the beginning, when he was saying all the right things to you, when it was just him and me, he made it quite clear he wasn't interested in me. I suppose, being at uni and meeting different people . . . I don't know. It makes you look at things differently.'

'Everyone's different. Everyone's relationships are different.' I protest, uncomfortable, trying not to show the effect her words are having on me. 'The only people who really know what a relationship's like are those who're involved in it.' Noticing Jess staring at me, I break off.

'I don't know how you're so calm.'

She's right. I'm unnaturally calm, with a chemically induced numbness. 'I'm taking something. Just short term – it helps.' I hesitate. 'I've been seeing Sonia again, too.'

'Your therapist from before? That's really good, Mum.' Jess looks relieved.

'Jess.' I'm struggling for the right words, but really, it's simple. 'I'm so sorry.'

'Why should you be sorry?' Jess looks outraged.

'I'm sorry you've been dragged into this. That I didn't know how you felt about Matt. That you're worrying about me instead of getting on with your own life back at uni.' For a moment, the veil the drugs have drawn threatens to lift. I force myself to take a deep, shaky breath. 'Maybe it was my fault. Maybe if I'd done something differently, this wouldn't have happened. I'm not saying what Matt's done is excusable, but I can't help wondering.'

Her eyes flash. 'You are joking, right? I honestly can't believe you said that. Matt's the one who should be sorry,' she says angrily. 'He shouldn't have cheated on you.' A frown crosses her face. 'Are the police sure it isn't this other woman who's lying?'

'The same thing's occurred to me.' I shrug. 'But for whatever reason, they seem to believe her. They say they have proof – CCTV, photos. The other thing is . . .' I pause. 'Even if she was lying, you have to ask why.'

'She could be a psychopath. People think it's just men who

get obsessed, but it isn't always. I wasn't going to tell you, Mum, but there's this girl in my hall who's just been arrested. She's been stalking her boyfriend, doing sick things like sending him dead birds and spreading all these lies about him. She seemed so nice. Everyone thought she was lovely. None of us had any idea.'

'God.' The thought of Jess being exposed to someone like that shocks me. 'There was something else that happened. Actually, two things.' After telling her about the old woman in Brighton, I tell her about the bouquet of flowers.

Jess is clearly horrified. 'That's disgusting, Mum. You should have told me. It must have freaked you out. What kind of person dreams up something like that? Could there be . . .' She breaks off, fear in her eyes. 'You don't think there's anyone who wants to hurt you, do you?'

Slowly I shake my head. 'The police asked me that, too. But honestly, I can't think of anyone.'

While I'm grateful for Jess's company, it's a Christmas I could do without, but I make an effort for her. We decorate a tree, buy nice food, while Jess tells me about a boy she's met.

'His name's Rik – without a c. He's really cool. He's studying sports journalism – and he surfs, Mum. He's going to teach me.'

I want to tell her to be careful. Not about surfing, but about Rik. When she barely knows him, how can she trust him?

She reads my mind. 'He's OK, Mum. I think you'd like him. He's nice to me. Otherwise, I wouldn't be with him.'

'I'm really pleased for you, Jess.' I force myself to sound enthusiastic, while the truth is I want to hold her close, tell her to keep her wits about her. To not make the same mistakes as I did. 'Have you told your dad?'

'No.' The single word tells me all I need to know.

'Have you seen him at all?' I speak quietly. Dominic's complete lack of responsibility is a controversial subject.

'He came to Falmouth a while ago and took me out for dinner.'

'That's nice – that you had some time together.'

'It was OK.' Her face is tight. 'But he doesn't really know what's going on in my life. He wouldn't think to ask if I had a boyfriend.' There's hurt in her voice. 'It's like spending time with a distant uncle, rather than my dad.' She shakes her head. 'Mum? On one of my courses, we've been learning about where our behaviour comes from – like from parents, families, friends. I've wondered.' Frowning, she shakes her head. 'About your childhood. Only you don't talk about my grandparents. I know they're dead now, but what were they like?'

As I think of my parents, my insides feel knotted. 'They were strict – and loving. They were a different generation. We didn't talk the way you and I talk, but life was very different then. Then of course, my sister died.' Swallowing, I break off, as a memory of her comes back to me. Hardly a day has passed that I haven't missed her. 'Your grandparents . . .' Shaking my head, my voice wavers. 'They were devastated.'

'It must have been terrible, Mum.' There are tears in Jess's eyes.

'It was.' I break off, waiting for more questions, but they don't come.

*

Over the days she's home, Jess and I fall back into the way we used to be, before Matt moved in, watching movies and reality TV shows, Jess lying on the sofa with her feet up, dipping into the packet of crisps beside her. As I watch her, something niggles at me – about myself, because when Matt was here, all of this stopped and until now, I hadn't noticed. Meanwhile, the other woman Matt was seeing obsesses me. Maybe she is the liar. Maybe she is deluded. Maybe Matt was trying to break it off with her, rather than me.

Far from the celebration I'd imagined, the arrival of Christmas only brings more pain. The house is too empty, heavy with the weight of Matt's duplicity, the knowledge that if he hadn't disappeared, he'd have been with *her*. I buy a tree that Jess and I decorate, fill the fridge with festive food, for the most part trying to hide my feelings from her – but unsurprisingly, she sees through it.

Wise beyond her years, she sits next to me, and takes my hand in hers. 'It will get better, Mum. When something like this happens, it always does.'

At some point over the fortnight Jess is home, I know the police will want to talk to her. They arrive one rainy morning early in January. After showing them in, I pull on a coat and go to my workshop, leaving them to talk. It's an hour later, after they've left, that Jess comes to find me. Huddled in one of my coats, her face is anxious. 'They asked questions about Dad. You don't think he would have done anything to hurt Matt, do you?'

I'd worried that talking to the police would stir up doubts, creating more questions there are no answers for. 'No. I really don't. I've told the police that, too. Don't worry yourself. There are just questions they have to ask, to rule people out.'

She's quiet for a moment. Then she frowns. 'It was weird. When they asked me what I knew about Matt, apart from where he worked and how long he's been with you, I realised something. He never really talked about his life before he met you, did he?'

Knowing Matt could be private about a number of things,

I try to gloss over it. 'Maybe not to you, honey. But he and I have talked about all sorts. I know about his past relationships and all that kind of stuff.' But I'm not being entirely truthful. How many times did I dig beneath the surface, only for Matt to change the subject? I know only fragments of what came before. He talked about his previous relationship, a woman called Mandy, but that's all. I keep my voice light. 'Did you tell the police?'

'I didn't.' Jess hesitates. 'Do you think I should have?'

Hesitating, I shake my head. 'It probably won't make much difference to anything. But if you talk to them again, if it's bothering you, maybe you should.'

But Jess is frowning again. 'This Mandy . . . Maybe we should try and talk to her.'

Shaking my head, frustration fills me. 'There's no point. Whatever's happened, Matt's gone. Whoever we talk to, nothing will change.'

Chapter Eleven

All the time Jess is home, I endeavour to put on a brave face, but when she goes back to uni, my mood dips. Unless it's the police or Jess, I let my calls go to voicemail, wanting to be left alone. When Cath unexpectedly turns up, I'm less than happy.

When I open the door, she stands in the doorway, the frown on her face indicating she's clearly irritated. 'I've been worried about you. You could at least have let me know you're OK.' She sounds more annoyed than sympathetic, but then she has come all the way from Bristol.

I close the door behind her. 'You know how it is. Jess was home over Christmas. Since she went back, I needed some time alone.'

'How can I know when you don't talk to me?' Her voice softens. 'I may not have wanted your help, but you were on my case the whole time I was going through it.'

I shake my head. 'You don't know what's been going on.' I pause, looking at her – she's my friend, she'll want to know. And I can't go on keeping it to myself. 'I've found out Matt's been leading a double life.'

'What?' Her eyes widen, then she frowns. 'No. I can't believe that.'

'I'll fill you in.' As I start walking towards the kitchen, Cath follows me. 'Around the time he disappeared, the police received a call from another woman – reporting a man missing. She had photos – of him, of them together. It was definitely Matt. Apparently, he told her he was about to leave me for her.' I can't keep the bitterness out of my voice. 'He was waiting to find the right moment – at least, that's what she told the police.'

'Oh, Amy . . .' Cath's voice is full of sympathy. 'No wonder you went to ground. But I wish you'd told me. Honestly, I can't believe he'd do this to you.'

Nodding, I swallow the lump in my throat. 'Right now, I've no idea what to believe. There've been so many lies – about the night he disappeared, the time he'd been taking off work, presumably to see *her*. He'd even insured our wedding without mentioning it to me. He'd obviously known we were going to be cancelling it. And in all this, I still don't know where he is. I don't even know if he's alive.'

'He really is a bastard.' Cath's silent for a moment. 'Do you have any idea who this woman is?'

Feeling my jaw clench, I shake my head again. 'The police won't tell me.'

'You need to find out – perhaps they could bring the two of you together? Between you, you might be able to work out where he is.'

'I've asked. But the police won't give out her identity.' Not knowing who she is, eats away at me. Filling the kettle, I switch it on. 'Tea?'

'Thanks. This woman . . . she must know who you are – from Matt.' Cath speaks bluntly. 'Maybe she'll turn up here – in fact, I'm surprised she hasn't. She must be as curious as you are.'

'It doesn't change anything, does it?' Fetching a couple of mugs, my voice is bitter. 'If she's telling the truth, he was planning to leave me.'

'If?' Cath sounds astonished.

I hesitate, but only briefly, because I no longer have doubts. 'To start with, I wondered if she might have been lying. She could have been obsessive – or a stalker even, doing whatever it took to get between us. But the police were never in any doubt that her story was more believable than mine.' I shrug. 'And now there's too much evidence that she's telling the truth. He was definitely cheating on me.'

'What kind of evidence?' Cath looks puzzled.

'Photos and CCTV that corroborate her story,' I say bleakly. 'Plus there's the time he's taken off from work.' I think of the lies he told me about seeing clients. My voice hardens. 'But until he turns up, I'm stuck without answers. Hardly fair, is it, when I'm the one he was supposed to be marrying.' As my words tail off, there's a lump in my throat.

'Stop being such a victim.' Her words are tinged with annoyance. 'If this is true, he's a complete shit. You're better off without him.'

My hackles rise. It's too close to what Jess said. It's also the first time she's ever talked about Matt like that. 'I'm realising that. But no-one actually knows the whole story yet.'

'He's cheated on you. That tells you all you need to know about him.' Getting up, Cath starts piling dirty plates and glasses into the sink. 'I can't understand why you're not furious with him.'

'I have been angry. I still am.' My voice is sharp, but she doesn't understand my rollercoaster of emotions; how I swing from fear and grief, to shock and denial, to raging anger.

'You should be,' she says pointedly. 'You know more than enough to decide never to have any more to do with him.'

But she's missing something. 'Cath. What if he's dead?'

'He's still cheated on you.' She pauses. 'Let the police deal with it. Move on. Get over him.' She glances around the kitchen. 'I suppose all his clothes are still upstairs?'

I nod, thinking of the clothes left in piles after I finished going through them, as I make two mugs of tea and take them over to the table.

Coming over and sitting down, she shrugs. 'Get rid of them – put them in the loft or something. Or burn them – he deserves it. If he was about to shack up with this woman, he probably has more clothes at her place. It's not like he's ever moving back here. If he tries to, you're going to tell him where to go, aren't you?' She searches my face. 'He deserves no sympathy whatsoever from you.'

As I sit opposite her, I remember something else she doesn't know. 'The day after Matt disappeared, remember you came here for lunch? After you left, I went for a walk and while I was out, someone left a bouquet of flowers on the doorstep. It was massive, wrapped in layers of paper with the stems tied in a water bag – or so I thought. I took them inside, thinking they might be from Matt. Anyway, they slipped off the worktop.' I pause, recalling the smell that reached me. 'It wasn't water in the bag. The police took a sample away. It was a pint of human blood.'

'Jesus.' Cath looks horrified. 'Do the police think it's Matt's?'

'They don't know yet – they're testing it.' I look at her bleakly. So much blood. What kind of person would do that?

She shakes her head. 'I had no idea what you've been going

94

through.' She pauses. 'You should come and stay with me for a few days. It would be good for you to get away from here.'

For a moment, I'm tempted. But while so much remains unresolved, it isn't the time. 'I can't – not right now.'

I wait for her to try to persuade me otherwise, but she seems to understand. 'Amy? You need to keep reminding yourself, that even if the worst thing has happened and he is dead, he's still treated you abysmally. It's incredible that you had no idea what he was getting up to. He must be bloody good at covering his tracks. You'd think there'd have been clues.'

'I know.' My voice is tight. 'But I'd always thought I could trust him. That he loved me. I was stupid.' But as I say that, her eyes shift slightly. Frowning, I stare at her. 'What have I said?'

But when her eyes don't meet mine, I know there's something she isn't saying. 'Nothing. Nothing at all.'

In the past, I wouldn't have questioned her, but with everything that's happened, my instincts are heightened. 'Cath?' There's a hollow feeling inside me as I ask her. 'Did something happen between you?'

Cath sips her tea. 'No. Of course it didn't. I'm your friend. I was in love with Oliver the scumbag, remember?'

'You have to tell me.' My voice cuts through the silence. 'My entire life has fallen apart. If there's something you know that I don't, you owe it to me to tell me what it is.'

'Jesus.' Her face is ashen. 'Alright. I will, because it will help you realise what a complete jerk he is – but it really was nothing. I came round here one afternoon to see you – it was after the first time Oliver hit me. You were out, but Matt was here.' She pauses. 'He asked me in – he could see from my face what Oliver had done. He was sympathetic, overly so, but I didn't realise at the time. Inevitably, I got upset. He seemed so concerned. Then he put his arms around me.' From the way she hesitates, I know there's more.

'He kissed you.' I'm filled with disbelief.

'He tried to, but I moved away in time. I was shocked that he'd even tried – it was the last thing I needed – or was expecting. I told him I wasn't interested and to fuck off. Then I left. Talk about taking advantage of me at my lowest.' She pauses. 'Amy, I promise you nothing happened. You must know I'd never do that to you.'

I believe her, but I'm staring at her green eyes and pale skin, the soft haircut, imagining Matt touching her. 'But you never told me.'

She looks stricken. 'I thought it was a stupid mistake on his part. A misjudgement or a one-off. You seemed so happy. I wasn't going to ruin the rest of your life for a fumbled kiss that didn't happen.'

But it's not the point. If she hadn't stopped him, it would have. How many other times, with other women, didn't he stop? Getting up, I fold my arms tightly around myself as I walk over to the window, staring out across the garden before turning to face her. 'You still should have told me.'

'You're right. Of course I should. And it's not an excuse, but at the time, I was a mess, as you know. Love makes people act irrationally.' She looks at me pointedly.

*

An uneasy truce falls between us. But after she leaves, more doubts kick in. She only told me what Matt did because I pushed her to. If I hadn't, if Matt had been here, if our wedding had gone ahead, I would be beginning married life naïvely believing that I was the only woman in the world for him.

The foolish woman, who still hasn't learned from her mistakes.

Already I'm regretting that I didn't ask Cath more. Maybe something else happened between them. How would I know? When I used to trust instinctively, after Matt's lies and Cath's silence, I can no longer trust anyone.

1996

The scorching heat, those blameless blue skies, the banks of wildflowers, none of them assuaged your jealousy. Instead it grew like the bindweed in the hedgerows, spreading its stranglehold. Unmoderated. Unchecked.

For a while, you held it to yourself. Welcoming the stabbing pain you felt. It came from loving. Such agonising pain that could only come from such great love. But he didn't see you, did he? Instead he only had eyes for Kimberley. You couldn't bear it, could you? The new pain that racked you, of rejection, twisting your guts until you couldn't breathe.

You'd waited so long. Been so patient. Waited for him to see you. But when he didn't, you had to do something. In your world, people fought for what they wanted. Everything about your childhood had been a battle. It was how exam results were achieved, careers forged, relationships built. If you wanted them enough, you fought for them. But you forgot one thing. You can't take love. Like the soft summer breeze, it has to be given.

Jess

It was easy to see why my mother was drawn to Matt. Good looking, he had charm; took her out for pub meals and to the cinema. Poured flattery onto her after she'd been alone, for so long. But as he inched his way into our lives, I was an annoyance, visible only when it suited him, incidental to his cause.

When he came round to take my mother out, while she was upstairs getting ready, I'd catch him wandering around the house. If my mother was within earshot, he'd make an effort to engage me in conversation – about college, my friends, watching my mother brighten, flattered by his interest, taken in by the façade of his seemingly considerate ways.

It was after he moved in that the changes started. The brands of cereal in the larder, dairy milk and cheese in the fridge suddenly appearing when my mother and I were vegan. Our comfy old sofas replaced by new expensive ones, the ugly painting he loved hung over the fireplace, the walls now country house shades of paint. The meat I was prepared to tolerate. Neither of us expected everyone to be vegan. So I kept quiet, until the day Matt cooked steak.

Excusing myself, I went outside. I could cope with him eating it, but the smell of seared animal flesh revolted me. Even ten minutes later, when I went back in, the kitchen stank. Opening the window, I heard my mother say behind me, 'She doesn't like the smell.'

'That's a shame,' Matt's voice was smooth. 'You should have some, Jess. It's ethically produced. You never know, you might like it.'

'No way.' I flinched at his suggestion that any slaughtering of animals could be described as ethical. After serving myself some veggie casserole, I went and sat down, but something made me glance in my mother's direction. My mother, who had sworn off meat since as long as I could remember, was cutting into a steak. 'Mum?' Incredulous, I watched her eat a piece, before cutting off another.

For a moment, she looked mildly discomfited. But only for a moment. 'Matt feels very self-conscious about the fact that he's the only one of us who eats meat. I thought . . .' Breaking off, she glanced at him. 'I thought I'd try eating it again – only now and then. And Matt's going to try more vegan meals. Aren't you, honey?'

'That's right.' He stared as I started eating. 'In the circum-stances, Jess, I'd suggest it's only reasonable you do the same.'

He had to be joking. But when I glanced at him, his face was deadly serious. 'You are kidding.' Putting down my fork, I glared at him. 'I can tell you right now, that for the rest of my life, I will never eat anything that's suffered in order to be shrink-wrapped in plastic before being served up to the ignorant masses.'

'Jess, don't you dare speak like that.' I rarely saw her angry, but pinpoints of red appeared in my mother's cheeks. 'Matt isn't ignorant. He's no different to anyone else we know who eats meat.'

'I think you'll find he is.' Shaking my head, I knew she was wrong. Matt was trying to control, manipulate, both of us – not because he cared about what we ate. That she couldn't see it made it even more wrong. Getting up, I picked up my plate, sweeping the leftovers into the recycling, before storming out. On the way, catching Matt's eye, I saw rage flicker.

It was his first attempt to impose his will on me, the first wedge he tried to drive between me and my mother. The next morning, I waited for some kind of fallout. I couldn't remember the last time I'd spoken to anyone in that way. But it wasn't just Matt's attitude that had riled me. It was the change of my mother's heart he'd forced. No matter what her reasons were, I felt betrayed.

The next day, Matt wouldn't look at me. When I spoke, he blanked me. Shocked, I started to wonder if I'd gone too far. A couple of days later, and you'd have thought I was his best friend. I watched him do the same with my mother, treating her with contempt, punishing her with his silence for something she allegedly hadn't done, then after a day or so, buying her a lavish bouquet of flowers, apologising exaggeratedly. It hadn't been a good day. He was under so much pressure at work. He promised he'd never do it again.

It was a pattern that recurred, so that you couldn't tell what was coming. Calm Matt or raging Matt, or almost jovial Matt the best friend. It was impossible to predict, while over time, it took less and less to trigger moods that grew progressively extreme, until in the end, we were walking on eggshells.

I learned about change. When it's gradual, you don't notice it. Not at first, as it gently twists invisibly, pulling you in. It was only when I came back from uni that first Christmas, Matt's behaviour shocked me, more so because my mother seemed blind to it. His criticism and expectations of her; the blow ups

103

and rows over nothing of any significance that left her tiptoeing around him, terrified of upsetting him, of the unleashed anger that would follow. The fabricated accusations he would hurl at her, her protestations that went unacknowledged. Ludicrously emphatic apologies that reeked of insincerity. While I wasn't there, the spiral had tightened.

I could forgive her the first few times. Understand when she made allowances – told herself it was a one-off, an aberration; an overreaction after a tough day at work; that it was all her fault: she pushed him too far and it was her who should apologise, not him. It would pass. Tomorrow was a new day. How deluded she was. Oh, the lies we tell ourselves.

Then the day came when she seemed to retreat inside herself, bled dry. Matt's cruel words; narcissism, opportunism, self-interestedness, control, all of them steel grey shades that had merged into the bewildering blackness I saw reflected in her eyes. But even then, she kept repeating habitual, fatuous excuses. He can't help it. He doesn't mean it. He loves me. I know he does. The world has been cruel to him, too.

Feeding on her soul, each time diminishing her, it always passed. And for a fleeting moment, even though she was empty inside, the rain would always clear and the sun would come out. A sun that was progressively weakening, but still bright enough to remind her how good they were together, how much she needed him; an illusion briefly painted that couldn't last.

Her conviction that he loved her never faltered. Love takes many guises, after all, and her belief never wavered. There was always the hope that maybe one day, things would change. It was enough to keep her holding on, to this cruellest, most desperate love that illuminated her darkness, out of fear of losing him, of once again, being alone.

The paradox of what it means to love.

Amy

Chapter Twelve

Even after what Cath said, I can't yet bring myself to pack Matt's clothes away. Having been through his pockets several times, as well as the drawer where we leave old letters and bills, I've searched every corner of the house. The police have been here and searched too, but even so, we're still missing something.

The more time passes, the more I think about Jess's comment, about the way Matt concealed his past. I'd always told myself that at our age, it could take years to share our life stories, but I can't deny that there's too much about his past I don't know. If only there was someone I could ask. A tap on the window at the side of the kitchen startles me. Looking up, I see Lara's face. Waving, she carries on round the back of the house and comes in through the sliding doors.

'Hey.' She looks anxious. Her cheek is cold as it brushes against mine. 'Any news?'

I shake my head. 'Nothing. There's still no sign of him.'

'The police have been in touch. They asked if I thought he'd taken off.' Lara's clear blue eyes hold mine. 'But you know I don't believe that. I know Matt well enough to know that if he hadn't wanted to marry you, he would have been straight with you.'

'Thank you.' I keep my voice level. 'It helps to know you think that, if only because it's what I believed. I told the police exactly the same.'

Her hand is cool as it touches my arm, her eyes full of concern. 'I've racked my brains, Amy. I can't think of a single reason why he'd deliberately do this to you. You have to hang in there. Life can be surprising and we still don't know what's happened to him.' Then it's as if she reads my mind as she adds, 'Someone, somewhere, must know something. People can't just disappear, not in this day and age. Don't you think someone must be hiding something?'

But like Cath, Lara doesn't know everything. 'It's got more complicated since I last spoke to you.' Pulling out one of the kitchen chairs, I sit down, and Lara does the same, putting her car keys on the table. 'After he went missing, another woman reported her partner missing. Another man called Matt. Their descriptions are the same.'

A look of shock crosses her face. 'A coincidence, surely? It isn't an unusual name.'

But I'm already shaking my head. 'It's definitely him. She knew where he worked. She knew about me, too. The police have photos and CCTV footage. For ages, I tried to tell myself it was a mistake.' I gaze blankly at her. 'It was easier than believing the truth, which is that he's a lying bastard. I still don't understand how he could do this to me.'

Her eyes widen in alarm. 'Have you seen the photos?'

I shake my head. 'The police won't give me any details about her – data protection, or something. But she told the police he was planning to leave me for her. It explains why he took out the wedding insurance, doesn't it? And why he didn't tell me?'

'I don't believe it.' Lara looks shocked.

'I didn't, either. But I have to. And I don't know where that leaves me. I'm hurt. Angry that he's betrayed me. I can't tell if this woman's lied about him planning to leave me. Would he really have left it so close to the wedding to tell me? And no-one knows where he is or if something's happened to him.' With so many loose ends, so many lies, my reference points have gone.

'I know Matt had a bit of a past, but since he met you, I thought he'd turned a page. He really seemed determined to make it work with you.'

But I'm frowning. 'What do you mean? About him having a past?' How come Lara knows more about it than I do?

'For a while, there were a lot of women in his life. All casual . . .'

'Hold on a minute . . .' My mind is racing as I work out what she's saying. Matt's never mentioned any of this. I frown at her. 'How do you know about this?'

Looking awkward, her eyes shift slightly. 'Nothing, really. It was a throwaway comment. I mean, everyone makes mistakes, don't they?'

Suddenly I see her with a stranger's eyes, noting her slim figure, her smooth fair hair and radiant skin, as. my brain starts pulling the threads of what I know together, in some warped way, tying knots I can't untangle. The calls. The way Matt would stop by to see her on his way home from work. He tried it on with Cath. Why not Lara? I stare at her in shock. 'You and Matt . . . You have to tell me, Lara. I know you were friends. But was there ever anything more between you?'

A look of horror crosses her face. 'Of course there wasn't. I've been planning your wedding, Amy. Nothing's happened between us. Look, you're upset and it's not surprising . . .'

But I interrupt her. 'You and Matt,' I repeat, my voice danger-ously quiet. 'I've never asked him. I never thought I needed to.' I shake my head. I have to know. 'You have to tell me, Lara. It was more than friendship between you, wasn't it?'

She stares at me, smoothing a long strand of hair behind her ear. When she doesn't speak, my stomach turns over. It's like it was with Cath, as suddenly I know. Pushing my chair back, I stand up. 'How could you?' I'm rigid, my voice tight as I look at her.

As I watch her face, her eyes shift sideways. 'It isn't what you're thinking.' She speaks quickly. 'It happened about a year before he met you. We had a fling. Sex, Amy. Just once. I was one of several women in Matt's life at that time.' Lara looks uncomfortable. 'He made it very clear he wasn't up for anything more than that. We both knew it was a mistake. Matt and I were only ever meant to be friends.'

It's like with Cath. I want to believe her. But as I imagine them together, Matt touching her, kissing her, Lara's long, pale hair against his skin, my suspicions run away with me. 'It changes things. Can't you see that?' My teeth are gritted. If Matt had been honest when we first met, before I let Lara get close to me, before any of this started, maybe I would have felt differently. But finding out now puts a different perspective on it. 'When you have sex with someone, it changes things. You should have told me. *He* should have told me. Otherwise, it becomes this big secret between the two of you that I don't share. I thought we were friends and friends are supposed to be honest with each other.' I break off, upset. 'I want you to leave.'

For a moment she doesn't move. Then she stands up. 'This is insane. You're overreacting, Amy. As far as Matt and I are concerned, it should never have happened. I'm sure you're no different. You had sex with people before you met Matt, but it doesn't demean what exists between you.'

I look at her, filled with disbelief that she doesn't understand. What happened in my past has no bearing on anyone who's in my life now. I haven't lied or kept secrets, the way she and Matt have. It makes all the difference in the world. 'How am I supposed to know whether I should believe you? For all I know, it wasn't over. All the time I thought you were helping plan *our* wedding . . .' I break off, defeated, my mind running haywire. 'For all I know, you were trying to sabotage it. How do I know you're not the other woman who reported Matt missing? Or if it was you he was with that last night?' Whether it's the stress or the antidepressants, my head is spinning as I stare at her. I know how irrational I sound, but something stops me believing a word she says.

Lara looks outraged. 'This really is insane, Amy.'

'I've no idea if it is. That's the problem.' As I speak, my hands are shaking. 'Don't you see, I can't tell? I've just found out Matt tried it on with another woman – someone I thought was a friend.' There could be anything in Lara's past that I don't know about. How well do I really know her? But I don't want to. Not now. 'Surely, on top of everything else that's happening, you can understand why I feel like this?' I watch her face for any flicker of compassion, but it doesn't happen. 'It's best you go.'

Lara's silent for a moment, then she gets up. 'Amy, please . . . You're wrong about this. I'm as worried about Matt as you are. And I'm your friend. I want to help you.'

'*Friend*?' My laugh is hysterical. 'Friends can trust each other. To find this out now, after so many lies, can't you understand it's too much?'

'I'm so sorry.' As she picks up her keys, her face is white as a sheet. 'I thought he was making it up. But I can see now exactly what Matt meant.'

'What do you mean?' The blood drains from my face. 'What exactly did Matt say?'

'Only that when you were upset, you became irrational.' Her voice is suddenly deathly calm. 'I wasn't going to say anything, but he came round to see me – after one of your rows. He told me . . .' Shaking her head, she breaks off. 'Never mind what he said. He didn't mention it again. When the wedding was still on, I assumed you'd reached an understanding.'

Her words leave me completely blindsided. 'And you believed him?' When I went out of my way to avoid rows, it was another lie. I was never irrational. There were occasional rows, but they were short-lived. 'What else did he tell you?' I demand. But Lara doesn't answer. As she starts walking towards the door, I follow her. 'Don't you think I have a right to know?'

When the police talk to her again, she tells them that Matt had told her I was unstable. That once, I became so aggressive towards him, he was frightened for his life. That my thoughts were irrational and I'd been aggressive towards her, too. She doesn't tell them how she and Matt had been keeping a secret from me.

At the door, she stops, then turns to face me. 'I'd be careful, Amy, if I were you. You need to calm down. If you carry on like this, no-one's going to believe anything you say to them.'

She walks out, closing the door hard behind her. Seconds later, I hear her car start, listening as she revs the engine and drives away. Though my face is a mask of calm, underneath my emotions are boiling. She has no right to suggest my behaviour is in any way unreasonable. And it might have been just a fling between her and Matt, but that isn't the point.

After she's gone, I angrily pull on my coat and go outside. Looking across the garden towards the Downs, my breath freezes in small clouds and my anger starts to dissipate. Glancing down, I take in tiny white cyclamen unfurling, their leaves still coated in frost, as a tentative sense of calm comes back. Maybe I did overreact. Maybe I shouldn't have spoken so angrily, or accused Lara of having an affair with Matt. Maybe it was just a fling – I've no way of knowing. But whichever way I look at it, I come back to one fact. Both of them lied.

But it isn't her I'm angry with. It's Matt. It was him who'd always been so adamant that we should tell each other every-thing, that there should be no secrets between us. It's further proof I'd rather not have, of how one-sided our relationship was, of my commitment versus his betrayal, my honesty and his lies, as he kept things from me. It's like I ask the police next time we talk, *what else didn't I know?*

*

My afternoon is interrupted by a call from PC Page. 'We've found his phone.'

Chapter Thirteen

The faintest of hopes flickers, that at last there will be answers. But if they have his phone, where is Matt?

'Where was it?' I say urgently to PC Page.

'In a street in Brighton. Luckily for us, someone handed it in. I'll let you know if we find anything out.'

After the call ends, I imagine the police downloading his calls and messages, his photos of us; wonder if they're mixed with photos of *her*. Yet more damning proof that he isn't who I thought he was.

I think about Lara. If she was still having a relationship with Matt, it would have made no sense for her to come here yesterday, letting slip about the fling they had. But I can't be certain there weren't more flings. And if Matt had been seeing another woman, why not two, or more than two? My brain goes full circle. Why not Lara?

★

At least now the police have Matt's phone, means they must be coming closer to finding out what happened to him. Later that afternoon, PC Page comes over.

When she comes inside, I've already decided to tell her about Lara. 'Have you found anything out from his phone?'

She shakes her head. 'It's being looked at as we speak.'

In the kitchen, I switch the kettle on, my voice tight as I tell her what I've found out. 'It seems Matt had a fling, just before we were together. But it isn't that in itself. It's the fact that he didn't tell me, because she's still in his life.'

PC Page looks puzzled. 'Go on.'

Placing two mugs on the table, I sit down. 'She's known Matt a long time. Since we met, I thought she'd become my friend too – it's Lara. Our wedding planner.' I break off. How did Matt have the nerve to do that? Frowning, I remember him saying the idea of helping to plan our wedding had come from her. Another lie? 'It came out yesterday that they'd had a fling.'

PC Page frowns. 'And that was the first you'd heard of it?'

I nod. 'She's known Matt longer than I have. She said it was a one-night stand, but I don't know whether to believe her.' I pause. 'It was a big thing that I felt I could trust Matt.' I watch her face for signs that she understands, before telling her what I found out from Cath. 'I've also discovered that Matt came on to another friend of mine. She swears nothing happened. But I had absolutely no idea. It would never even have occurred to me that he'd behave like that.'

'He really is a serial cheat. It must have come as quite a shock for you.' PC Page shakes her head. 'But all of this demonstrates what he's capable of.' After a moment of silence, she goes on. 'I can only imagine how hard this is for you, but it's building a picture of him. We still have no reason to doubt the other woman who reported him missing. When you take her photos

114

and the CCTV footage, the time Matt's taken off work, now there's the fact that he insured your wedding without telling you.'

All of which I've already thought of. 'I want to know if it's her,' I say slowly. 'Lara, I mean. If you were in my shoes, wouldn't you?' There's a long silence between us. 'Her name is Lara Carmichael.' I feel my heart beat faster, as I watch her face, suddenly panicking again. 'God. I was right. It's her, isn't it?'

PC Page looks reluctant. 'Amy, you know I can't tell you.'

'But you can tell me if it isn't her?' I persist, feeling my face flush. 'Can't you see what this is doing to me?'

Putting her coffee down, PC Page gets up. 'Alright. I'll tell you. For what it's worth, whatever was going on between Matt and Lara, it wasn't her who reported him missing. But I'd like to speak to her again.'

A sense of foreboding comes over me, as already I'm wishing I hadn't mentioned Lara, dreading what she's capable of saying about me.

'I should be going.' As she starts walking towards the door, her hand reaches for the latch, then she turns to look at me. 'Amy, I will be in touch the minute I find something out. I know you're upset, but you must understand, we're doing everything we can.'

I stand there, irritated, reading between the lines. *Don't waste our time* is her clear message. But she visited *me* today. I didn't ask her to.

To my surprise, she changes the subject. 'There was one more thing . . .' She pauses. 'It looks as though it wasn't a heart attack that killed your neighbour. She died from carbon monoxide poisoning – most likely from an unswept chimney.'

'What?' I'm taken aback. She was always so organised – and something like that is completely avoidable. But it could have been caused by a combination of factors, the removal of any one of which might have meant she'd still be alive. The consumption of too much gin, which might have meant she nodded off to sleep, combined with the chimney that hadn't been swept. Perhaps when she lit the fire, the smoke couldn't get out, and she hadn't noticed because of her poor eyesight and sense of smell.

PC Page continues. 'People die every year from carbon monoxide poisoning caused by open fires. You wonder why she didn't have a detector. You'd have thought her daughter would have made sure of it.'

'It does sound unlikely, but I don't think her daughter came here that often. Most of the time, Mrs Guthrie was alone.'

PC Page frowns. 'I keep asking myself the same question. When an old woman keeps her garden meticulously, when she cooks proper meals, how come the fireplace was so neglected? Her daughter was sure she had it swept regularly. Apparently the chimney cowl was completely blackened.'

'Her sight wasn't good. Maybe she forgot?' I fall silent, thinking of the dark rooms, the windows that need cleaning. 'I suppose it could have happened gradually, so that she didn't notice the room filling with smoke.' I pause. 'Are you treating her death as suspicious?'

'No. It was a tragic accident that could have been avoided.' She glances at her watch. 'I really should be going.' As she turns to open the door, she pauses briefly. 'Take care.' Her voice is kind, but I flinch. They're the same words Matt said to me the last time I spoke to him.

Jess

Tall with lightly tanned skin, a ready smile, he always asked the right questions, had an apparent shared interest in whatever he thought I'd be into. At the beginning, flattered by his attention, just for a while, I fell under his spell.

When there'd been so much sadness in my mother's life, I wanted her to be happy. After her sister died and my father left, for years it had been just her and me. And now I was about to go away. It was the perfect time for her to meet someone.

Even when the façade slipped and I saw his other side, I kept quiet. But it nagged at me, that too dazzled by the Matt she wanted to see, my mother was blind to the shadows and hairline cracks behind the illusion she trusted. Matt's criticism was justified, he knew better than she did. And all relationships had their blips. Giving more of herself, Matt taking every last piece of her. But it was never enough.

I wonder if that's how it was when she and my father were together. If she'd always wanted to see the best in people, had the same child-like need to feel validated. Whether she turned away from her problems, seeing them as failures, but I was too young to remember any of it.

Whether or not there was a pattern, Matt fooled her, just long enough, for her to see a different side to him. The thoughtful Matt given to grand gestures. When he gave her the ring that belonged to his grandmother, she was blown away. 'I can't believe he gave me this. Isn't it beautiful?'

Made of dull gold, it was unlike the other jewellery she wore. Too heavy for her delicate hands. I wanted so much to love it, to share her joy, but as I looked at the ring, it reflected back an aura of coldness.

'We're getting married on a beach.' Her eyes were shining and I felt my heart twist as she shared her dream, of wearing a simple dress, her bare feet in the sand. 'Matt and I have been looking at Caribbean islands. I've found the perfect setting, Jess. It's a small guesthouse on a Jamaican beach, with white sand and palm trees. Matt loves it too! It's going to be so special! You and I need to go shopping for dresses!'

It sounded magical, but her excitement seemed unnatural and I couldn't feel it. 'Have you decided what colour, Mum?'

'I'm not sure . . . Not white, but otherwise, I'm open to ideas. I want a dress that makes me feel like a princess for the day.' Her eyes were far away. Knowing Matt represented the fairy tale, I felt myself shiver. Fairy tales were for children, not for women of my mother's age. And there was no way Matt was a prince.

'We'll go shopping. I'll help you.' For her benefit, I tried to sound excited.

On the way to the shop, I tried to talk to her. Asked her if she was sure Matt made her happy. I'll never forget her silence, before she answered. *Happy enough, Jess. I never expected to meet anyone. I'm lucky.* For a moment, I tried to see it through her eyes, to weigh up life with Matt versus life without him. Whether or not I liked him, it was her life and maybe it wasn't my place to argue, if being with Matt was better than being alone.

So that day, I helped her pick out her fairytale dress in shades of dusky pink, mine simpler in soft grey. When we got home, her eyes were shining as she told Matt where we'd been; how we'd found perfect dresses for a beach wedding but how he'd have to wait until the big day to see them.

I remember watching the lines deepen across his forehead, then the look of incredulity that washed over his face, as he shook his head. I'll never forget what he said. 'Amy, we've talked about this. A beach wedding's out of the question. We agreed. I can't believe you've done this.' A worried look on his face, he'd stood up and come over to her, putting his arms around her. 'With so much on your mind, you've forgotten, that's all it is.'

I watched her body turn rigid, before she pulled away, a look of confusion on her face. 'Matt, no. The picture. Surely you must remember? We were looking at it only last night – of that beach in Jamaica – the guesthouse where they hold ceremonies under the palm trees. I emailed them to reserve the date. You were there when I did it. They emailed back, confirming the date. I'll show you.'

Going over to the table, she got out her laptop, bringing up her emails, scrolling through them, her frown deepening. Then as she turned towards us, there was a look of confusion on her face. 'I don't understand. The emails aren't there.'

'Amy . . .' Matt shook his head. 'Try not to worry about it. Really. You've obviously forgotten the conversation we had. We definitely agreed. A beach wedding isn't practical.' But this time, his voice was firmer.

Then as he went upstairs, she looked at me. 'I didn't imagine it. I'm sure I didn't.' Her voice was quiet. 'We'll have to go shopping again – for shoes!' Feigning brightness, masking how she was really feeling. 'He's probably right. The beach wedding was a nice dream, but it's not practical.' Behind her smile, her eyes were bleak.

The twisted dance between the narcissist and victim, both equally convincing. I didn't want to believe that he'd set her up. But something told me that Matt was capable of anything. I wasn't sure I'd ever forgive him, not just for breaking the magic of her fairy tale, but for lying. Lies my mother chose to ignore, because she loved him. And as she always said, if you loved, you could forgive anything.

But he didn't know how to love her back. Once or twice I caught him texting on his phone, a look I couldn't decipher on his face. Unable to hide his shock when he saw me watching, before glossing over it with one of his lies, about how he was helping an old friend who was having some problems. But when there was no evidence of any old friends in Matt's life, I knew he was hiding something.

While I tried and failed to catch him out, in the background of our lives, distant thunder continued to rumble, now and then erupting into a storm, as Matt kept pushing my mother to sell our house and move to Hove or Brighton.

The memory of my mother's voice, upset, is clear in my mind. '*I don't want to move. This is my house. I need the garden for my work.*'

From upstairs, I heard the sound of broken china. I couldn't tell if the plate smashed by accident or design, as he raised his voice. '*For fuck's sake, Amy. We're getting married and you're talking about "my" house.*'

My mother's desperate reply. '*I love this house, Matt. Everything I need is here.*'

'*Don't lie, Amy. You hate this fucking house. I thought we'd agreed we were going to share everything. I want to sell it and get away from here, but you don't care what I want. It's all about you.'*

My mother didn't hate our house. But my hands were over my ears, unable to bear hearing him speak to her like that, so that I missed her whisper in response.

The exchange unsettled me, as I applied reverse logic to what Matt had said, about it not being her decision to make, because it certainly wasn't his. It had happened repeatedly, Matt bullying, my mother resisting, the situation spiralling, deepening my mistrust, until slowly it all started to make a warped kind of sense. If he forced her to agree, if they bought somewhere together, it would be in their joint names. That was the moment I understood it wasn't her he wanted. It was her money.

I waited until Matt was out before confronting my mother. 'You can't go on letting him speak to you like that.'

Her face was ash-white as she shook her head. 'You only hear part of the story, Jess. He gets upset easily. I don't mean to, but I always seem to make things worse.' Her eyes were troubled; unable to hide how upset she felt.

'That's outrageous,' I cried. 'You don't do anything of the sort. Love shouldn't be like this. He should be on your side. He should want you to be happy. But instead, he's completely vile to you.' I broke off. 'Don't sell the house. Not if you don't want to. It's your home. It isn't up to Matt to decide. You have a say in what happens too.'

Seeing her stricken face, I wondered if a part of her agreed with me. But when she spoke, she sounded defeated. 'I can't sell the house.' A look I couldn't read had flickered in her eyes. 'It's our home. It's where I work. It's taken years to create this garden. If we moved, I'd have to start again.'

Why do you put up with this? I wanted to shout at her. *Can't you see how wrong it is?* But I couldn't hurt her more, not after what Matt was already doing to her. Instead, I made her a silent promise.

I was under Matt's spell – but not for long. I'm stronger than my mother. One day I'd catch him out. Then I'd do whatever it took to get her away from him.

Amy

Chapter Fourteen

Two days pass when I see no-one, days during which my mind frets about what the police are finding out, from Matt's phone and more disturbingly, from Lara. After cancelling another appointment with Sonia, I'm on edge, watching from the sitting room window as the For Sale board goes up outside Mrs Guthrie's gate. It's the wrong time of year to sell a house that's dark and cold, that still holds the echo of her presence. Even from here, the house reeks of emptiness, its windows unlit in the fading light, the curtains left open. Shivering, I think of the ambulance that came, when her cold body was found a day too late.

Soon, the house will be sold. New people will move in. More people I won't be able to trust, because until they prove themselves, no-one is trustworthy. It's why I go over there one evening, letting myself into the back garden that had been hers for fifty years — to say goodbye and close a door in my mind.

Looking around, I'm reminded that we are only ever custodians of a garden; our influence fleeting. Already hers is diminishing, the edges of the path losing definition as the grass encroaches. Weeds are starting to take over, while there are gaps in the borders where someone's been in and dug up some of her plants. As I stand there, I wonder if her soul is here. But I feel nothing, not even a whisper. Every last part of her seems to have gone.

When I glance into her greenhouse, pots are planted with early sweet peas, that without her daily watering, have withered and died. Alongside are the broad beans she's always grown from seed, to carefully pick months later, just as she always harvested the apples from her tree. It's clear she hadn't expected to die. I wonder if the police have taken note, that she must have imagined at least another year here.

As I stand there, the memory of her voice comes to me. *My Japanese anemones are still in flower . . .* Gazing at the last remaining petals, I whisper back. *I'm sorry . . .* Trying to imagine how it felt when smoke overwhelmed her, when there wasn't enough oxygen in her lungs; hoping she'd drifted into unconsciousness, so that when it came, death was painless. *I'm sorry I hadn't known. I wish there was something I could have done to save you.*

'Why are you sorry?'

The voice startles me. Spinning around, I notice Sonia standing in the lane, the other side of the hedge, a curious look on her face. Realising she must have heard me and wondered what I meant, my face colours. 'I was thinking out loud. Mrs Guthrie, the old woman who lived her, died recently – at home.'

'Can I join you for a minute?'

I nod in the direction of the hedge. 'The gate's just there.' I wait as Sonia opens it and walks towards me, then glance towards the house. 'I suppose I came over to say goodbye. She lived alone and I was wishing I'd kept more of an eye on her. She was kind to me and Jess when we first moved here.' I pause for a moment, remembering. 'She used to let Jess pick her strawberries and raspberries. Jess used to love her homemade cakes. But that was years ago. More recently, we used to wave at each other in passing and I'd bring her any spare plants I had. But as my business grew, there was never enough time. I'm just sorry I didn't do more to help her.' Then I realise I'm trespassing. 'I shouldn't really be here. The house is for sale, but I wanted to come here, one last time, before it's sold.'

'It is sad.' Sonia pauses, glancing around the garden. 'Sad that an old lady should die alone like that. She certainly kept the garden in order, which must have taken a lot of work. She's pruned everything perfectly.'

I glance in the direction Sonia's looking, taking in the clump of shoots poking up through the earth, the neatly cut-back rose bushes, which by summer will be covered with blowsy pink blooms. 'She did. There are cuttings and seeds in the greenhouse, too. She reminded me of my grandmother. She lived alone, too – and looked after herself – and her garden.' I remember vases filled with cut flowers, the trays of seedlings and cuttings on her kitchen windowsill. 'She knew so much about plants: which ones needed shade, those that thrived in full sun. I suppose that's where my interest came from. She died years ago,' I add hastily. 'Life had become too much of a struggle. In the end, I suppose it was a blessing.' I look at Sonia more closely. 'I didn't know you were coming to see me.'

'I've just called in on a friend in Steyning.' She sounds matter of fact. 'When you cancelled, I thought I'd stop by and make sure you were OK. You didn't answer when I knocked, but then I saw you over here.' Glancing towards the house, she frowns. 'Do you know how your neighbour died?'

'The police said it was carbon monoxide poisoning.' Then I

follow Sonia's eyes as she glances downwards to a cluster of dark leaves and tiny white flowers.

'I used to know, but I've forgotten what they symbolise. Cyclamen, that is.'

'Goodbye. Resignation,' I tell her, struck by how oddly in keeping with our conversation it is, frowning slightly, surprised that she's interested in flower meanings.

Sonia glances around the garden. 'It interests me how so many flowers and herbs have a significance we've lost over the years. You must be so aware of it in your line of work. I've often wondered if you can read a life story from a garden – take your neighbour, for example. Given how long she's lived here, many of these plants could have been significant to her in some way, maybe as gifts or as memories. Those roses, for example. They're old, aren't they? Maybe a celebration of her children – or anniversaries, perhaps. Her herbs, too. There's rosemary for remembrance – and in a garden like this, there must be snowdrops. They mean hope, don't they?'

I look at her in surprise, because she's right. 'Actually there are snowdrops. Over there, under the shade of that tree.' I point in the direction of an oak in the far corner, before turning back to her. 'You know a lot about flowers.'

'I used to enjoy helping my sister. She's a florist. But like you, what really interested me were herbs.'

I had no idea she shared the same interest. 'I started learning which herbs to use to treat Jess. You can use herbs individually, but it's a whole different thing when you combine them.'

As the breeze picks up around us, her single word is almost lost. 'Alchemy.'

I'm startled, because it's the same word I've always used. 'Most people don't realise, but that's exactly it.'

Both of us are silent for a moment. Then she turns to look at me. 'And how about you? How are you?'

'OK.' I shrug. 'Getting used to my new normal. Accepting I've been betrayed and cheated on. But life goes on.' Bleak words belying how hard I'm finding this. 'The police have picked up Matt's phone. I'm hoping that will mean more answers.' I turn to stare at her. 'Whatever else has happened, that's the worst of it, Sonia. All I have is what other people have said, when I need Matt's version of what he did, and why he treated me so badly.' I pause, because that's what lies at the heart of my turmoil. 'Until he's found, I can't move on.'

1996

Even when you followed them, he didn't know how you felt. Laughing, he nudged Kimberley, who turned around and told you both to go home. But it was like the wood nymphs had got to you, or the elder witches. There was a gleam in your eyes as they carried on walking. Then when they next looked around, you'd gone.

It wasn't enough for you to harvest lemon balm, mint, rose petals; make forget-me-not memories. Back at Gran's, with the place to yourself, you had a new agenda; freedom to open the curious locked door, behind which Gran distilled nature's magic.

On a dusty shelf, you found the rows of tiny bottles with faded labels, filled with the elixir of life. Next, you sought the small black book, the wisdom on its pages headed love, luck, providence, prosperity. The love spell that was on the first page, of pink, red and white rose petals, the essence of rosemary and hazel; about sage and lotus flowers for wisdom and purity. The essence of digitalis and belladonna that was darkness, the words scrawled in Gran's spidery handwriting; the bottle, waiting for you to find it, out of sight.

Kimberley told him about Gran's fury as she snatched the book from you. Her face white with rage, her hands shaking. How dare you . . . Don't you know you can't steal a gift that doesn't belong to you?

But you can't return a gift that's been carved into your mind. One that would stay with you always. But there was more you didn't know. About the alchemist's curse, about the significance that lay not just in essence, but in intent. Meant to heal, to soothe, with only the best of intention. Not arrogantly, misguidedly, selfishly, tipping alchemic scales, that would go on swinging until one day, what you'd done would be redressed.

Amy

Chapter Fifteen

It's another cold morning when the air barely moves, the sun silvery behind a thin layer of cloud, as I stand in limbo amongst frozen banks of chamomile and creeping thyme. The silence broken when my phone buzzes with a call from Jess.

'Mum, I'm worried about you. I can't stop thinking about what's happened.' Jess sounds flustered. 'Nothing makes sense. I'm coming back at the weekend. I need to talk to you.'

The sense of urgency in her voice fills me with alarm. 'Jess, there's no need. You've only just gone back to uni. And I'm fine. The police are still investigating, and it's time for me to start moving on.'

'It isn't just that.' She hesitates. 'We've been studying a book about a psychopath. He pulled the wool over everyone's eyes – like his wife, the police, his whole family . . . Mum, I know you won't like this, but in so many ways, he reminds me of Matt.'

I'm stunned, then horrified. 'I know you mean well, Jess, but this isn't helpful. Cath's Oliver . . . maybe. But whatever Matt's done, he's no psychopath. If he was, I'd have noticed.'

She's silent for a moment. 'I'm not so sure. Don't draw any conclusions. Not until we've talked. I'll bring the book.' Her voice is small as she adds, 'Be careful, Mum.'

Her words take me by surprise. 'Of course I will. You too, honey.'

Her call unsettles me, then as I look around the kitchen, a memory blazes into my mind, of when Matt first moved in. The walls had been ochre, the floor covered in green carpet. After ripping them up, he'd wanted to repaint the walls in neutral colours, insisting on his choice of rug for the newly sanded floorboards, replacing them in the kitchen with dark slate. He had clear ideas about furniture, too, changing the sofas Jess and I had had for years, for expensive new ones. I'd been slightly shocked at how emphatic he was, how easily he spent money, but I'd told myself change was good. I'd got too used to it being just me and Jess. Now, it was his home too.

But no matter how I try to rationalise things, Jess's words play on repeat in my mind. Matt pulled the wool over my eyes, there's no question. And she's trying to help, I know that, but being a liar doesn't make him a psychopath.

Looking across the garden, taking in the leaves scattered on the ground, I get my coat. Since Matt disappeared, my usual motivation has been absent and my garden has been somewhat neglected. Going outside, after raking them up, I fetch the wheelbarrow, loading it up from the mountain of recently delivered compost.

By the time I wheel it to the new flowerbeds, my hands are cold from the frost on its handles, that's melted and re-frozen, sticking my gloves to them. But I go on. Digging is hard work, but I force myself to the point it hurts, only the fading light stopping me, when I'm too exhausted to go on.

★

That evening, while I'm heating up my supper, Jess calls again.

Picking up my phone, I force an air of brightness. 'Hi, Jess. Is everything OK?' It's unusual to hear from her twice in one day.

'It isn't me I called about.' She sounds agitated. 'I wanted to check you're OK.' She hesitates, before adding, 'Have you heard anything more from the police?'

'No – but they said they'd be in touch if they find anything.'

'I've been thinking, Mum. We ought to start our own investigation – into Matt's past.'

I interrupt her. 'It's in the hands of the police, Jess. It's best left to them.'

'I know you think that.' Jess pauses. 'But I've thought about this. It really is seriously weird that after you two being together for two years, all I know about him is where he works and that he loves Indonesia . . . And I don't even know if he's been there.'

'Jess, we've talked about this. He's talked to me about stuff.' I'm slightly exasperated. 'There's nothing weird – I promise you.'

'Why do you always do this?' Jess's voice is fierce.

'Do what?' I'm not sure what she's getting at.

'Underplay things. It's not normal that he doesn't talk about his past. OK.' She challenges me. 'You tell me. What do you know about him?'

I hesitate. 'Before we were together, he lived on his own. He'd just broken up with a woman called Mandy. It sounded like she was a bit of a psycho when they split up. I think that's why he lived alone for so long.' But already I'm thinking of what Lara told me, about the women in his life – wondering what else he'd hidden from me.

'What about his family?' Jess demands. 'Any siblings? Old school friends? I know you were going to meet his parents at your wedding, but there must be other family members. I can't believe you haven't tried to find them.' There's a slightly accusing tone in her voice.

'I tried to call his parents, but I had the wrong number. There isn't anyone else to find.' I rack my brains. 'There was a cousin who was coming to the wedding, who cancelled a couple of weeks before. But there was no-one else in his family he was in contact with. Not all families are close, Jess, for all kinds of reasons.'

'Don't you think it's odd you never met his parents?' She fires the question at me.

My blood runs cold, as I tell her what Matt had told me. 'They live in Edinburgh. They were going to come and stay a couple of months back, but Matt's dad was ill and they had to cancel.'

'You've got to admit, that's neat and tidy.' She sounds disbelieving. 'How do you know he didn't cancel them? Or if they were really coming in the first place? Have you heard from them at all?'

I shake my head. 'I've emailed them − twice − to tell them the wedding was cancelled, then to ask them to contact me, but they haven't replied.'

'He probably gave you a false email address.' Jess looks distrustful. 'He's got it all covered, hasn't he? If you ask me, he's a piece of work.'

My sigh is reluctant. 'Even if you're right, none of this changes anything, Jess. And like Cath said, maybe it really is better that he's gone.'

'Right.' Jess is defiant. 'But don't you want answers? I'm going to start digging around. Rik's offered to help me. There's a Mandy in Matt's Facebook contacts, so we'll start with her.

You should email the cousin who was coming to the wedding, too.'

All I know about Rik is the course he's studying and his passion for surfing. I'm not sure how I feel about him getting involved, when we haven't even met. 'There is someone who knows more,' I say slowly. 'Lara. She's known Matt for years. They had a fling – ages back, before he and I were together.'

'When did you find that out?' Jess sounds amazed.

'Recently,' I say shortly.

But Jess is immediately on to her. 'So she and Matt kept their secret? I thought Lara was supposed to be your friend, too. She's hardly reliable, is she?'

'No.' But apart from Jess, no-one is. I'm silent for a moment.

'There's another thing.' Jess pauses. 'I've been thinking about his obsession with the house. I think he was after your money.'

This time, it's a step too far. 'Look, Jess, can we talk about it at the weekend? I'd really rather you didn't do this.'

But she refuses to let it go. 'Think about how many times he went on at you about selling the house. He wouldn't leave it alone, Mum. He had a reason, I'm sure of it.'

'Jess, please. I really don't want to have this conversation – not now, OK? We'll talk, if you really want to, when you're home.'

She gives in, albeit reluctantly. After she goes, I let my mind wander back to an evening shortly after Matt moved in. It was the first time he tried to persuade me to sell the house. But that hadn't been about money. It had been about lifestyle – at least, that's how he'd sold it to me. Had I been blind to what was right in front of me? He'd always liked beautiful things – well-cut suits, pristine shirts, smart furniture, his car, all of it expensive. But he'd had a well-paid job. If he'd had money problems, it wasn't obvious.

Unable to settle, my mind is restless, turning things this way and that, getting nowhere. Later, when my mobile rings again, I glance at the screen, surprised when I see it's PC Page.

She gets straight to the point. 'I spoke to Lara Carmichael yesterday.'

I feel myself freeze, wondering what Lara's said to her. But if it's anything controversial, PC Page doesn't say.

'She was clearly as shocked as you were when she found out about Matt's double life. We've also been studying his calls and texts.' She pauses. 'They're clear evidence of his relationship with this other woman. I find it increasingly hard to believe he didn't give himself away. There must have been calls he hid from you, or texts flashing up on his screen. Surely you must have had your suspicions?'

I shake my head. 'There honestly weren't any.' It's true. I never saw anything that made me question him. Matt and I didn't look at each other's phones and messages are private, anyway. Suddenly cold, I feel myself shiver. It almost sounds as though she doesn't believe me.

But the conversation with Jess is still in my head. 'Actually, there's something I thought I should tell you.'

'Go on?' PC Page's voice is crisp.

'Jess called me earlier today. She was talking about how little we both know about Matt's past. She thinks he might have been hiding something. But she was right about one thing. He was evasive, deliberately changing the subject if you asked him anything he didn't want to talk about.'

'It does seem rather odd.' She pauses. 'But surely you must have known him well enough if you were going to marry him.'

She's right. I should have wanted to know more, but he had this way of smoothly changing the subject, so that before long, I'd forgotten what it was I'd even asked about. Feeling stupid, I backtrack. 'I thought I should mention it. That was all.'

I'm about to go to bed when my phone buzzes again. This time, it's a number I don't recognise. I almost don't answer it, but curiosity gets the better of me. 'Hello?'

'Hello.' It's a woman's voice — clear, mocking, precise.

My heart starts to race, the phone falling from my hand, as I'm catapulted back to the past. Snatching up my phone, I switch it off, then block the number before she can call again. How does she have my number? And why is she calling me now, of all times? She's the last person in the world I want to speak to. There really is nothing to say to her.

She doesn't belong in my life. It has to stay that way. But unsettled, that night I lie awake, scrolling through faces from the past on my closed eyelids as unwanted memories come flooding back, trying to work out why she'd want to talk to me. There can be only one reason, one I can't tell the police. And apart from me, she's the only person who knows.

Chapter Sixteen

It's early, the trees silvery in the mist. After a sleepless night, I watch from an upstairs window as the police car pulls up and PC Page gets out. This morning she's in uniform, her shoulder-length hair clipped back. Then I notice she isn't alone – she's with an older uniformed officer I haven't seen before. My heart lurches as I try to imagine why they've come here, dreading the worst kind of news.

I must have been right about her call last night. She was setting the scene, preparing the ground for whatever it is they've come here to tell me. By the time I reach the bottom of the stairs, there's a knock at the front door. I'm shaking as I open it, filled with dread.

'Amy. This is DI Lacey.' PC Page holds my gaze. As she introduces her colleague, her air of formality disconcerts me. I've shared so much with this woman, her brusqueness takes me aback.

'May we come in?'

Standing back, I let them in, a hollow feeling churning inside me as I close the door behind them – my nerves on edge, my instincts sharp. Whatever the reason they've come here, I sense it isn't good. Even before I turn around, I feel their eyes on me.

Looking from one to the other, I falter. 'It's Matt, isn't it?' My voice is husky. 'Oh my God. You've found him.' I'm light-headed, my legs weak, as I turn towards the kitchen, my heart hammering in my chest. But before they can answer, I hear another car pull up out on the road. Glancing behind me, through the window beside the front door, I catch sight of several officers getting out of a police van. I turn to PC Page, suddenly cold. 'What's going on?'

The gate through to the garden clicks open, distracting me, and I walk towards the kitchen. Pulling back the curtains, through the glass doors the garden is clearly visible, the early sun cutting through the mist, as several figures slowly make their way across the garden. In what seems like a nightmare, I watch as one of them tramples across a bed of herbs. 'NO . . .' My hands cover my mouth, the words out before I can stop them. My plants are my livelihood. It's too much to watch an ignorant stranger trampling them. Hearing footsteps come up behind me, I spin around. 'They're killing my plants. You have to stop them.'

But my cries go unheard. As DI Lacey goes outside to join them, PC Page's silent. Then she says, 'What really happened that night, Amy? When Matt came back late and told you he was leaving you?'

My eyes widen as I gasp in shock. 'I've told you. He didn't come back that night. The last time I saw him was before he went to work.'

Her eyes don't leave mine. 'I think he did come back and you had an argument. One that escalated when your temper got the better of you. You couldn't bear that your dream wedding wasn't going to happen, that he was leaving you for someone else. You lost control and then you attacked him.' She glances through the window towards the police officers walking across the garden. 'They're looking for the murder weapon. They have metal detectors – they know what they're doing. But you could save us all from wasting our time and tell us where it's hidden.'

As she speaks, I'm dizzy. She doesn't believe me. She doesn't believe a single word I've said to her. 'I could never have hurt Matt. I'm not that kind of person. I'm a healer, you know I am. I'm not a killer . . .' My voice desperate, urgent, willing her to think again.

'What about the messages you bombarded Matt with? They were all there, on his phone. You couldn't have imagined we wouldn't find them. They make for some reading. You'd obviously found out he was leaving you. It's all there – you begging him to stay, threatening him that if he left you'd come and find him.'

My mouth falls open. 'I don't know what you're talking about. I didn't send him messages. I called him several times and asked him to text me when he could, but nothing like you've just said.' I break off, incredulous, because they're not my messages. 'Are you sure it's Matt's phone?'

'It's pointless you denying it.' PC Page's voice is abrupt. 'Your number is listed against your photo.'

'But I didn't send them. I really didn't.' I stare at her, unable to believe the way the police are speaking to me, desperate for her to believe me. 'Someone must have set it up to look like it was me. But it wasn't.'

'So where's your phone?'

I glance around for my iphone, cursing that I've never bothered to lock it. 'I don't know. I need to find it. You'll see there aren't any texts on it. I don't know how this has happened, but someone's setting me up.' But my heart sinks, because I know what she'll say, that it was me who could have sent the texts and deleted them afterwards; how she won't believe me when I tell her I didn't write them in the first place. When she doesn't reply, I follow her gaze across the garden. His hands in his pockets, the DI is walking back towards the house.

Suddenly I'm terrified. 'If they find anything, it's because someone's planted it.'

Her voice is sharp. 'Who would do that?'

I stare at her aghast. Any sympathy she's shown in the past has vanished. Instead, she's brusque, forthright. What's changed? Wretchedly I shake my head. 'I don't know. I don't know why any of this is happening. I don't know where the flowers came from, or the blood, but someone's trying to get at me. Please. You have to believe that.'

As DI Lacey comes back in, he nods towards PC Page. Her eyes flicker briefly away from me, as his fix on mine. 'Amy Reid, I'm arresting you in connection with the disappearance of Matthew Roche. You do not have to say anything. But, it may harm your defence if you do not mention when questioned something which you later rely on in court. Anything you do say may be given in evidence.'

His words are lost as blood rushes in my ears. Dazed, I shake my head, trying to take this all in. 'This is wrong.' I stare at them, imagining some kind of sick joke. 'I haven't done anything to Matt.'

'Please, Amy . . .' PC Page's voice is firm. 'Don't make this harder than it needs to be.'

'No.' This is insanity. When she doesn't respond, I repeat it, louder this time, my voice panic stricken. 'PC Page, no. This is a mistake. You know it is.'

But DI Lacey's voice is firm. 'Ms Reid, you need to come with us.'

PART TWO

Fiona

Chapter Seventeen

In the weeks since Matt disappeared, my life has been on hold. One day he was moving in, the next there was no trace of him. Instead, I find myself waiting, aware that the more time passes, the more unlikely it is that he'll be found alive.

As I contemplate life without Matt, sadness fills me. Then anger, at the universe, for giving me a glimpse of something magical, before taking it away. What the hell was the fucking point? Why couldn't I have just carried on as I was, my life undisrupted? Why deliberately screw things up for me, yet again?

Nothing has ever been easy. From starting out without a penny to my name, hard work and determination have got me where I am today. In ten years, my entire life has changed beyond recognition. Not just my clothes – the real deal instead of cheap and make do – but my flat in Regency Square, with its elegant proportions and sea view. But in building a successful career, the greatest reward has been the credibility I'd for so long been seeking. Instead of being dismissed as I was in the past, I have a voice now. People listen to me.

Grabbing the mirror out of my bag, I check my make-up and add a sweep of the same red lipstick I've always worn, then pick up the pile of paperwork on my desk. On top is a file, entitled Lucinda Mills. It's a high-profile, high-stakes divorce case, where she left him but still wants to take him for everything he has. With whisperings of domestic abuse that he obviously denies, it isn't straightforward. A long afternoon lies ahead. Taking a deep breath, I get up. I'm ready as I'll ever be.

★

It's a gruelling three hours later that I come out of the meeting. Back in my office, I ask my assistant to hold my calls, then slip off my shoes and walk over to the window. In the street below, life goes on as it always does, regardless, as I think of Matt's unresolved disappearance.

At my desk, I check my emails, then sit back, thinking of how many times I've sat here, exactly like this, checking for missed calls on my phone, waiting to hear from Matt. Hating feeling so powerless, but telling myself that until he was free of Amy's clutches, this was how it had to be. I knew he loved me; that I had a choice. I could either leave him or let things run their course between him and Amy. I hadn't let myself dwell on it, until that morning came when I absolutely knew something was wrong.

★

When Matt and I first met three months ago, I'd no idea he was living with anyone. I was in a Brighton bar just off the seafront, catching up on case notes over a gin and tonic, when I noticed him. He was good looking, but what impressed me more was his air of confidence as he walked in. He was with a man, who I assumed was a client. The body language gave

148

them away. Every so often, I became aware of his eyes glancing towards me.

An hour later, after the client left, he came over. 'You look like you could do with a break.' He nodded towards my laptop.

'You know how it is. New job . . .' I decided to show off. 'I'm a partner with Hollis and James. And it's a man's world out there.' Then I paused, because that was unfair. 'Actually, they're not too bad in that respect.'

Vague amusement registered in his eyes. 'Can I get you another drink?'

I hesitated, my eyes flickering to his left hand, noting an absence of a wedding ring, then at my almost empty glass. 'Why not?'

While he went to the bar, I finished what I was writing, then put my laptop away just as he came back carrying two glasses. I remember him holding out his hand. 'Matthew Roche.'

'Fiona.' He'd need to do more than buy me a drink if he wanted to know any more about me.

His eyes were steady as he took my hand in his and I'd felt electricity spark. Racking my brains, I tried to think if we'd met before. As we talked, it became evident how eerily similar we were. Both of us were ambitious, wanting to create a comfortable life, but we'd both known adversity and broken away from unsupportive families. Matt had hinted at his, but about mine, I'd remained silent.

'So, Matthew Roche. Are you married?'

'No.' But he said it too quickly. 'And it's Matt, by the way.'

'Single? Attached?' I watched his demeanour change, as he seemed to close up.

Then he sighed. 'It's complicated.'

Folding my arms, I sat back. 'Right.' Then I got up. 'Thanks for the drink. But I don't do complicated, I'm afraid.' It was one of my rules. Single men only. Life was too short, time too stretched, for anything else.

'Please don't go.' His eyes blazed into mine. 'Hear me out. I want . . .' He sighed. 'I really want to talk to you.'

I knew I should be walking away, but something struck a chord with me and pulled me back towards him. There was an honesty in his gaze, my gut instinct telling me Matt wasn't a selfish, conniving man – over the years, I'd met enough of them.

'OK.' Slowly, I sat down again. 'Tell me.'

So he did, about the woman he was involved with, who he was marrying in three months. How he was only beginning to realise he'd made a mistake.

I still couldn't be sure he wasn't spinning me a line. 'What are you going to do?'

He looked miserable. 'I have to tell her.' He hesitated again. 'But it's not that simple. She has problems.'

'You still can't pretend.' I was shocked. 'You can't marry someone just because you're worried about them. Unless you love her . . . then of course, that's completely different. And it means there's no point in us having this conversation. But it sounds as though she needs professional help.'

But he was already shaking his head. 'I don't usually talk about it, but she's unstable. You wouldn't think it was possible if you met her, and I know it sounds extreme, but I'm really worried she'll try to kill herself.' He sighed. 'I really thought I did love her. But things have changed between us. If we argue . . .' He broke off.

'What?' I was insistent. If he wanted me to hang around, I needed to know everything.

'She does need help. She can get really fucking angry. I mean, smashing-things-screaming kind of angry. And the trouble is, if

150

I told anyone, they wouldn't believe me. They think she's gentle, quiet Amy who's had it tough since her bastard of a husband left her.' I remember his hollow laugh. 'Her ex was one smart guy to get away from her, believe me.'

'And I should believe you because?' Only half-teasing, I looked him in the eye.

'If you don't, this is a waste of time.' His voice was abrupt as putting his drink down, he stood up.

'Hey, I wasn't entirely serious. I'm a divorce lawyer. Believe me, I've heard everything.' I also knew better than most people that you can't judge anyone based on appearance. But I was curious about this Amy. I'd grown up around here. I might have known her. 'What's her family name?'

'Reid. She has a daughter, Jess. Nice kid. Really nice – another thing that makes this so difficult.'

I didn't know any Amy Reids. He clearly wasn't faking how badly he felt. It was coming off him in waves. But I knew too that you can't build a life on something that doesn't exist. And I found myself liking him. The way he had strength, yet compassion. That night in the bar, as I walked away, I knew that whoever Amy was, this man deserved so much more.

*

For some reason, I wasn't altogether surprised when I saw him again – in my office. 'Mr Roche.' I was overly polite as he walked in. 'I had a feeling it was going to be you.'

'I hope you don't mind. I thought that as you were a lawyer, you might be able to shed some light on something – in a legal capacity, obviously.' Even though he was hedging, he clearly knew what he wanted to talk about.

I watched his face. 'I can try. You do know I'm a divorce lawyer?'

As he shook his head, I wasn't sure if it was an act or not. 'You did tell me. I can't believe I've forgotten. I'm an idiot. Look, I won't worry you with it.'

But I was curious. 'You might as well ask me, I might be able to point you in the right direction.'

'This is strictly in confidence . . .' He hesitated. 'I wouldn't want Amy to find out I've come to see you, but it's her house. She refuses to discuss selling it. She always says she needs the garden for her work. But it's made me think. If there is a reason she can't sell it, would you have any idea how I could find out?'

'It doesn't sound very likely. If the house is in her name, it's up to her what she does with it.' It's an impossible question to answer. 'Where does she live?'

'Steyning. It's stuck out in the middle of nowhere and I'm trying to persuade her we should move somewhere with a little more life around us.'

As he spoke, an unwanted memory flashed into my head, of somewhere else in Steyning, up a narrow lane that snaked into the middle of the Downs. I pushed it from my mind.

'I know Steyning quite well. But as to why Amy can't sell . . . I couldn't comment. She's the person you need to talk to about this.'

When he said no more about the house, I wrote it off as a convenient excuse to come and see me. I had a feeling it wasn't going to be the last time I saw him. The next time we bumped into each other, we went for a coffee. The time after that, coffee turned into dinner, when Matt told me about how he and Amy met. He admitted that he'd thought quite quickly she was the one. It was why he proposed so early in their relationship. They valued the same things, seemed to share a vision of what they wanted from life. He knew she loved him, that she wouldn't betray him. He'd even given her his grandmother's engagement ring.

Were they happy, I asked him. When he looked evasive, I added, *Your grandparents?* When I told him that a ring conveys the joy or sorrow of its previous wearer, a shadow crossed his face. Clearly they hadn't been. If you believe these things, as far as his marriage went, he'd already signed its death warrant.

All the time I listened to him talking about her, the penny had yet to drop that I'd once known Amy. I found out one evening, when he went to the bar to order drinks. At the table, I was deep in thought when my phone buzzed. But when I glanced at it, I'd realised it wasn't coming from my phone. It was Matt's.

When the face flashed up, shock washed over me. Recognising the woman, I felt the past come flooding back. I had never imagined she was *this* Amy. We'd been close at one time, until the end of one summer, when she'd suddenly dropped me without warning. Since, I've seen her only once. As a lawyer, I'd come across many unbelievable coincidences, but this one was too much – even for me. In an instant, everything fell into place. The behaviour Matt had described; that her ex-husband had left her. I had a feeling I knew where their house was, too. Even the thought of it fills me with dread. But what I didn't know was how much Matt knew – about her past.

Once I'd discovered who she was, I became obsessively curious, unable to understand how someone like him was living with a woman like her. As our relationship developed, I was still wary, but his compassionate side drew me in. Then the day came when he told me how he felt. 'You and me,' he whispered. 'Isn't this how it should be?' His eyes were earnest as he looked at me. 'Until I met you, I didn't know.' Coming closer, his arms had gone around me and my deep frozen heart had started to thaw. To meet a man who wasn't like the others, a man I liked, who wanted me, meant that I broke my own rules. Something told me Matt was worth waiting for.

But it hasn't been at all easy. So many times he mentioned his reluctance to leave her, how he dreaded what state he'd find her in when he got home. He'd already told me how often he'd gone home to find her after a few drinks, lost in her own world, loud music blaring across the garden. He needed me to trust him, be patient. For a while, I was, but as more time passed, my patience wore thin. I'd listened to enough of his endless excuses about poor frigging Amy. So much so that I reached the point of no return.

After calling Matt and asking him to meet me after work, I knew exactly what I had to say. In the same bar off Brighton seafront where we always met, I waited for him, filled with sadness at the thought of what I had to say to him. When he came in, I watched his eyes light up as he walked towards me. A light that left as I started talking. 'I can't do this any more, Matt. You and me . . .' I shook my head, not wanting to do this but knowing for my sanity that I had to. 'I think we've come to the end of the road.'

In silence, he reached across the table, taking my hands in his. 'This isn't what I want.'

The look in his eyes was hollow, empty. 'But I can imagine how you feel. It must be impossible for you.'

I'd hoped to shock him into action, but any hope I had of him seeing sense evaporated into the ether. There was no point in dragging it out. Getting up, I kissed him on the cheek, my heart aching as I walked away. But underneath, there was a much deeper sense of injustice that burned. Not for the first time, Amy had one over on me.

For a couple of weeks, I avoided Matt, before he called me again, asking if we could meet. Against my better judgement,

I agreed. This time, he told me, he wasn't spinning me a line. He knew now: he wanted to be with me.

The night he disappeared, he'd come to my flat. Fobbing Amy off with a story of a non-existent client, he told me he'd reached the end of his tether.

'You were right – about what you said at the beginning.' As I looked at him quizzically, he went on. 'You said you can't marry someone because you're worried about them. There has to be love.' He hesitated again. 'It isn't Amy I love. It's you. I think I always have, right from when I first met you.'

As he spoke, I felt victorious. Walking over, I put my arms around him, claiming my prize. 'I love you, too. So what are you going to do?' But already, I knew the answer.

He kissed me, a drawn out kiss that went on and on, until he gently pulled away. 'I'll tell her when I get home.' He kissed me again, more urgently. 'She won't like it, but it can't be helped.' His mouth was on my neck, as he spoke into my hair. 'I'll pack first thing and bring everything over in the morning, before work.'

Ever practical, I pulled away, then went to one of the kitchen drawers, rummaging around until I found what I was looking for, holding it out as I walked towards him. 'I'm out early tomorrow. And if you're moving in, you'd better have a key.'

Something flickered in his eyes as he took it from me. 'Maybe tomorrow night we can go out and celebrate!' When I didn't reply, he added more soberly, 'It's a new beginning, Fiona. It's going to be good.'

As I started to let myself believe that this was really happening, I felt a weight begin to lift. He stayed a couple of hours longer, talking about the future, making plans, only falling silent as our bodies became entwined.

When the time came for him to leave, I kissed him goodbye at the bedroom door.

'I'll call you in the morning, when I'm on my way.' His dark eyes were thoughtful as he lingered a moment.

Standing there, I watched him go downstairs, knowing that leaving Amy wasn't going to be easy for him, yet filled with a sense of anticipation. I still have an image of him, his hair dishevelled, his shirt button undone, his smile as he turned to look at me before he went outside, thinking about him going back to sad, mad Amy one more time. I couldn't have known it was the last time I'd ever see him.

1996

It takes time for seeds to be nurtured. Blue sky days during which an idea takes root, form, definition, fed with your hatred. The most shocking of thoughts becomes less so, the more you think about it.

It's where it started, isn't it? With thoughts. Such a simple act, you told yourself. People did far worse. This was nothing. An anti-love spell to break two people up, it wasn't much more than a practical joke. Each time you thought about it, the idea grew stronger. What harm was there in a benign spell? The world's a battlefield, remember?

But you had no right to change the course of nature; to intervene in the purest of love. You didn't stop to think about how what you were doing might become complicated; that there was always going to be an explosion of consequences. You can't interfere with destiny and expect to get away with it. No question, one day, it would catch up with you.

Fiona

Chapter Eighteen

The next morning, as I left for work early, to prepare for a court case, I was on alert for Matt's call telling me he was on his way. By late morning, when I still hadn't heard from him, I called his phone, leaving a voicemail, before trying his office. When they told me he hadn't been in, I was filled with apprehension. I couldn't believe he'd had a change of heart – not when he'd seemed so decisive. But when I called him several more times, on each occasion it went to voicemail.

Another uneasy night passed, as I waited to hear from Matt, unable to sleep. Imagined all hell had broken loose when he told Amy, her talons digging into him, drawing blood as she refused to let go of him. At work, I tried to concentrate. But I couldn't get it out of my head that something had happened to him. The following morning, in between calls and client letters, I thought about our last conversation. He'd been distracted, talking about how Amy's moods were all over the place; how he was worried about what she'd do when he told her – not just to herself, but to him.

As I considered calling the police, I couldn't rule out him

changing his mind about us, deciding that when it came to it, he couldn't leave Amy. If he was cosily back at home with her, I was past caring if the police turned up and embarrassed him. But if he genuinely was missing, I needed to be sure the police knew.

Halfway through the morning, having still heard nothing, I called them. A male voice answered. 'Brighton and Hove Police. Can I take your name and the reason for your call?'

'Fiona Rose. I wonder if you could help me. It's about my partner. We don't live together, but I haven't heard from him since the day before yesterday. It's completely out of character and I'm worried about him. Is it possible to check if anyone else has reported him missing?'

'Can I take his name?'

'Matthew Roche.'

'Can I take your contact details?' After giving them to him, he took more information: Matt's description and when I last saw him. Then for the rest of the morning, I tried to concentrate on work. In between calls, I thought about our last conversation. He'd been distracted, talking about how Amy's moods were all over the place; how he was worried about what she'd do when he told her – not just to herself, but to him.

It wasn't until lunchtime that I got the call back from the police.

'Ms Rose? It's PC Page – Brighton and Hove Police. I understand you reported a missing person earlier today?'

'That's right – my partner. Matthew Roche.'

'Can I ask you when you last spoke to him?'

'The night before last. We spent the evening together.'

She pauses briefly. 'What makes you think he's missing?'

I frowned. 'Partly my instincts. He came to see me the night before last. He was supposed to call me yesterday and I haven't heard from him. Usually he texts or calls several times a day.

I've tried him several times. I've tried him at work too, but they haven't seen him.'

'You say Mr Roche is your partner?' There was uncertainty in her voice.

'Yes. It's complicated. We don't live together. He lives with a woman called Amy Reid. I'm guessing she will have reported him missing.' If she hadn't, she certainly should have, I wanted to add, but I bit my tongue. It was still possible I'd got this wrong and they'd reconciled their differences, Amy persuading him to cut off contact with me, after he'd decided to stay with her. But a sixth sense told me that wasn't what had happened. 'Matt was going to leave her. The night he disappeared, we spent the evening together. When he left my flat, he was going back to tell her. He was worried about how she'd react. That was the last time I saw him.'

There was a moment's silence. 'We are aware of him. Go on.'

So Amy had been in touch. 'I'm not sure what else I can tell you. It was obvious Matt had been restless for some time. Living a lie was getting to him. Matt isn't a compulsive liar – he's just not the type. I'm a lawyer. I can see the signs coming a mile off.' It's true. At the start, he'd been so weighed down with guilt, I thought he was going to break it off with me. 'He was dreading having to tell Amy, but it wasn't fair to keep leading her on. Their wedding is only a couple of weeks away. He knew he wanted to be with me. He meant every word.' I paused, swallowing. 'He was about to move his things into my place. Yesterday.'

'I see.' As she paused, I'd imagined her reconciling the Matt I was describing with Amy's Matt. She went on. 'Do you have a photo of him?'

'Several. Would you like me to send them to you?'

'We'll come and collect them – I have a photograph I'd like

you to identify. If you give me your address, I'll get onto it straight away.' After I gave her the address, PC Page hesitated. 'There is one thing I do have to ask. If you'd guessed Ms Reid would report her fiancé missing, why did you feel the need to call us?'

'In case she hadn't . . .' I broke off for a moment, gazing through the window at a seagull perched on a rooftop. 'This is difficult, because I only know what Matt's told me about her. But what I do know is he worries about her. That's why he kept putting off telling her he was leaving her.'

Her voice was sharp. 'What exactly was he worried about?'

I sighed. 'He described several times how her behaviour could be erratic. She could be quite aggressive towards him. They had violent rows where she'd end up smashing things.' I broke off, worried. What if she'd attacked him? 'He wanted to pack his stuff and get out of the house while she wasn't there, but the problem is she works from home. She's always there. It's meant he hasn't had the chance. I just thought you should know what he said.' I paused. 'I'd rather Amy didn't know about me. From everything he's told me about her, I really don't want her trying to find me. I have my career to think about – I've just started working with a new law firm. I don't want her coming here and screwing it up.'

'It might be helpful if the two of you were to meet at some point, but I take your point, Ms Rose. She won't find out from us. As I'm sure you're aware, we're legally obliged to maintain confidentiality.'

As a lawyer, I was fully aware, I just wanted to be sure the police knew I was. 'What happens now?'

'We'll continue our enquiries. In the meantime, if you think of anything else that might help, can you contact us?'

'Of course.'

'Thank you.' She paused, as if there was something she wanted to ask, then thought better of it. 'Someone will be round to see you shortly. And if we need any more information, we'll be in touch.'

After the call ended, I scrolled through my photos until I found what I was looking for, selfies of Matt and I in the grounds of a country house hotel in the Lake District, the first weekend we spent away together, before printing them off in readiness for the police.

It had been a magical weekend, tainted only by the knowledge that he'd told Amy he was going to Dubai for work. He hated the subterfuge. It was what I hated too – living a lie.

An hour later, I get a call from one of our receptionists. 'Fiona? There's an Officer Walker here to see you.'

'Can you show them in?'

Minutes later, there's a knock on the door, before it opens. The young uniformed officer looks uncertainly at me. 'Ms Rose?'

'Yes.' I get up. 'Come in. Close the door behind you, will you?' As he does what I ask, I pick up the photos I've printed off. 'I imagine you've come for these?'

'Thank you ma'am.' Hesitating, he takes a brown envelope out of his pocket, then pulls out a couple of photos. 'Would you mind taking a look?'

Taking the photos, I quickly glance at them. 'That's Matt. The woman . . .' I hesitate, staring at Amy's face. 'I'm fairly sure I saw her. The evening Matt disappeared. I was on my way home. She was walking quite near to where I live.'

Frowning, he takes out a notebook. 'About what time would that have been?'

I shrug. 'Somewhere between six-thirty and seven-thirty. Approximately.'

Chapter Nineteen

Another day had passed, during which I didn't hear from Matt, while I wondered if the police had made any progress. Leaving the office behind, I walked slowly along the crowded street towards the seafront, stopping at a Costa for a herbal tea.

Taking my drink with me, I crossed the road, then took the steps down onto the beach. Finding a quiet spot on the shingle, I sat down, glad to be alone. Not minding the cold, I gazed at the calm, grey sea, feeling the tang of salt on my skin, assailed by memories. Cradling my tea in both hands, I closed my eyes, remembering another evening, less cold than this, when Matt and I had sat here for hours, long past sunset, until the sky above us glittered with stars. He'd told me how stupid he felt. How he hated letting Amy down, betraying her trust, but he couldn't go on pretending, when it wasn't right between them. Her obsession with her house was just the start of it. Then he'd told me how he could envisage a completely different way of life – with me.

All the time I've known Matt, there's always been Amy, her presence in the background of everything. The woman he didn't love, but who for reasons I could never understand, he put before me. After he disappeared, I couldn't help wondering if, stricken by guilt, he'd decided to take off and spend some time alone. Back then, before I knew more, anything, everything was possible.

I stayed on the beach until the grey sea darkened – as the swell picked up, the cold eating into me – before I got up and started to walk back towards my flat. Though I was tired, restlessness filled me. I even considered calling Amy. I'm not sure why, but on impulse, I'd copied her number from Matt's phone. To hell with maintaining anonymity. But I knew it would have created more problems than it would have solved.

Back home, after a bowl of soup and a couple of glasses of wine, I'd been no less agitated. Switching on my laptop, I'd started going through Matt's social media profiles, something I hadn't done since we first met. Having studied the backgrounds of a large number of acrimonious divorce cases, I'd become adept at identifying what people tried to hide.

On Facebook, his profile photo was unchanged, the same shot of him as when we first met. Staring at it, I'd frowned, wondering if I'd missed something and all along, he really had been spinning me a line. For a moment, doubt had crept in. Two weeks before their wedding was short notice to call it off. Maybe it was me he'd been lying to? Maybe he had no intention of cancelling it.

While previously there'd been certainty, increasingly I was becoming paranoid, as I scrolled through his photos, not knowing what to think, questioning everything. They were the same photos I'd seen before – mostly selfies of Matt, a few of him with other people, with one or two messages about their wedding as it hit me how ridiculous this was. If he wasn't getting married, God only knew why he hadn't told Amy by now. The whole thing was insane. Suddenly nauseous, I'd hurried to the bathroom just in time before being violently sick.

★

I slept fitfully that night, on alert for a call or message from Matt – or even the police; my emotions like a pendulum, swinging back and forth between hope and fear. Still nauseous the next morning, I skipped breakfast. Under pressure, my imagination was in overdrive. On the way to work, I passed a man the same height as Matt on the other side of the road. His hair a similar colour, he had Matt's way of walking. Even his coat was familiar. For a moment my heart hammered, until he turned and I saw a profile that was nothing like Matt's.

Trying to pull myself together, the more I thought about it, the more obvious it was – Amy was key in this. From everything Matt had told me, it was clear her problems had escalated. Maybe even to the point where she'd attacked him.

Chapter Twenty

It hadn't taken long before the police were back in touch –
namely PC Page, who from the start, seemed unnaturally
preoccupied with the case. Or maybe she was more conscien-
tious than most of the police I'd dealt with. When she came
round to see me, she'd got straight to the point.

'We've spoken to David Avery, Matt's employer. He's shared
a list of dates when Matt wasn't at work, which his fiancée
seems unaware of, so obviously . . .'

'You wondered if they were days he spent with me?' My
voice cool, I appraised the list of dates she passed me, astonished
at how each was imprinted on my mind. A lunch that went
on forever, a day in Hastings, the first time he came back to
my flat – and other times since. After checking my diary, I
looked up at her. 'You're right.'

'All of them?'

I checked the list again, then frowned. 'There's one date he
wasn't with me. I was in court that day.' Another memory
indelibly etched. It was one of the rare cases I'd lost.

She frowned. 'You're sure?'

I nodded. 'Absolutely. Why?'

She shook her head. 'A hunch. It seems Matthew Roche has a history of infidelity.' She paused briefly. 'Look, there's no easy way to ask this, so I'll come right out with it. How sure are you that Matt wasn't seeing anyone else?'

'A third woman?' I was incredulous. It hadn't crossed my mind. 'You're suggesting he might have been cheating on me, too?'

'Is it so implausible? He's clearly very skilled at deceiving people – women. The way Ms Reid talks about him, she paints a picture of a couple very much in love, certainly not a man who's having an affair.'

Suddenly I felt hot. 'She would, wouldn't she? If you were her, wouldn't you hate it being public knowledge that your world was falling apart?'

'It's clear there had been other women.' She paused again, thinking. 'Can I ask you another question?' Her eyes bored into me. 'How much do you know about Matt's past?'

I shrugged. 'He often talked about Amy. There was a lot to talk about. Before her, he was with a woman called Mandy. Before that . . .' I felt a frown cross my face as I realised, there was stuff I didn't know, but whenever we'd seen each other, caught up in the moment, there'd never seemed to be enough time. 'We'd only just started. I suppose it takes time to get around to all these things,' I said at last. 'But I honestly don't think he was hiding anything.'

'You can't be sure, though.'

My eyes swivelled to meet hers. It was impossible to answer, but I'd become more adept than most at reading liars. 'Of course not. But because of my job, I'm a fairly astute judge of character and to the best of my knowledge, he was straight with me. There's another possibility you seem to be missing.'

170

I paused briefly. 'Maybe Ms Reid isn't what she makes herself out to be.'

PC Page's frown sharpened. 'What do you mean?'

'Well.' I shrugged. 'You're saying that Matt was adept at deceiving people – which I have to say is a side of him I'm unfamiliar with. Isn't it equally possible that Amy – Ms Reid – is just as adept? I'm a divorce lawyer. I've seen people stoop to all kinds of tactics to get what they want.' When she didn't comment, I went on. 'Have you considered that maybe she knew Matt was seeing me? That when he told her he was leaving, she lost it with him? Maybe she killed him – even by accident. Playing the helpless victim means everyone will think she's the last person in the world capable of hurting him.' Speculating, I had no way of knowing these words would come back to haunt me.

'There's a problem with your theory.' PC Page's voice was quiet. 'And that's proof. Because there is none. Whatever's been going on between Amy and Matt, there's absolutely nothing to suggest that she's a killer.'

I hesitated. 'The most unlikely person can have a past.' The police needed to consider that Amy wasn't the innocent victim she portrayed herself to be.

Her eyes were fixed me. 'What are you suggesting?'

I held her gaze for a moment, then shrugged. 'Nothing in particular.'

'Right now, it's Mr Roche we're more concerned about.' But as she got up, I could see her thinking about what I'd said.

After she'd left, seeds of doubt had taken root. It was impossible to know what to believe. From a lawyer's viewpoint, both Matt and Amy were equally plausible and implausible. If it wasn't for the fact that I knew Matt and trusted him, it would be difficult to call.

I think of another time Matt was talking about Amy. He'd never actually shown me a photo of her. Of course, I'd seen her face flash up on his phone by then, but I couldn't tell him I'd recognised her.

I kept my voice casual. 'I still don't know what Amy looks like. Do you have a photo of her?'

Silently he unlocked his phone, then scrolled through his photos. 'Here.' He passed it to me.

Her looks contradicted everything Matt had said about her. On the screen, Amy's face looked back at me, her fair hair glinting in the sun, no hint of instability in her eyes. Instead, she looked calm, striking, composed, self-possessed. I hand the phone back, hating that I can't tell him what I know about her. How he doesn't know that all this time, Amy's been hiding something from him.

Amy

Chapter Twenty-One

In the back of the police car, I'm in a state of shock until slowly, I start to rationalise what's happening. I've been arrested in connection with Matt's disappearance. It can only mean they've found evidence linking it to me – but what? As the police car drives towards Brighton, I'm numb, the roads and hills I know so well suddenly unfamiliar, my landscape changed forever, as I confront the fact that somehow the police think I'm responsible.

Gazing outside, a feeling of dread hovers over me. Anger too – not just with Matt, but with the police for wrongfully arresting me. But my overwhelming emotion is fear. What if no-one believes me? 'I need to call a lawyer.' The words out before I realise, I don't have one.

Jess. My desperation is stepped up a level as an image of her face flashes into my mind. She'll be devastated. Who will tell her? 'Someone needs to tell Jess.'

Without meeting my eyes, PC Page nods. 'You'll be given the opportunity to make a call once you've been taken into custody.'

Custody. Until now, it's a thought that hasn't even entered my head. But that's what happens when someone's arrested. It's the next step. After taking my fingerprints, I'll be in a cell, like a common criminal. When I'm innocent.

I have to make sure Jess knows – before she hears from someone else. She'll be upset and worried, but she'll know there's been a mistake. Someone needs to go to Falmouth and tell her in person what's happened, protecting her from any backlash. To look after her, until I'm out of here.

Her father, Dominic, is the obvious person to ask, but, lacking in empathy, what will he say to her? Will he make sure she knows I'm innocent? These and a million other questions flash through my head, while a new reality tenuously settles around me.

The police clearly think Matt's disappearance is suspicious. Tears fill my eyes as out of nowhere, that morning in Brighton comes back to me. The woman who stopped me. Her words. *He isn't who you think he is . . . You're in danger. Get away . . . before it's too late.* And now it is too late. Blankly, I stare outside across the misty landscape, as the first raindrops snake down the closed window. Then, utterly powerless, I close my eyes, my thoughts fraying like string.

*

The custody centre has white walls and a cheap blue carpet. Inside, I'm led into a small room where they take my finger-prints and a DNA swab. Forcing myself to stay calm, I tell myself it's only a matter of time before they realise their mistake. Her eyes avoiding mine, PC Page waits with me, while the custody sergeant completes the necessary paperwork, then I'm asked to hand over my personal belongings. When they ask me for my phone, suddenly I realise I haven't brought it with me. 'I need to call someone – a lawyer.'

174

PC Page nods. 'As soon as we've finished the paperwork.'

'This is so fucking ridiculous.' I know I'm not helping myself, but a cocktail of anger and helplessness fuels me as I imagine the police in my home, going through my things, even picking up my phone, scrolling through my calls, putting their own interpretation on my personal messages. As a suspect, even though I'm innocent, I have no privacy. 'I haven't done anything. I shouldn't be here.'

'I understand you're upset.' As PC Page speaks, for a moment, I look for a hint of compassion. But there is none. 'Do you have someone in mind?'

It's the million-dollar question. I've never needed a lawyer before. Shaking my head, I shrug. 'I don't know anyone.'

'We can arrange a solicitor if you need us to.' PC Page's voice is matter of fact. 'This quite often happens.'

Nausea sweeps over me, as I hear myself casually referred to as similar to any other suspect. 'I need a glass of water.'

For the first time I notice another uniformed PC near the door, as PC Page glances towards him. 'Could you fetch a glass of water?'

I'd thought about calling Dominic, but as I think of Jess, I know he isn't the right person to tell her. 'If I'm allowed to make a call, I need to speak to my daughter. She should hear what's happening from me.'

PC Page nods, passing me a phone. Taking it, I start dialling Jess's number with shaking hands, then changing my mind, I call Cath.

★

An hour later, apart from the CCTV camera monitoring the cell I'm being held in, I'm alone. Calling Cath was the right thing to do. When I spoke to her, after she got over the initial shock, she took charge, immediately offering to drive down to Falmouth to see Jess. In Bristol, she's closer to Jess than Dominic is. She'll also be more supportive. I'd imagined Jess's reaction if I called her, the shock that she wouldn't have been able to hide from her fellow students – for all I knew, she might have been in the middle of a lecture. I don't want her painted as the daughter of a suspected criminal, especially when I'm completely innocent.

Knowing Cath will make sure no-one overhears, that she'll protect Jess, is some comfort. On the narrow bed, I wrap my arms tightly around myself, thankful that she is on her way to Jess. At last away from everyone, tears scald my face, as the indignity and injustice of what's happening to me close in.

Only now that it's been taken away do I appreciate the basic liberty that freedom is. As my tears subside, an urgency grips me; to demand to be heard. To be told how long I'm being held here. But then a cold, logical part of me takes hold. The police clearly have enough evidence to convince them I'm a suspect. I have to stay in control, keep my wits about me, in order for them to realise that I'm not.

Sitting in the cell, I scrutinise everything I know about Matt, trying to imagine what someone might have told the police. Maybe something Lara said; what evidence may have been planted, as I take in the unfamiliar sounds around me. Briefly raised voices, the opening and closing of doors, footsteps coming closer, but not close enough, knowing twenty-four hours of this could lie ahead of me, though unless they find evidence that proves my innocence, it could be longer.

If you're suspected of a serious crime, you can be held for up to ninety-six hours. The thought of ninety-six hours feels interminable, as words keep repeating in my head. *Serious crime. Matt. Matt's disappearance.*

Chapter Twenty-Two

Alone, I lose all sense of how much time passes before I'm escorted to the interview room. As I sit at the small table, I imagine those who've sat here before, echoes of their fear, desperation and anger rebounding off the dingy walls. They're tangible, seeping into my skin, then into my blood, tainting me with their crimes; unwanted, when I'm innocent.

Consciously, I steel myself as the solicitor appointed to me, Andrew Nelson, sits down. Short-haired and clean shaven, he wears a middle of the road suit and polished shoes. Catching sight of the time on his expensive watch, I'm shocked to see only two hours have passed.

Across the table from me, PC Page sits beside DI Lacey. 'Amy, I'd like you to tell us what you did the day that Matt disappeared.' There is no trace of her former friendliness. Instead her voice is matter of fact, her blank eyes those of a stranger.

'I drove to Brighton to deliver some orders. Then on my way back to my car, this old woman called after me.' I stop suddenly, frowning. 'I told you about her. I think she was some kind of a clairvoyant – at least, that was what she wanted me to think. She told me that Matt wasn't who I thought he was. Then she told me I was in danger. I dismissed it at the time.' But however implausible it sounds, she was right – about absolutely everything.

'Ms Reid, could you start again from the beginning, and take us through exactly what you did when?' DI Lacey's voice is loud, his eyes boring into me.

I stare at him, my gut feeling kicking in, instantly not liking him. For whatever reason, I sense he wants to find me guilty. Swallowing, I force myself to stay calm. I have to be logical, careful to state my case clearly to him.

'I got up at around seven. Just after Matt.' Already, it feels like a lifetime ago. 'We had breakfast together, then at about eight, he left for work. I did a bit of clearing up and put on some washing . . .' I pause. 'Then I drove to Brighton to deliver two orders.'

'You're a herbalist, I understand?' His voice is questioning. 'But you don't have a shop. Can you tell me exactly what's involved with your work?'

His manner is dismissive, but I'm used to the reaction of people like him, none of whom understand the power of herbs. I meet his eyes. 'I make herbal remedies – tinctures, teas, creams – from herbs and flowers I grow myself. They're organic – more and more people want natural, locally sourced products. I have regular clients and I also supply some local businesses.'

He raises his eyebrows before frowning slightly. 'I understand you told PC Page that you started by treating your daughter's eczema with herbal remedies you made yourself, before studying at college. That was quite a responsibility to undertake. It's a good thing you didn't get it wrong.'

I shake my head, because it's clear he has no idea. 'They were simple treatments. There is a wealth of information available. I used herbs I'd grown myself, so I knew they were pure. I learned what strengths to use, as well as the healing properties of each of them.' I look from one to the other. 'Later, I studied herbalism at college. I have a qualification.'

'What do you grow?' For the first time, he sounds as though he's interested.

'Common or garden herbs that many people grow – rosemary, bay, oregano, mint, lavender, calendula, echinacea, several types of sage. The list goes on.'

'Do you use berries?' He stares at me.

'Sometimes.' I pause. 'Herbalism isn't limited to leaves and flowers. Some preparations use the root and bark and seeds . . .'

'But you said you use berries.' He repeats it too quickly.

I frown. 'That's correct.'

He nods slightly. 'I was just thinking about how many poisonous plants there are out there. It wouldn't be hard would it – if someone wanted to kill a person.'

I stare at him, aghast, then turn to Andrew Nelson. 'I can't answer that. It's like admitting I've done something.' Then I add slightly accusingly, 'I thought you were supposed to be helping me.'

'It isn't a trick question, Ms Reid.' The DI interrupts. 'I'm asking if it would be possible, that's all.'

His words shock me. *Do they think I've poisoned Matt?* 'The whole world knows about plants like deadly nightshade or hemlock, that can kill people. Others can be dangerous and like any reputable herbalist, I'm aware of them.'

'Tell us more about the old woman in Brighton.'

'I was walking through the Lanes – after making a delivery.

On my way back to my car. The first I knew of her was when she called after me.'

PC Page's voice is sharp. 'Can you tell us about her?'

I shake my head. 'I don't know who she was. I'd definitely have remembered her if I'd met her before. She said she had a message for me. I assumed it was to do with Matt.' I shake my head, remembering. 'She told me I wasn't safe. To get away. She said Matt wasn't who I thought he was. Then she told me I was in danger.'

'You give this any credence, Ms Reid?' The DI's eyes are locked on my face.

'Truthfully? I don't know what to think. But after everything that's happened, what she said makes sense.'

'Did it resonate with you at the time? Perhaps tap into any unvoiced suspicions you might have had about Mr Roche?'

Frowning, I shake my head. 'I didn't suspect Matt of anything – not then. At first, I wanted to dismiss what she said as nonsense. But she was insistent.' I pause, thinking. 'It was the same day all of this started.'

'What do you mean?' The DI frowns.

'It was after she stopped me that Matt disappeared.'

The DI sounds mildly irritated. 'Would you say you're the kind of person who believes in clairvoyance?'

Beside me, Andrew Nelson seems to stir into life. 'I'm not sure that question is entirely relevant.'

'Thank you,' I mutter towards him, then turn back to the DI. 'Should I go on?'

'If you would.'

I continue. 'I drove home and carried on working. Later that morning, Matt called me.' My voice wavers. At that point, as far as I knew, our wedding was going ahead. 'He said he was taking an American client out for dinner. He sounded

180

flustered – and apologetic – we were trying to organise the last minute details for our wedding.' My voice wavers again. 'He said he didn't have a choice.' I pause. 'He told me he needed to speak to me later – he didn't say what about. Then he said, *take care babe.*' I look from the DI to PC Page. 'That's when I suspected something was wrong.' Watching the DI's puzzled face, I explain. 'Matt never called me babe. And he never said take care. Not ever. When he called me that morning, something was different.'

'Let me get this straight.' The DI frowns. 'Your fiancé says take care, babe . . . and you interpret that to mean he's in some kind of trouble? He didn't give you any clue as to what it was you needed to talk about?'

'No.' My throat is dry, my voice husky.

'From what we've been told, presumably he was planning to come home and tell you he was leaving you.'

'Maybe.' I stare at the table.

DI Lacey looks confused. 'So what happened next? I've been going through the case notes. With regard to the meeting your fiancé had with an American client – that was later discovered not to be true, wasn't it?'

PC Page leans forward. 'For the record, David Avery, Mr Roche's boss, said there was no American client. Amy knows this.'

I swallow, remembering how alien the call had seemed. 'At the time I had no reason not to believe him.' I stare at him, then at PC Page, because it's true. 'No-one's proved he didn't,' I object. 'It's still possible there's a client nobody knew about.'

'According to our notes, he went for a drink with a work colleague, then spent the rest of the evening with the other woman who reported him missing. It checks out – we've spoken to the colleague who confirms he went to a bar with Matt.

And a cab driver has also confirmed driving Matt to the woman's address. You are aware of this?'

I shake my head. 'I didn't know you'd spoken to Matt's colleague.' But I know about the cab driver. Humiliated by his reminder, I fall silent.

'It's a pity your neighbour isn't alive.' The DI sits back. 'She might have been able to vouch for your whereabouts.'

I nod. 'She would have confirmed what I've told you.' I often used to see her face behind unwashed windows. Then my skin prickles as I realise I've played right into his hands. What if he thinks Mrs Guthrie was murdered? That I had something to do with it? Suddenly nauseous, I'm desperate for the glass of water on the table in front of me, but I'm terrified they'll see my shaking hands. 'If she could actually see,' I add bleakly. 'Her eyesight wasn't good.'

'But she could have seen well enough to notice if your car was there or not.' The DI doesn't give up. 'She noticed a van, didn't she? Quite probably the one that delivered the flowers?'

I nod. 'Yes.'

There's an uneasy silence before he changes the subject. 'So, the last morning you saw Mr Roche, what did you do after you spoke to him?'

'Apart from making a sandwich for lunch, I was in my workshop most of the day.'

'Can anyone vouch for this?'

I shake my head. 'I didn't see anyone – though my neighbours might have noticed my car parked at home.'

'Can you tell us who your clients in Brighton are?'

'Serenity – it's a business in the Lanes.' I watch as PC Page notes it down. 'And Davina Osborne – she works from her home.' I give her Davina's address. 'Both have known

182

me for years. They'll be able to tell you what kind of a person I am.'

He glances at the notes on the table in front of him. 'We have the names of two of your friends – Lara Carmichael and Catherine Bowers. Is that correct?'

'Lara was our wedding planner – Matt had known her for years.' I break off, not sure whether to mention how, in different ways, both of them had let me down. At least Cath is on her way to Jess. At the thought of Jess, tears prick my eyes. Summoning my strength, I pull myself together. 'Cath is my oldest friend.' My voice wavers.

'We've spoken to Lara Carmichael before. She said that your behaviour had become quite unstable, a fact that Mr Roche had also mentioned to her. Latterly, she said you accused her of having an affair with him. Is that correct?'

It's what I'd dreaded her saying. Leaning forward, I rest my head in my hands.

'Ms Reid?'

I look up. 'It's true. I'd just discovered that she and Matt had a fling a while ago – something both of them had hidden from me.'

'Long before the two of you were together, according to Ms Carmichael.' DI Lacey's voice is sharp. 'From which you made the assumption that it must have been her who was the other woman now in his life.'

'After she'd gone, I realised, I'd completely overreacted. It came on the back of Cath telling me that there was an occasion Matt came on to her. I was upset that she'd never told me. Then I found out about Matt and Lara . . . I wasn't thinking straight, but my life has been turned upside down.' I break off. 'All I want is answers, but there aren't any. You must understand why I'd be upset?'

'From what Ms Carmichael said, your reaction was somewhat excessive.' The DI stares at me. 'It sounds like you were having trouble accepting what Mr Roche had done.'

'Maybe I was,' I say bitterly. 'Our wedding was a couple of weeks away when he disappeared. I thought we were going to spend the rest of our lives together. I didn't want to believe he'd betrayed me. I wanted to blame anyone else, other than him.'

DI Lacey doesn't comment. 'What did you do that evening, Ms Reid?'

'After I finished working, I delivered an order to Brighton. It came in at the last minute and the woman sounded desperate, so I agreed to deliver it that evening.'

He nods. 'This was to a house in Brunswick Square, I understand?'

'Yes.'

'What time would that have been?' The DI frowns.

I remember the roads being clear, that it hadn't taken long to get there. 'Around six-thirty, seven o'clock.'

'Can this woman verify what you were doing?'

I stare at him, realising that I haven't told them the whole story. I shake my head. 'When I got there, I realised she'd given me the wrong address. Flat 5, 13 Brunswick Square, doesn't exist. It's a heritage centre.'

The DI's frown deepens. 'You're saying you made a mistake?'

'I don't think so.' I hesitate. 'It was definitely the address in the email she sent me. I emailed her again, asking her to confirm it, but when she replied, she cancelled the order – something to do with her husband not liking the idea of herbal remedies.'

'How convenient.' The DI folds his arms. 'So you never saw her and the address doesn't exist. Correct?'

'That's true.' I stare at him. 'Why?'

But he ignores me. 'Can you tell us what you did after that?'

'I drove home. When I got back, I went upstairs to change.' I pause, remembering the events of that evening. 'I picked up on an unfamiliar scent. It was faint. It definitely wasn't anything I recognised. Then I went downstairs, checked my emails, looked at the seating plan Lara had sent over.' As I mention Lara's name in conjunction with the seating plan, I feel naïve that I never suspected anything. 'I spoke to Cath. That was about it.'

'What time did you speak to her?'

I look at him incredulously. 'I can't remember. Maybe around ten.'

'You didn't speak to anyone else after that?'

'No.' I'm frowning.

'Or go out again?'

'No.' My frown deepens. 'Like I said, I was in Brighton early evening, but I didn't go out again after that.'

In his chair, the DI pulls himself upright. 'Even if you were at home when you phoned your friend at ten, you would have had plenty of time to drive to Brighton. You didn't believe Mr Roche, did you, when he told you he was having dinner with a client? You'd done your homework. You knew exactly where he was going and who he was meeting. You knew where she lived, too. That so-called order gave you the perfect excuse to be in Brighton. The delivery address was convenient too, only a street away from where Mr Roche would have been. Parking out of sight, I think that after allegedly trying to make your delivery, you hung around that evening, watching him go into the woman's flat, then waiting for him to come out again. In that time, you spoke to your friend. She'd never have been able to tell you weren't at home. Then Mr Roche came out of the flat and there you were. Knowing all that time he'd been with the woman, I can guess how you must have felt. Angry wouldn't begin to describe it, would it? I imagine he got in the car with you to avoid a scene. Then you drove home, where you had the mother of all rows, which ended up with you losing control, maybe even attacking him.'

'No . . .' I'm shaking my head, stunned. 'That's wrong. None of that happened.' Then realising the futility of trying to argue with them, I'm silent. But it's like with everything I've told them. I can't prove any of it is true.

Chapter Twenty-Three

After the interview is over, I'm led back to my cell. Standing just inside, as the door is locked behind me, the phrase *innocent until proven guilty* comes to mind. But in the eyes of the police, I'm not innocent.

Fear fills me that I'll never get out of here, while I wonder if Cath has reached Falmouth and talked to Jess. As I think of my daughter, I'm filled with a new sense of urgency. Getting up, I press the call button. When no-one responds, I press it again as a disembodied voice comes through. I interrupt it.

'I need to talk to PC Page.'

But at the other end, there's silence. Filled with frustration, I wait.

★

An hour passes, in which my mind runs wild with possibilities. By the time I'm led back to the interview room, I know exactly what I'm going to say. When I go in, Andrew Nelson, my solicitor, is waiting for me.

'Do you really think the police believe I'm a suspect?' I speak quickly. 'Or where are they going with this? If they don't have evidence, they can't keep me here, can they?'

'If they have reasonable grounds, they can hold you for up to twenty-four hours – but it could be longer. I will query them.' Hearing footsteps outside, he nods towards the door. 'That's them. Let's see what they have to say.'

'Please . . .' I mutter desperately. 'Do anything. Just get me out of here.'

But as the door opens, he looks at me awkwardly. DI Lacey and PC Page walk in. Without any preamble, they start the tape.

'Can I say something?' They have to realise that I'm the one person who can help them. I take a deep breath. 'I'm the last person who should be considered a suspect. I don't know why you think I'm connected to his disappearance, but I can assure you, I'm not. I know Matt better than anyone. If you were to tell me exactly what you think's happened to him, I might be able to help you.'

'Ms Reid, that's exactly why we have brought you here.' DI Lacey glances at PC Page. 'To help us with our enquiries.'

'Yes, but I still don't know why you've arrested me,' I say agitatedly.

But he ignores me. 'Ms Reid, can you tell us what happened the following morning? By which time twenty-four hours would have passed since you'd last seen Mr Roche – that's correct, isn't it?'

'Yes. When I woke up, I tried him several times. Then I had another delivery to make – to Brighton, again. I drove to my client's house, then on the way home, I kept trying Matt, but there was no reply. After that, I called his office, where I left a message with the receptionist.' I try to think back. 'That was when I first spoke to you.' I look at PC Page. 'I kept calling his mobile all morning, then my friend – Cath – turned up at lunchtime.' So much has happened, I'd forgotten Cath turning up that day. 'We'd arranged to have lunch – before Matt disappeared.'

'This would be Cath Bowers?'

I nod, then frown. 'If anyone can tell you how happy Matt and I were, it's Cath. She commented on it, only recently.'

'This is the same Cath who you told us Matt tried it on with?' PC Page looks disbelievingly at me. She glances at the DI. 'I'll talk to her.'

'I believe her when she said nothing happened between them. She told him where to go. It was a one-off that he never repeated – at least, that's what she told me.' I look at the DI. 'She knew how happy I was. She didn't want to ruin it.'

'Ms Reid,' the DI pauses. 'After the conversation with PC Page, what did you do for the rest of the afternoon?'

'I went for a walk.' I remember the damp, the swirling wind when I reached the top of the hills; coming home as dusk was falling. 'Then when I got back, there was a bouquet of flowers on the doorstep.'

'Go on.'

'I took them inside. It was a big bouquet. I assumed it was from Matt. I didn't unwrap them straight away. At some point they fell over.' As I relive the moment, nausea rises in my throat. 'You know those bags of water bouquets are delivered in?' I watch him frown slightly. 'They're hidden beneath the paper wrapping, tied around the stems – to keep the flowers fresh. Only . . .' I hesitate. 'It wasn't water in the bag. It was blood.'

189

Chapter Twenty-Four

'Do you have any idea who might have sent the flowers, Ms Reid?' Across the table, DI Lacey is a formidable presence.

'No.' I shake my head.

'Then there's the card. The quotation, if that's what it is. *Kill one man and you are a murderer.* Does that mean anything to you?'

Again, I shake my head. 'No.'

'According to our records, after you called PC Page, she came over and collected a sample of the blood. We sent it away and the results have come back. It was human blood – type B positive. Not one of the more common types, but it turns out it's the same type as Mr Roche. He used to give blood.'

Shocked, my hands go to my mouth, at the possibility that the blood could have been Matt's.

PC Page frowns at me. Then she stares at me intently. 'You didn't know, did you? That he used to give blood?'

Suddenly, I feel trapped. 'Of course I did. Matt and I told each other everything.' Worn down by their seeming suspiciousness of everything I say, the lie slips out.

'I think we all know quite categorically that isn't the case.' DI Lacey sounds disparaging. 'It's here in black and white – in the case notes.' He pauses a moment. And I know it's coming – the million-dollar question. 'When did you find out your fiancé was having an affair?'

I look at him, not sure who he's talking about. 'Are you talking about Lara?'

'I hardly think a fling, which happened before you and Mr Roche met, constitutes an affair.' DI Lacey looks irritated.

I sit there, and a rush of blood surges to my face, because surely they know this. 'When PC Page told me.'

DI Lacey looks at me suspiciously. 'You genuinely had no idea before then?'

'You don't understand.' Blinking away the tears suddenly filling my eyes, I gaze at PC Page. 'If there were warning signs, I didn't see them, but I wasn't looking for them. Our wedding was two weeks away. My dress was upstairs. We'd written our vows . . . I thought we were happy.' I tail off. Every word is true. 'When he first disappeared, I suppose I was hoping there was an understandable reason. It was before I knew about Lara – and Cath. Obviously, now, the reality has sunk in.' Sipping my water, I try to work out how to explain how I felt. 'No-one is perfect.' I hold her gaze. 'If he had come back, I would have forgiven him. If you're lucky enough to meet that person you love with all your heart, don't you think you would make allowances for that? Yes, there might have been reasons for what he'd done, if other people had screwed him over, or things had happened in the past that meant now and then he made an error of judgement.' I pause for a moment. 'Everyone makes mistakes. I suppose it all comes down to one thing – how much you love.'

'I honestly don't get it.' PC Page looks at me blankly, but I already know. She's never loved the way I have. If she had, she'd be able to understand.

'That's how I felt,' I say simply, looking at them both.

'You say the two of you had written your own vows? Where are they?' DI Lacey frowns at me.

'Mine were on my laptop, but I've deleted the folder.' Remembering the day of the bonfire, when I'd printed them off, then burned them with my dress, I shake my head. 'Matt printed out his vows before he disappeared. I've looked for the piece of paper since then, but I couldn't find it. The only person who might have a copy is Lara.'

'What did you write, Ms Reid?'

At what seems the ultimate invasion of my privacy, I feel myself tense. 'I can't remember, word for word.' There's no way I'm repeating words written for our wedding in here, in front of them. My voice wavers as I go on. 'I can't bear much more of this. My fiancé's betrayed me. No-one knows where he is and the life we were looking forward to has been ripped away . . . And now, I've been wrongly arrested.' With tears pouring down my cheeks, I reach into my pocket and pull out a tissue, before turning to my solicitor. 'I need a few minutes.'

'My client would like a short break.' Beside me, Andrew Nelson sounds nervous.

'Very well.' Pushing his chair back, DI Lacey gets to his feet, then checks his watch. 'Five minutes, Ms Reid. Then we'll continue.'

Once DI Lacey and PC Page have left us alone, Andrew Nelson gets up and walks across the room. After a few minutes, he turns back to me. 'I don't understand.' He frowns. 'How you had absolutely no idea anything was wrong.'

I look at him, remembering how I'd felt when I found out. 'When you love someone, it's the last thing you expect. Can't you see that? And I would have forgiven him at the beginning. I thought if he loved me enough, we could have left it in the past. I loved Matt.'

'There are limits, though, surely?' He sounds disbelieving. 'When you knew he was seeing someone else, a woman he was allegedly leaving you for.'

'That was where I had to draw the line.' But I shake my head slowly, because I don't think he gets it. Not everyone knows how many kinds of love there really are. I know *his* kind – the kind that comes with conditions. A one-sided trade-off – *I love you as long as you meet my expectations of what love should be.* 'Have you ever loved someone so totally that you'd do anything for them?'

The look of bewilderment crossing his face, as he shakes his head, tells me he hasn't. But I hadn't either. It was only when Matt and I met that everything changed. And changed again, when he betrayed me. 'That's how it was,' I say briefly. 'But not now.'

'And you have no idea who might have sent you those flowers?' Andrew Nelson has an expression of distaste on his face.

I shake my head. 'I can't think of anyone.' Then I'm thinking of the blood again. 'It was horrible.' My voice is suddenly quiet. 'The flowers, I mean. To think it was human blood, too.' Possibly Matt's. I fix my eyes on Andrew Nelson. 'You have to find out what evidence they have against me.'

*

The interview is terminated early when PC Page gets called away to a traffic accident. It's then that I realise I might be spending a night here. I wonder if the police are at my house – what they're looking for, what they've found. If they're searching through drawers and cupboards, rifling through

194

private messages on my phone. Having never bothered to lock it, I've made it easy for them. Then I think of the garden. The flowers and herbs I've nurtured, knowing the police won't care if they damage them.

Exhausted, every fibre of my being craves a hot bath, the comfort of my own bed, while I try to stem the relentless flow of thoughts through my mind, imagining what evidence the police have. Lying back on the narrow bed, I gaze at the ceiling.

Slowly I'm realising how much has changed since Matt went missing. At the start, if he'd come back, even if I'd had the chance, I wouldn't have confronted him. Already that seems unbelievable, but the Amy I used to be would still have been holding on to everything we'd dreamed of, terrified of losing it. Only now he's gone can I admit the truth, if only to myself, about the other side of Matt. One I don't like to think about. One I've never talked about, to anyone.

1996

Your efforts were futile, because there was no-one else for Kimberley or Charlie. They wanted to live together, wherever that was going to be. Forever. You didn't know they were planning to go to the same uni, that they wanted to live in a modern apartment in Brighton or a warehouse flat in London. They had it all mapped out. Holidays around the world, three kids. They'd work hard, then retire early while they were still young enough to live.

But they could never have told you that. They knew how you felt, though, your jealousy a noxious, foetid cloud that followed you, its odour pervading everything that surrounded you. You couldn't bear that Kimberley loved Charlie. Not when you wanted him for yourself. But you didn't love him. People like you don't love. It was about possession. Obsession. Control.

It consumed you, didn't it? While the plan in your head grew bolder. Enough for you to commit one deadly act that tipped the scales, consciousness becoming intoxicated, innocence turning to evil, as you stopped at nothing; destroying a life you decided was simply dispensable.

Starting a ripple effect that even now, hasn't stopped.

Jess

When I open my bedsit door and see Cath standing there, I instantly know something's wrong. 'Oh God.' My heart misses a beat as I start to panic. 'What's happened? Where's Mum?'

Cath's voice is low. 'Let me come in, hun.'

'You have to tell me.' Fearing the worst, my voice is hysterical, my head filled with all kinds of terrible scenarios.

Squeezing past me and closing the door, she turns to face me, both her hands grasping my arms. 'Listen, Jess. Your mum's OK. But the police have arrested her.' She pauses. 'In connection with Matt's disappearance.'

Shocked into silence, my mind is racing as I shake my head. 'No.' I stare at Cath. There's been a mistake. It can't be happening, not to my mother. 'When? Where is she?'

'I don't know any details. She has a lawyer, but the police are holding her in custody in Brighton. They must think they have proof that she's involved, otherwise they couldn't have arrested her, but I've no idea what it is.'

Already I'm hurrying around my room, gathering a few clothes into a bag. 'I have to go there. Oh my God . . . *Poor*

Mum . . .' After what Matt's done to her, now this. 'How can they even think that?' Tears blur my eyes as I stare at Cath. 'I need to go there. Now.'

She's nodding. 'I thought you would. And it's OK. I'll take you.'

'You're sure?' I follow her gaze to where she's staring across my room.

'What are those?'

She's looking at the montage of images I've printed off and crudely stuck on a section of wall. 'I started looking into Matt's past. I don't trust him. I never did. There's too much that doesn't ring true.'

Cath frowns. 'Like what?'

'He never talked about his life before he met Mum – other than the woman he was with before her. I started going through his Facebook friends – and their friends. His Facebook is weird – it's only been going about three years. He's always with rich-looking women, but never for very long. I'm sure he was up to something. I need to find out to help Mum.' A sense of urgency grips me. 'Do you think we could leave now? I need to get to Mum.' I glance around the room, checking I haven't forgotten anything important. 'Have you spoken to her?'

Cath nods. 'Briefly. It was she who asked me to come here and tell you. I said that if you wanted me to, I'd take you home with me, but I thought you'd want to go to Sussex. There must have been a mistake. We have to believe that, Jess. I can't believe she could have done anything wrong.'

'But the police must think she has.' My eyes are wide as I stare at her. 'What has she actually been arrested for?'

'I think in connection with his disappearance. Presumably that means they're still investigating.'

Anguish fills me, as I think of everything she's been through.

'Mum hasn't been herself. Not since she met Matt. He's a shit. Sorry . . . But he is.'

'I know he is.' Cath shakes her head. 'He had me fooled at the start, though. And he completely fooled your mum. She always told me how happy she was.'

'I think they were happy – at the start.' I stare at Cath. 'Why else would they have been together? It's why I put up with him. But he could be horrible to her. Cruel. And before he disappeared, it was like he hated her.'

'I have an idea how these things work.' Cath frowns. 'After all, I stayed with Oliver, letting him drag me down, when I should have moved out months ago. But I never imagined it happening to your mum.'

'There's something else.' I glance back to the montage of Facebook pictures stuck to my wall. 'It's creepy. All these friends of his – they're connected. Each connection brought him closer to Mum – until that party where they met. By then, they knew a whole load of people in the same circle. I actually watched him make his move that day. And the rest is history.'

'But why?' Cath looks mystified.

I shake my head. 'That's the bit I haven't been able to work out yet.'

★

As we leave Falmouth behind, the leaden skies lighten, but only slightly. It's one of those days that knows only half-light, the drive seeming endless, while my brain tries to pull together the little I know and make sense of it. On the way, I text Rik, wanting him to know what I'm doing. *Something's going on with Mum. I'm on my way home. I'll call you and fill you in later xxxx*

The further east we drive, the busier the roads become. The

closer we get to Brighton, the longer the journey seeming to take; my frustration building as roadworks mean the city centre is gridlocked.

Gazing out of the window, even the sea is different here, the same steel shade as the sky. Our speed reduced to a crawl, I wish none of this was happening; that Mum was at home and I was back in Cornwall – my hatred for Matt growing with every minute.

Eventually we reach the custody centre. As Cath turns into the car park, I'm nervous suddenly, my stomach knotting up as she finds a parking space. As we go inside, the custody sergeant looks up from behind a desk.

'I'm Jess Reid. You have my mother here – Amy Reid. I want to see her.'

He nods towards a few chairs set in a corner by a window. 'Can you take a seat over there?'

As Cath and I do as he says, she looks at me anxiously. 'You OK, Jess?'

'Yes.' There's no point in saying I'm anything else. But how can I be, when I'm here instead of in Falmouth, with my mother being held on suspicion of committing a crime. It's nothing other than a living nightmare.

Only a few minutes pass before a policewoman walks over to us. Instantly, I recognise her. 'Hello, Jess. I'm PC Page. We spoke before, at your house.' Questioningly, she turns to Cath.

'I'm Cath Bowers. We spoke on the phone.'

A flicker of recognition crosses the policewoman's face. 'Yes, of course.' She turns back to me. 'Before you talk to your mother, do you think you and I could have a chat?' She glances around as if looking for somewhere.

Not sure I have a choice, I shrug. 'OK.'

'Would you like me to come with you?' Beside me, Cath sounds uncertain.

I shake my head. 'I'll be OK.'

'Right. Shall we find somewhere quieter?' As PC Page starts to walk along a corridor, I follow behind, then she shows me into a small room, with white painted walls and a small window. 'We shouldn't get disturbed in here. Have a seat, Jess.'

The plastic chairs remind me of uni classrooms. Pulling one out across a table, I sit down opposite her. After organising the papers she's holding, she gets out a pen, then looks at me. 'I know we talked before, just after Mr Roche disappeared, but I wanted to ask you more about his relationship with your mother. Can you describe how they were together? From the beginning?'

I try to cast my mind back to a time when my views were untainted, to when Matt was new in our lives. When my mother was the same as she'd always been – before I'd noticed things change. 'They seemed happy together, to start with. He used to pick her up and take her out for dinner. But after he moved in, I missed quite a lot of what went on because I started uni. She never said anything to me, but when I came back that first Christmas, things seemed different.'

'In what way?'

I try to work out how best to explain it. 'Her excitement had definitely gone. It was like they'd skipped a couple of decades and had turned into a middle-aged couple who sniped at each other. Except . . .'

'Go on,' she says quietly.

'It was always Matt who did the sniping, like she irritated him. It was like he looked for reasons to criticise her. It didn't make sense, because they were still planning to get married.

My mother almost seemed blind to it. She was convinced he loved her. She was always saying love was about compromise.' I pause, knowing I should have seen how bad things had got, how warped her perception had become.

'This is difficult to ask . . .' PC Page hesitates. 'Your mother seems fragile. In the circumstances, it's understandable – the events since his disappearance have clearly caused her immense distress, let alone anything else. I didn't know if she'd had problems in the past?'

I hesitate, not wanting to say the wrong thing. 'I know she suffered from depression – a long time ago. But she did tell me she'd recently been seeing her therapist again.'

PC Page's pen hovers above her notebook. 'Do you happen to know her name?'

'Sonia.' I stare at her as she starts writing it down. 'Sonia Richardson.' Adding more urgently, 'Will you talk to her? She'll be able to vouch for the kind of person Mum really is.'

For a moment, PC Page doesn't reply. 'Was it depression that led your mother to start seeing her the first time?'

I shake my head. 'I'm not sure. It was when I was quite a bit younger. It may have been, but Sonia would be able to tell you. I think it was after my dad left her.' I watch as she makes another note.

A frown appears on her face. 'There's another thing I wanted to ask you about your mother, because I'm not sure Mr Roche hasn't been playing mind games with her.'

'That's exactly what he does,' I say angrily, feeling my hands curl into fists, relieved she understands. 'We've been studying psychopathic behaviour at uni. He ticks all the boxes. Matt definitely plays – or played with her head, I'm sure of it.' An example comes back to me, which at the time, I hadn't known what to make of. 'It happened when they started planning their

204

wedding. Mum had this dream of getting married on a beach and Matt had completely gone along with it – or at least, that was what she told me. She and I went dress shopping and bought the perfect dresses for a beach wedding – without shoes, because we were going to be barefoot . . . Mum had it all planned out. She was so excited, but when she told him, he convinced her they'd discussed it the night before and changed their minds. He couldn't believe she'd *forgotten*.' I shake my head. I hadn't been able to work out if he was making it up or if she really had forgotten. 'She was sure she'd provisionally booked it. She said they'd confirmed over email, but when she went to check, the emails weren't there.'

'It hardly seems likely she'd have forgotten a conversation about their wedding.' PC Page frowns. 'The only other explanation is that he deliberately deceived her.' She pauses for a moment, looking thoughtful. 'Actually, there's a name for this sort of behaviour, where someone is consistently undermined until they reach a point where they question their own sanity.'

'What is it?' I ask her. 'Because that describes exactly what he's been doing to her.'

'Gaslighting.' She looks at me. 'It looks as though Matt's been gaslighting your mother.' Sitting back, she speaks quietly. 'It explains so much about how she's behaved and what she's said to us about him. It's a form of emotional abuse. A constant wearing down as a means of control. Psychopaths are often very smooth operators. From what you've told me, it sounds as though Matt would have known exactly what he was doing to her.'

As she speaks, I feel myself shiver, thinking of the way Matt used to talk to my mother. It wasn't just his words, but the way he used them – to manipulate. Like when I learned about Walker's cycle of violence in one of my uni lectures. About the build–up, explosion, remorse, denial, that keep people caught in relationships they'll never leave. The way love breaks down, becoming abuse, leading to unimaginable consequences. My eyes stare into hers. 'I'm sure he knew what he was doing. Sometimes, it was like he wanted me to share the joke, behind her back. Except there was no joke.'

'For whatever reason, it seems you managed to see through him when your mother couldn't.' PC Page shakes her head.

Mystified, I nod. 'But it still doesn't explain why he was doing it.'

PC Page shrugs. 'It can be unconscious. A defence strategy, to prevent emotional intimacy. But given what we know about Matt, I'd say he was up to something.'

'I think it was deliberate. There's more you may not know,' I tell her quickly. 'I've been looking at his Facebook profile. To start with, I thought he was targeting women who had money. I've been reading about men who do that kind of thing. Anyway, right from the start, he's tried to persuade my mother to sell her house and she really doesn't want to. It's caused so many rows between them. Sometimes, he wouldn't speak to her for days. But he never gave up.'

PC Page looks confused. 'Do you know why she was so determined to hang on to it?'

'It was her home.' I shrug. 'It's taken years to get the garden the way she needs it – for work. I think Matt wanted to get his hands on her money. I've been studying his Facebook friends and the way they're connected. I'm fairly sure that for some time before they were together, he was building a network, making it easy for them to meet.'

PC Page frowns again. 'That sounds incredibly contrived. Can you prove anything?'

It docs sound unlikely, unless you've seen what I've seen. 'I can show you what I've found, but that's the trouble.' I fold my arms. 'I'm still looking, but so far, other than money, I can't find any other reason.'

PC Page looks thoughtful. 'Where are you going when you leave here?'

'Home. Cath said she'd stay tonight.'

PC Page shakes her head. 'I'm afraid you won't be able to go back to the house. It's been taped off. Sorry, Jess, but it's a potential crime scene.'

It's a blow I hadn't been expecting. 'Where do I go?' I look at her helplessly. It was the thought of home that kept me going as we were driving here. I don't have anywhere else.

'Maybe Cath will know somewhere you can stay. I'll come with you and explain to her.' She pauses. 'Jess, can we talk again tomorrow? I'd be interested to see what it is you've found on Facebook.'

'OK.' I hesitate, then blurt it out, the only question that really matters. 'When are you letting her go? My mother? She hasn't done anything.'

'I'm sorry, but right now, I don't have the answer to that. It depends on all kinds of things.'

But I need to know how they can go on holding her. 'You must think you have evidence. You need to tell me what it is.'

'I'm afraid I can't discuss any more with you.' She sounds brusque suddenly. 'We'll talk tomorrow. Come on. I'll walk with you back to Cath, then we'll find someone to take you to see your mother.'

*

After finding out about the house being taped off, Cath doesn't seem surprised. 'I had wondered. Don't worry. I've a friend we

207

can stay with, Jess. I'll call her while you're talking to your mum.'

'OK, Jess?' PC Page looks at me. When I nod, she adds, 'I'll find someone to take you to see her.'

A few minutes later, we're approached by a uniformed officer who doesn't look much older than I am. Then at last I get to talk to my mother. After following him through double doors, he leads me along a different corridor into another small room, where I wait a couple of minutes, until my mother comes in.

She looks grey, defeated, her eyes anxious. As I hug her, tears fill my eyes, a new determination gripping me to do whatever it takes to prove her innocence. 'Mum . . . it will be OK. I know you haven't done anything. We'll get you out of here.' As we sit at the small table, seeing her eyes fill with tears, I lean forward, lowering my voice. 'Matt was after something. I thought it was your house, so that he could sell it, but I'm not sure now. But I've told the police.'

As I mention the police, her expression changes to one of alarm. 'No,' she whispers. 'I don't want them to start digging around.'

'It will be OK.' I try to reassure her, wondering why she's so agitated. 'Try not to worry.'

Clearly upset, she bites her lip. 'Is Cath with you?'

I nod. 'She's waiting outside. Mum, I'm just trying to think why anyone would want to hurt you – or Matt. Is there anything you can think of that's happened? Anything at all?' I pause. 'There has to be someone from his past – or maybe this other woman? It could be, couldn't it? If she was jealous enough?'

For a moment I think she's going to say something, but then what little colour her face has drains away, leaving her swamped with an air of hopelessness. Resting her hand on my arm, she shakes her head. 'You shouldn't have come here, Jess. I can't bear you seeing me like this. You should go and find Cath.'

As she speaks, instinct tells me she's hiding something. Then a terrifying thought occurs to me, that maybe she knows what happened to Matt. But before I can protest, she gets up and walks over to the officer at the back of the room, waiting for him to open the door and close it behind her, leaving me alone.

Amy

Chapter Twenty-Five

Seeing Jess leaves me stricken with pain and heartache, hating that she's been dragged into a place where common criminals are held. She should be carefree, living her own life at uni, studying the subject she's passionate about, being with her friends. She belongs outside, by the sea, the wind in her hair, her lungs filled with salty air.

My heart bursts to see her, the same heart that breaks when she goes. It's me who asks to go back to my cell, imagining Jess leaving with Cath. Grateful that she has someone supportive rather than her father, who wouldn't be able to give her what she needs.

Back in my cell, the long night stretches ahead of me. It offers too much time, mentally allowing me to go over all that's happened since Matt and I met. My initial reticence, before he won me over. It seems impossible to think he was the same person who'd reminded me how good it was to enjoy life, to have fun. To feel attractive again.

When he moved in, he seemed so different. I'd looked forward to there being someone with whom to share day to day life, especially with Jess about to go away. But it hadn't taken long before I'd seen another side to him. The first time he lost his temper, I'd been taken aback by the force of it. Profuse apologies had followed. Warily, I'd listened, believing him when he told me what a strain he'd been under, prepared to forgive and forget almost anything. But from that point on, it seemed that more and more of what I did was wrong in his eyes, his outbursts perfectly timed so that Jess never got wind of them. There had been another scene – most likely the one Lara referred to, a week before he disappeared. Ratcheting things up to another level, he hit me.

The blow to my stomach had knocked the breath out of me, leaving me slumped on the floor, doubled up in pain as I waited for the next. I'd wanted to tell PC Page, back at the beginning. But fear prevented me. Fear of what Matt might do, if he came back and discovered I'd told them. My bruises were hidden. I was afraid of the police, too. What if they didn't believe me? Or saw it as a motive, twisting the truth to use against me?

A month before he disappeared, there was another day that stands out for all the wrong reasons. The day everything moved to another level. Matt had come home from work, earlier than usual. After closing the front door, instead of coming to find me in the kitchen, he went straight upstairs. Almost immediately, I could hear drawers being opened and closed, the pad of his feet as he went through to the spare room; the sound of wardrobe doors being opened and closed. I remember my skin prickling with goosebumps. Then silence.

Tiptoeing to the bottom of the stairs, I'd called up. 'Matt? Honey, are you OK?' When he didn't reply, a feeling came over me that I couldn't describe. I tried again. 'Matt. Are you there?' The bottom two stairs creaked as I started to make my way up, then at the top, Matt appeared from one of the bedrooms.

'Amy. I assumed you were in the workshop. I came home early. I wasn't feeling well.' His annoyance obvious, his eyes didn't meet mine.

'Are you OK? Can I get you anything?' As I carried on up the stairs, he stepped forward.

'I'm fine. I'm coming down in a minute.' His voice sharp, his behaviour was strange, too, with no explanation as to why he was going through drawers and cupboards.

'I just want to make sure you're alright.'

As he spoke through gritted teeth, I shrank back. 'Amy, get the fuck away from me. I want some quiet. Leave me, OK?'

Not wanting to upset him further, I did as he asked. But there was something about the expression on his face. As he headed back towards our bedroom, I hurried up the rest of the stairs, but before I could get there, he spun around and stood in the doorway, blocking it.

'What's going on?' My heart was fluttering, my stomach twisting as I took in the look in his eyes. Then I glanced past him, at the piles of clothes on our bed, feeling the blood drain from my face. 'What are you doing, Matt?'

For a moment, he didn't speak. 'I'm looking for something.' His voice was icy. 'A jumper. Now for Christ's sake, leave me in peace.'

'Which one? Maybe I can help.' I was trying to sound calm when inside I was anything but, desperate to know what he was hiding from me.

This time he shouted. 'You can help by leaving me to get on with this. Fucking hell, Amy. Just go downstairs.'

Numb, I shook my head. 'I can't.' A frantic whisper, my plea for this to be anything other than what it looked like. 'What were you doing in the spare room?' Turning, I started to walk towards it, when I felt Matt painfully wrench my arm, pulling me away. But not before I'd seen an open suitcase piled with clothes.

★

By the time I'm next interviewed by the police, I've decided to tell them about that episode. As I'm escorted back to the interview room, I've rehearsed in my head what I want to say. When PC Page and DI Lacey come in, before either of them speaks, I take a deep breath. 'There's something I should tell you about.' Seeing both of them looking at me intently, I go on, as they start the tape. 'I should have mentioned it before, but Matt didn't always treat me well.' My voice shakes slightly. 'I wasn't intentionally hiding anything, it's more that it didn't seem relevant. I suppose I wanted so badly to believe everything was OK between us. I didn't want to admit that anything was wrong. Once you do, even to yourself, you have to do something about it. And I didn't feel strong enough to face that.'

PC Page frowns at me. 'When you've gone to such pains to say what a great relationship you had, even with evidence to the contrary, it's quite a surprise to hear you admit it was anything but.'

Resigned, I shake my head. 'It was a good relationship – at the start. But more recently, Matt would hurt me. When I first spoke to you, I was worried that if he found out what I'd been saying about him, he'd hurt me again.'

DI Lacey interrupts. 'Ms Reid, from what we've learned about Mr Roche, his behaviour can only be described as intimidating and bullying. It's hardly what most people would call a great relationship. So what happened on that day you were going to tell us about?'

'He came home early from work and went upstairs. I heard

him opening and closing drawers.' My voice shakes. 'When I went up to see what he was doing, there was a suitcase he didn't want me to see. But they weren't his clothes he was packing.' Remembering, I shake my head. 'They were mine.'

PC Page stares at me. 'Why on earth would he have been packing your clothes?'

Forcing myself to focus on the table, I try to keep my voice steady as I go on. 'He said he'd arranged for me to go and stay somewhere. Just for a while. Apparently, he was worried about me . . .' I break off. 'Matt was always so considerate. He'd thought of everything, you know.' My words are laden with sarcasm. 'He'd even timed it to perfection so that Jess would never know. He told me I had problems, so he was doing what he could to help me.'

'Ms Reid, I'm not sure what you're saying.' DI Lacey's voice cuts into the silence. 'Had you seen a doctor?'

I shake my head. 'He said I didn't need to. He'd found somewhere for me to go. He was paying for it. Somewhere I could rest and get help.'

'Did you go?' The DI frowns.

'Yes.' I pause. He hadn't given me a choice. 'He said that if I didn't, it proved I wasn't as invested in our relationship as he was.' It had been a small private hospital that had felt like a prison. 'He said my problems were the reason things weren't right between us. Apparently I didn't think straight, especially when it came to my house. He kept trying to push me to sell it – he said it didn't make sense that I wouldn't. But he didn't understand.'

'What didn't he understand, Amy?' PC Page's voice is low.

'I can't leave that house.' I look at them both.

'You've said this once before. Why can't you?' PC Page's face seems to loom towards me.

'It's the only thing I have. And my business relies on it. It's just as well I didn't sell, now that he isn't here.' Suddenly I'm lightheaded. Then as the room starts to spin, I grip the edge of the table, trying to focus.

'Have some water.' A hand pushes a glass into one of mine. As I drink, my vision starts to clear. 'I'm sorry. This happens sometimes. One of the many things Matt thought I needed help with.' It's another lie, but a plausible one. I'm risking giving them a motive, but I need them to know how erratic Matt would be. I'm trying my hardest to sound in control. But I'm wishing they'd stop asking questions, because yet again, I haven't told the police everything.

★

It's only when I'm alone in my cell that I allow my mind to confront what followed.

'Why are you packing, Matt?'

He looked coldly at me. 'You're going to stay somewhere for a while. They can look after you. I can't do it any more. I've spoken to the staff and told them about your behaviour. You refuse to see a doctor, you refuse to talk to a shrink. It's irrational.' Breaking off, he punched the wall. 'If you really want to know, each day you're on your own, I'm worried you're going to kill yourself.'

'That isn't true.' Shocked, I stared at him. I had no idea where this was coming from. 'And I'm not on my own, Matt. I have you.'

'Amy . . .' There was anger in his voice. 'It's too much to expect me to go on like this. That's the whole point.' Taking a breath, he spoke more calmly. 'If you were in your right mind, you'd know it's what you need to do.'

216

'But I'm fine.' I looked at him, bewildered. 'I really don't need to go anywhere.'

'You don't get it, do you?' His expressionless eyes gave nothing away. 'You don't know anything. It's like living on a knife edge where either I give you what you want, or you lose your temper and I'm forced to suffer the consequences. You don't love me, Amy. You love the idea of me, slotting into your twisted little vision of how life's meant to be.'

I remember flinching away from him, then hunching over, as if protecting myself from his cruelty, shielding myself from the sting of his words. 'Don't,' I sobbed, turning, heading down the stairs. Feeling my legs give way, I stumbled over to the sliding doors, then opened them and walked into the garden.

Outside, I'd gulped air as if I couldn't breathe, as if the pain itself was suffocating me. Everything he'd said, all of it was backwards, every word. It was me who was perpetually on the knife edge. Me who had to slot into *his* world. Pain enveloped me, before I did what I always did and blanked it out.

'Amy.' Matt's voice came from behind me.

'Don't.' I cried out. 'Get away from me.' As I started heading across the garden, I heard him behind me.

'Amy, wait. Don't do something you'll regret . . .' Matt didn't want me to hurt myself. And in that moment, in my madness, I'd clung on to what I so desperately wanted to believe, that deep down, he still cared.

1996

That summer at your gran's cottage, Kimberley's spirit burned brighter. From your bedroom window at the top of the house, the two of you watched her and Charlie lose themselves in a night of a million stars; felt your capricious heart break into as many fragments.

It was a night when you couldn't sleep. Then the next morning, under a waning moon and rising sun, the two of you made a spell to a dawn chorus. Justice, you called it. Something to put out the stars, one of you giggled. Carried along on your wave of madness.

Dewdrops, cyclamen, marigold, yellow rose, salvia.

Then at the last minute, taken from your pocket. A few drops of Gran's bottle labelled DARKNESS.

Just briefly, you watched Kimberley's eyes burn brighter, darker, more hypnotic, the constancy of her heart suddenly erratic. Her love headier, giddier as she rushed outside to greet Charlie. At her most dazzling, a lifetime's brilliance condensed into her final moments. She stopped briefly, a look of confusion on her face before her body went into shock, before the world started to spin; before she lost control and staggered in front of the van.

Hitting her hard enough, that second by second, her life was ebbing away from her.

And the two of you watched, didn't you? As Gran brought out a cushion and placed it under her head, as Charlie knelt beside her, his face ashen white, helpless as her heart slowed, as her life faded, until the ambulance came.

But not before you'd stolen away to one of your hiding places.

It didn't end there, though. Violent, unresolved deaths don't dissolve conveniently into the earth. Gran was implicated, wasn't she? Kimberley's death was accidental, everyone said. Gran was the one who could have prevented it.

And you let everyone believe that. Let an old lady take the rap. Thinking you'd got away with it; that nobody knew what you'd done.

You gave no thought to what would come after. Not thinking, not caring that death changes the lives of those who are left behind. The heartbroken parents, siblings, lovers; the shock waves crashing through their lives. You didn't think about them, either. Kimberley and Charlie, who wanted to live together. You couldn't have known that they didn't want to live without each other. That there would be more shock waves. That after one went, it was inevitable that before long, another would follow.

Fiona

Chapter Twenty-Six

Through the legal grapevine I heard a woman had been arrested in connection with Matt's disappearance. From a distance, I gleaned more details from an indiscreet colleague, who confirmed it was Amy who was being held in custody. Then told me of her daughter's return from uni. Matt had told me about her. Jess – like her mother to look at, but ten times smarter.

I imagined the police seeing first-hand how Amy was volatile; Amy unravelling. The inconsistency, the aggressive behaviour she was capable of. I felt no sympathy for her. People like Amy didn't deserve pity. Not when they'd done what she'd done. But while Matt was still missing, I wouldn't let myself indulge my grief. Rule one was to maintain control at all times, meaning my grief was locked away with other painful memories, in a part of my mind that would forever remain firmly closed.

Amy doesn't deserve. Nothing should follow that sentence. To put a word there denotes that she deserves anything at all. I tried to talk to her, years ago. But she didn't listen, just got rid of me as soon as she could, when she had no right. We are bound together forever by the vow we made; by the mingling of blood. There is no undoing the past.

It seems bizarre that it's Matt who's unwittingly drawn us together again. She won't have told anyone about the friendship that used to exist between us. How after our drifting apart as teenagers, she'd gone out of her way to make sure I wouldn't find her – changing her name, moving away, making her social media profiles private. What hurt me most was that she'd got away with it. That she had her cosy life, while I struggled. Even as more time passed, I couldn't let it rest.

But unless they really want to remain hidden, it isn't difficult to find someone. Fifteen years ago, it took a private detective I couldn't really afford, who found her in days after discovering she'd changed her name. I wasn't sure what I was doing this for. An apology? A hint of our old friendship? Or just to remind her what she'd done . . .

After catching a bus, I walked to the street where I knew Amy was living. It was an autumn day, the blustery wind whipping up the newly fallen red-brown leaves, as I found the terraced house on a small housing estate in Eastbourne.

Knocking on the door, when she came to open it, from her look of astonishment, it was clear I was the last person she was expecting. Instead of asking me in, she stood in the doorway. 'What are you doing here?'

I wanted to tell her, *for you to make amends for what happened to me. For you to know how much I've suffered.* But instead, I watched her face. 'How about *hello, how are you, how lovely to see you after so long* . . . How long has it been?' Even though I knew exactly how long, I spoke sarcastically, pretending to consider. 'I think it's eight years, by my calculation. I thought I'd come and tell you about what's happened in my life, ever since you dropped me and didn't bother to get in touch.'

I watched her eyes flicker over me, knowing I'd changed from the teenager she remembers. After losing weight, I'd recently had my long hair cut into a chiselled style that accentuated my cheekbones. My make-up was minimal but dramatic – black mascara, red lips, my clothes well-cut, smart, as if I'd come from work. It was another of my rules – dress for the life you want to live, even if you don't have it yet.

In her ripped boyfriend jeans and faded sweatshirt, I wondered if she felt as frumpy as she looked. Folding her arms, she stood there. 'What's this about?'

'Can I come in? Let yourself go a bit, haven't you?' Without being invited, I walked past her, then stood there, looking around the hallway. When she didn't say anything, I prowled into her living room, poking around until I found something. 'The husband?' I waved a framed photo in the air towards her, deliberately goading her. Then without waiting for her reply, picked up another. 'Oh, a baby. How sweet. Let's hope history doesn't repeat itself. What's its name?'

This time I got a response. 'Put the pictures back.'

But I ignored her. 'Quite the nice life you have here, *Amy*. Does he know? The husband? About what happened all those years ago? About what kind of person you really are?'

She lost control the way I'd always known she would, rushing at me, trying to grab the photos. But as she wrestled them from me, one of them fell to the floor. When she picked it up, the glass had cracked.

'Never mind.' My words were loaded with cynicism. 'I'm sure you'll think up a way to cover yourself. Back to your question, as to why I'm here.' Dropping the act, I leaned towards her until my face was inches from hers. 'I've come to tell you what my life has been like, ever since your sister died. Ever since your bloody gran told my parents. They sent me away,

Amy. Not to some nice private school like you might have gone to, but to some vile prison camp where I was bullied. For three years my life was hell. After that, guess what? It got even better.' My voice took on a mocking tone. 'Did you hear they disowned me? Imagine – nowhere to go at Christmas, no birthday cards, no friendly phone calls, *just to see how you are, darling.*' Not just that, but they disinherited me, too. When the wealthy old bastards die, I get nothing.'

'And you blame me?' A look of contempt crossed her face. 'If you think it's my fault, you're talking rubbish.' She shook her head. 'No, I take that back. You're insane. You know as well as I do what actually happened that day. You can't walk in here and put it on me. Not when it was all down to you.'

I stared at her, unflinching, until she looked away. Then I laughed, a harsh sound, devoid of humour. 'You know, I've heard of this. People who convince themselves of something, when in actual fact it's a lie. But I've never seen it for myself before. You're weak, Amy. You could convince yourself of anything. You don't even realise you're doing it, do you? You're one of those people who actually believe their own bullshit.' Angrily, with a single hand, I swept a pile of letters off a shelf onto the floor. Then taking a deep breath, I tried a different tack. 'We need to talk, don't we?' I tried to sound persuasive. 'You need to face up to what you did. Then maybe we can both put it behind us – for good.'

'You have a nerve coming here.' Amy stared at me. 'We have nothing to talk about. I never want to see you again. Get out.'

'Ooo,' I was taunting her. 'Ever so slightly losing it, are we?'

'This is my house.' Amy's voice was hostile, her body rigid. 'Don't come here again. If you do, I'll call the police.'

I stood there for a moment, challenging her. 'I don't believe for one moment you'd actually do that.'

'Who do you think they'd believe?' Her eyes blazed into mine. 'My life is sorted. Yours clearly isn't.' As she speaks, her eyes deliberately linger on my hair, my clothes. 'You might wear the right clothes, but I wouldn't mind betting that underneath, you're the same as you always were. Reckless, acting first, thinking later . . .'

'You have no idea who I am,' I snarl at her. 'You just wait. One of these days it will be me people listen to – I'll make sure of it. You won't have a chance. You'll regret the way you treated me.'

'Are you surprised?' This time, she sounds outraged. 'After what you did?'

'You may have convinced yourself otherwise, but we both know who is the guilty one. But if you want me to, I'll go.' I hesitated. 'Just so long as you know you haven't heard the last of this.' Picking up my bag, I walked towards the door. Just before opening it, I turned around briefly. 'There are two sides to every story. Don't ever forget that.'

'But there's only one version of the truth,' I heard her call after me just before I slammed the door. As I walked away, I wondered if she'd sunk into one of her velour armchairs, with God knew what going through her head. I hadn't wanted to lose it, but for too long there'd been an imbalance between us, one it was time to redress. Sweet, innocent little Amy who got off scot-free, while my entire life had collapsed around me. Well, she wasn't getting away with it any longer.

Knowing she'd done everything in her power to prevent our paths from crossing again, I had no doubt my visit would have shaken up her cosy little world. She might have thought she was safely ensconced in her dull suburban life, that she held the trump card. But as I walked away, I swore on my life that one day, our roles would be reversed. It would be me holding the trump card. This time, it would be Amy no-one would listen to, Amy who ultimately suffered and who at long last, paid the price.

Chapter Twenty-Seven

With Matt still missing, my conviction grows that the police are right and Amy is connected with his disappearance. From speaking to Matt, I know exactly where she lives, in the house I know from way back, on a quiet lane. I don't think even Matt knew it was her gran's house. For a moment, I picture it as it was when we were teenagers; the thick walls with stories embedded in the age-old Chinese wallpaper; where overgrown hedges and flint walls guarded an alchemist's garden. I wonder if it's changed. Then I try to imagine how life is there, in a home tarnished by the memory of what happened all those years ago.

One evening before Amy's arrest, idle curiosity – or obsession, as no doubt some people would call it – took me to that house. *Amy's house*. As I stood outside, I couldn't believe she'd made it her home. It used to be a magical place with a wilderness of a garden. Now, the memory of what happened here is hidden behind the neat front lawn, the closed wooden gate, the curtains masking the glow from an upstairs window.

My idle curiosity satisfied, I drove back to Brighton, as

something Matt said came back to me. It was about Amy refusing to sell the cottage, and it causing endless rows between them. At the time, it had puzzled me, but now, knowing who she is and who it used to belong to, I wonder if there's more to it than she's letting on.

Back in my flat again, I was struck by the fact that that this was some coincidence. I'd thought about calling her to confront her about Matt, but also, because I was curious, to find out what she knew about me. Instead, I poured myself a drink, trying to ignore my conscience pushing me to do what I didn't want to: to tell the police what I knew about Amy and what she was capable of.

But seeing the house again stirred up memories of that day, twenty-three years ago, as I remember the teenager who died. The elderly woman who took the blame, a woman who was innocent. Amy and I knew that, just as Amy and I know the truth. But it's a truth that will remain hidden, like the vow we made, forever binding us, in silence.

Blood sisters.

Suddenly irritated, recklessness gripped me. Picking up my phone, I dialled the number I'd found online for Amy's business. Waiting as it rang, imagining what her reaction would be, irritated with the way she'd clung on to Matt, wanting to shake her up. At last, she picked up and I had my chance.

'Hello, Amy.'

There was more to say, but it was all I managed to get out before she hung up, then immediately blocked me.

Chapter Twenty-Eight

The first time PC Page calls and asks me to come in to the station, it's only days since Matt's gone missing. I try to keep the annoyance out of my voice, as we arrange a time that's supposedly mutually convenient; knowing I have no choice. But after the call ends, the pressure is palpable. Presumably it's to do with Matt, but I've no way of knowing what Amy's said to them. If she's said too much, who knows what conclusions the police may have jumped to.

It's early afternoon when I drive along the seafront towards the police station. The sea swell is a surging grey-blue, the sky scattered with white clouds. When I park and get out, I pull my jacket around me against the wind, before heading inside. A young officer leads me along a typically bland corridor with white walls and a brown carpet, until he stops outside a cracked-open door. As he knocks, inside, from behind an untidy desk, PC Page looks up.

'Please come in, Ms Rose. Take a seat.'

As I walk in, I take off my jacket, slinging it over the back of the chair, wondering why a phone call wouldn't do and why it's so important for me to come here.

'DI Lacey's joining us. He won't keep us long.'

Alarm flickers through me. I haven't been brought in for official questioning as such, so why the two of them? My disquiet obviously shows.

It's as if she reads my mind. 'It's nothing to be concerned about. It's just at this stage, it's helpful if we both hear what you have to say.'

'Sure.' My hands are clammy as I sit there, grateful for a few moments to compose my thoughts, telling myself Amy wouldn't have been rash enough to bring up the past. Like me, she has too much at stake. Trying to distract myself, I look around. It's a typical nondescript office; impersonal, untidy, unlike mine – with its elegant proportions, tall windows, and polished mahogany desk. Then the door opens and an older man walks in, with greying hair and pale skin.

'Sir.' PC Page looks at me. 'This is Fiona Rose.'

He nods towards me. 'Detective Inspector Lacey. Thank you for coming in. Has PC Page told you what this is about?'

'No.' I try to sound cool, confident, unfazed, wondering how long it'll take them to find out what's happened to Matt.

He pulls up another chair. 'We'd like to hear more about what Mr Roche told you, about his fiancée, Amy Reid. I take it you've never met?'

The question takes me by surprise, the lie out before I can stop it. 'No. Of course, I've thought about trying to talk to her. When Matt first told her about me, he didn't tell her who I was. But that night he disappeared, maybe he did tell her. I've no way of knowing.'

PC Page frowns at me. 'She hasn't said anything to us about you.'

DI Lacey's face is unreadable. 'As a divorce lawyer, I'm sure it must happen all the time that you're presented with two conflicting stories. On the one hand, the devoted fiancée, the wedding a fortnight away, the picture she paints of a loving partner – most of the time, that is . . .' Pausing, he and PC Page exchange glances. 'Then on the other, there's yours.' He frowns. 'Tell me. Apart from the fact that you're a partner with Hollis and James, a highly reputable firm who speak extremely favourably of you, why should your story be any more plausible?'

I stare at him, surprised that already, he's checked me out. Surely the facts speak for themselves – wasn't that the whole point? I certainly wasn't expecting to be challenged. 'I've told you the truth. Matt spoke to me at length about Amy's problems – her mood swings, her instability. I'm not sure what else I can add.'

'Ms Rose isn't the only person with accounts of Ms Reid's disturbed behaviour. Here.' As PC Page passes him what looks like a couple of witness statements, my ears prick up.

He shakes his head. 'But what we don't have is first-hand evidence. We need to check her GP records, find out if there were any referrals for mental health problems.' Pausing, the DI turns back to me. 'Going back, were you aware that Mr Roche wanted Ms Reid to go into a private hospital?'

It's the first I've heard of it, but doesn't surprise me. 'From what he said, it seemed obvious enough she needed help, but he didn't mention anything about a hospital.'

'Apparently he packed her case for her, then drove her there.'

I look at him. 'I honestly had no idea. Maybe it was before we met.'

'It's quite an extreme act,' the DI remarks. 'If he confided in you the way you've described, I'm surprised he didn't tell you about that.' He pauses. 'Tell me again. You last saw Mr Roche the night he disappeared?'

I nod. 'He came to my flat. I think you have CCTV footage of where he went that evening.' I glance at PC Page, relieved when she nods. 'It was late when he left me. He'd had a few drinks, so instead of driving, he called a taxi.'

'So apart from the taxi driver, that makes you the last person to see him.'

I'm frowning as I remember something I haven't thought of, until now. 'I saw him go outside and close the front door behind him. I didn't actually see him get in the taxi.'

The DI sits back in his chair. 'So if you and Ms Reid are both to be believed, somewhere between leaving your flat and arriving back home, he disappeared.'

After a brief silence, PC Page takes a deep breath. 'The day after Mr Roche disappeared, someone left a bouquet of flowers on Amy's doorstep. Red roses and white lilies. As you may well know, the two colours together symbolise blood and tears. Anyway,' she pauses. 'Amy took them into her kitchen, where she discovered that instead of water, their stems were encased in a bag of blood.'

As I gasp in shock, both of them stare at me. Then as she goes on, her eyes hold mine. 'We had a sample of it analysed. It was human blood – the same type as Mr Roche's.'

'God.' I'm silent, thinking quickly. I've had clients stoop to the lowest of low acts, especially where matters of the heart are concerned, but even so, I'm shocked. Then I look at them. 'You surely can't think I had anything to do with this? I don't even know what Matt's blood type is.'

'Apparently, neither did Ms Reid.' DI Lacey's voice is quiet. 'Clearly someone wanted to upset her. They succeeded.' He goes on. 'Ms Rose, what can you tell us about the other people in Mr Roche's life?'

I shrug. 'Not much. He talked about his boss, David Avery

– and one or two people he worked with. But I never had a chance to meet his friends. Even at its best, ours was a difficult relationship.'

'I can imagine.' DI Lacey's voice is dry. 'How did you cope with that?'

'It wasn't ideal. But I had a choice. Be patient and wait. If not, I could leave.'

'Did your patience ever wear thin, Ms Rose?' The DI's face seems to loom closer.

I know where he's going with this. Having seen his type in action, I'm not about to be intimidated by him. 'Of course it did. We broke up for a while. But since we got back together, no.' I speak coolly. 'I trusted him. He gave me absolutely no reason not to.'

Glancing at PC Page, DI Lacey sits back in his chair. 'Until now.'

Reluctantly, I nod. This time, I can't argue with him.

He doesn't comment. Shortly after, the interview ends and I'm free to leave. But as I walk away, I feel soiled, by the stale air in the office, by their air of suspicion. A stark reminder of how not being believed feels, it's one I could do without.

I don't go straight back to the office. Instead, I walk to the seafront, where an easterly breeze has picked up. As it chills my skin, I watch a couple of surfers catching waves, the spray briefly breaking the green water, feeling my mind start to calm. Casting off my sense of uncertainty, I have to believe the police will find Matt. That justice will be done and everyone will know I'm completely innocent.

Chapter Twenty-Nine

With the knowledge that she's being held in custody now, my obsession with Amy's behaviour grows, knowing she'll be playing a game, pretending she's vulnerable, a victim, when she's anything but. A scenario I can't allow to get to me.

It's taken years to build my life, reach where I am in my career. Achievements I can't let anything threaten, not even Matt's disappearance. Whatever happens from here on, I have to be ready, have my own game plan. But then I take a call that completely throws me.

As I drive, I'm irritated that yet again, I have no choice, cursing the traffic, thinking about the meetings I've had to cancel this morning at short notice. I plan my days at work carefully, prepare methodically. Disruptions have consequences, which is why it annoyed me when PC Page called again, most insistent that I went over there straight away.

It's a beautiful morning – the faintest hint of warmth in the winter sun. At the police station, I park outside, hesitating as I gather my thoughts. When I go in, I wait only a few minutes before PC Page appears.

'Good morning, Ms Rose. Would you come with me?' Her brusque, matter of fact, manner disconcerts me.

But there's no way I'm letting her see that. 'Sure.' I walk with her up the same corridor as last time. 'Can I ask what this is about?'

'I'd like to wait till the DI gets here.' She glances at her watch. 'He won't be long.'

The DI? Again? This time, alarm bells start sounding in my head. Then I'm annoyed. 'I've cancelled meetings to come here at such short notice. I hope this isn't going to take too long?'

She doesn't reply, as instead of her office, she opens a door into an interview room with a small table and plastic chairs. 'Have a seat. I'll just get rid of this.' Picking up an empty cup carelessly left behind, she takes it outside.

Pulling out one of the chairs, I sit down, before running through the well-rehearsed mantra in my head. *You are confident. You have done nothing wrong. You've got this*.

The door opens again and PC Page comes back in, with DI Lacey just behind her.

'Good morning, Ms Rose.' He nods briefly, before sitting down opposite me. 'Thank you for coming in. We've received some new information I'm hoping you can shed some light on.'

I hold his gaze. 'I'll do my best.'

Not expecting our conversation to be recorded, when she starts the tape and records the official preamble, I'm taken aback. As PC Page sits next to the DI, she puts down the papers she's holding. 'We've received an anonymous letter. Normally, they're a complete waste of police time, but this one is potentially rather interesting. It refers to the death of a teenage girl that happened twenty-three years ago. It was described as a tragic accident. The writer of the letter suggests that the truth has intentionally been hidden, then goes on to name you, specifically, as someone who might know what actually happened. As well as your name, they've given us your address. It doesn't say much more than that, other than the address where the accident took place and the date.'

As she speaks, my blood runs cold, a rushing sound filling my ears. It's as if I've been transported back to that house, the garden; a summer that lasted forever until it was abruptly cut short. As PC Page goes on, I try to concentrate. 'It's quite a coincidence, wouldn't you say? That you knew the house Amy shared with Mr Roche?'

Poised, I wait for their questions, already knowing I have to watch each word, every nuance; how imperative it is that they believe me.

The DI frowns. 'So you'll know the woman who owned the house was a Ruth Preston?'

I pause for a moment. It would be so much easier to tell them that it's Amy they should be talking to, but it could just as easily work against me. I have to take this step by step, so that the police can work it out for themselves. 'It belonged to the grandmother of a friend of mine. I only knew her as Gran.' Then because he's going to ask, I add, 'My friend's name was Emily Preston – so in answer to your question, I guess the answer is yes.'

He doesn't miss a beat. 'And it was her sister, Kimberley Preston, who died?'

I nod calmly. 'That's correct.' But my brain is racing. 'Why would someone send a letter like this now?'

The DI doesn't answer. 'Can you tell me what happened that day?'

Sitting up straighter, I try to wrestle back some control. 'Should I be asking for a lawyer?'

'I'm sure that's not necessary.' The DI leans back in his chair. 'How old were you when it happened?'

'I was fifteen. It was terrible.' My voice lowers. 'Kimberley was older – seventeen, I think. She didn't really hang out with us – she had her own set of friends. We all loved being at Kimberley and Emily's gran's house. She let us run wild. The garden was a wilderness and the lane led straight onto the Downs. We used to go off on our own for hours.' I break off for a moment, thinking back. 'Their gran used to make home remedies from the plants she grew. Now and then, we'd sneak in and try them. That's what Kimberley did, but unfortunately she consumed something poisonous. It hit her really fast. One minute she was running outside, the next, she was hit by a van.' An image comes back to me, of Kimberley unsteady on her feet, her eyes huge, her pupils dilated as she lurched into the road, before collapsing as the van hit her.

'There is one thing.' The DI looks puzzled. 'We looked the case up. Records mention Kimberley and her sister, Emily, and a third teenager called Alison Macklin. There's no mention of a Fiona Rose.'

'That's because I changed my name, Detective Inspector.' I regard him coolly. 'You can hardly blame me. I didn't want to forever be linked to what happened to Kimberley. Fiona's my second name. Rose came from my ex-husband.'

'I see.' While PC Page makes notes, the DI looks unfazed. 'It really was rather tragic, wasn't it? An accident, though the grandmother took responsibility. It's noted that she said her remedies had only ever been created for beneficial use, never for harm.' He studies me closely. 'You say you tried some of them? You and your friend?'

I shrug. 'Once or twice. They didn't have much effect, to be honest.'

He frowns. 'Unlike Kimberley's death. That must have had quite an impact on both of you – especially your friend, losing her sister like that.'

'Yes.' I'm rigid, trying not to show my irritation, because it was what everyone had said. *Poor Emily.* No-one thought about me. Nor did they care what happened to me, after.

DI Lacey looks thoughtful. 'Is the grandmother still alive?'

PC Page shakes her head. 'I don't imagine so. Ms Reid told us she moved there after the old woman who'd lived there for years died. We're trying to get hold of records of owner-ship of the house, but for some reason, there's been a hold up.' She pauses. 'Odd isn't it.' She looks straight at me. 'Like you said – why would someone send a letter like that after all this time?'

'Really odd.' I stare at the table. 'That family went through so much when Kimberley died. After all this time, it's hard to imagine why someone would want to stir it up.'

The DI frowns. 'This line, about how the truth has been hidden, but that you were the person who knows what really went on . . . Do you have any idea what they're getting at?'

I look up at him. 'Other than the grandmother shouldn't have felt responsible, not really.'

His frown deepens. 'Wasn't she responsible, though? If she stored potentially harmful substances somewhere teenagers could easily access them?'

I look at them both. 'She kept them in a locked part of the garden, behind a stone wall. It wasn't that easy to get into. You had to want to.' Realising it sounds as though I'm defending her, I add, 'But maybe you're right.'

When neither of them speaks, I stand up. 'Will that be all? I have another meeting I really can't miss.' I hold my breath,

239

waiting for them to tell me that's all for now, that if there's anything else they'd be in touch.

But he holds my gaze a little too long, speaks a little too lightly. 'Ms Rose. Sit down, please. We've only just started. I'm afraid you're not going anywhere.'

Chapter Thirty

For a moment, I'm silent. Then I shake my head. 'I'm sorry. I really do have to go. I'm already behind with meetings. I can come back another time. I haven't been arrested.'

'If you're determined to leave, you'll give us no choice.' PC Page is very calm, leaving me in no doubt she means it.

'On what grounds? You don't have anything, other than an anonymous letter clearly written by some kind of crackpot.'

'I think you'll find suspicion of perverting the course of justice would fit quite well.' The DI breaks off, his eyes not leaving me, as he adds, 'Would you kindly sit down?'

Uneasy, I do as he asks, my mind racing again as I try to think who might have sent the letter; wondering what's coming next.

DI Lacey shuffles through the papers in front of him until he finds what he's looking for. 'At the post-mortem, there were traces of a number of things in Kimberley's blood, most notably salvia, rose, calendula, none of which are dangerous, but there were also hemlock and digitalis. She suffered respiratory collapse caused by the hemlock, but even without that, the levels of digitalis would have affected her heart, eventually causing cardiac arrest. That's some cocktail to take by accident.'

I shake my head. 'Maybe one of the jars had been mislabelled.'

'Maybe someone mislabelled it deliberately?' DI Lacey's voice is misleadingly light. 'Maybe it wasn't an accident. Maybe it was done intentionally.'

I stare at him, a look of horror on my face. 'Why?'

Ignoring me, he goes on. 'Tell me about the sisters. How did Kimberley and Emily get on? Were they close?'

'Not particularly, but they didn't dislike each other, either. As I said, Emily and I used to hang out together. And Kimberley had a boyfriend . . .' I break off, silently cursing. Another mistake. No doubt DI Lacey will be straight onto it.

He is. 'Did that cause any problems between them? Jealousy, for example?'

I hesitate. 'Things were different, obviously, compared to before he was on the scene.'

'In what way?'

'Kimberley was quite obsessed with him. He came to see her most days, but like I said, Emily and I had each other. It wasn't a problem.'

'Are you and Emily still in touch?'

I shake my head. 'After I changed schools, we drifted apart – like so many teenagers do.'

PC Page looks at me. 'I would have thought something of the magnitude of her sister dying would have meant you'd stay in touch.'

I'm silent for a moment. 'If we'd stayed at the same school, I'm sure we would have.' Leaving out what I want to say, that it was directly because of Kimberley's death, then my parents

242

sending me away, that we didn't drift apart, our friendship was severed.

★

'We need to try to trace her.' I'm aware of their eyes scrutinising me. 'You genuinely don't know why the writer of the letter insists there's something you know about Kimberley's death?'

I shake my head. 'I've no idea.'

Neither of them comments. Then as they get up, just as I think the interview is over, PC Page stops and turns to look at me. 'It really is the most bizarre coincidence that all this took place in the house where Ms Reid now lives.'

Not wanting to pursue this line of conversation, I just nod, wondering if she believes in coincidence, because I don't. The timing of the anonymous letter is sinister, as well as far too inconvenient to put down solely to chance.

★

As I drive away, my sense of relief is temporary. If they question me again, there's only one plausible option. I'm going to have to come clean, and tell them exactly what happened. That Emily was jealous of her sister, that she'd tried to make a remedy to break her and her boyfriend up, that went disastrously wrong. I imagine their questions. *Ms Rose, can you explain why you didn't tell us about this?*

Making my way through the centre of Brighton, around me the streets are busy, stirred into life by the bright sunshine, people hurrying to and from work, or to the shops and bars. When I first moved here, I imagined staying for years, but already I'm thinking about moving away, maybe changing my name. Leaving the past in the past, for good.

Going on experience, I don't suppose it will be long before

the police are back in touch. There will be someone, somewhere, who will remember the family that was devastated by a death that should never have happened. Records of ownership of the house. It had been an error on my part not to tell them.

The more I think about Matt, the more certain I feel about what transpired that last night. After he left my flat, the taxi dropping him back at Amy's, he told her he was leaving her. A red mist would have fallen over her eyes as she overreacted, became furious, raging angrily as she lost control. She could have stabbed him, then he tried to get away. Maybe even drive away, desperate to get away from her. I haven't heard anything about his car.

Parking close to the office, I sit there for a moment. There's a sense of control sliding out of my grasp, of time slipping through my fingers like grains of sand. Knowing the police will be making enquiries into Emily's whereabouts, there'll be more questions. But this time, I have to be ready for them.

Jess

As we drive away from the custody centre, my head is filled with a tornado of thoughts – about my mother, Matt, how they met, why they met. What reasons Matt could have for trying to hurt her.

Cath's friend Zoe lives in a quiet street off Dyke Road, by chance not far from where Amy is being held. By the time we get there, it's almost dark, glimmers of light coming from behind closed curtains, where normal lives exist, undisrupted by police investigations. But as I know, appearances give nothing away about what's inside. As we reach Cath's friend's house, parking right outside, I climb out, feeling myself shiver as the first spots of rain start to fall.

'Let's get out of this.' Beside me, Cath is carrying the overnight bags I'd completely forgotten about. Taking mine from her, I follow her up the steps to the front door, then as she rings the bell, a light comes on inside.

'Cath!' The woman who opens the door has dark hair and warm eyes. Leaning forward, she hugs Cath. Then she looks at me. 'You must be Jess. I'm Zoe. Welcome. Come in, it's so cold out there. You've had a long day, haven't you?'

I nod, then think of Cath, whose day started in Bristol. 'Cath's has been longer.'

We follow Zoe along a light hallway into her kitchen. 'Come through. It's just us tonight. Nick is in the Algarve playing golf and Lizzie's away at uni. I've made pasta. After the day you've had, I don't suppose either of you have eaten. Come and sit down. I'll get you both a drink.'

After the events of today, her warmth and kindness is comforting. The kitchen is big but still manages somehow to be cosy, with a colourful rug on the wide floorboards and a large oak table surrounded by eight chairs.

As Cath and I sit down, Zoe brings over a bottle of white wine and three glasses. 'Cath told me about your mum, Jess. I'm so sorry. I can't imagine how upsetting this must be for you. You're welcome to stay here as long as you need to.' She glances at Cath. 'Both of you.'

'Thank you.' Touched by her kindness, I take the glass she offers me. 'I don't know what's happening. Do we?' I look at Cath.

'Not right now.' Cath takes a sip of her wine. 'Hopefully we'll find out more tomorrow.'

The wine is cold and crisp, and as I drink, I realise how exhausted I am. Zoe serves up a huge bowl of steaming hot pasta. 'It's with olive oil and herbs,' she says. 'Cath told me you were vegan, so I kept it plain. I hope that's OK?'

'Thank you so much. It looks wonderful.' In this warm house, in the company of a stranger, I'm grateful, but it's another stark reminder of Matt's lack of consideration. His arrival in our lives radically changed my own home until it barely resembled what it used to be.

'Let's eat. The food smells amazing.' Cath tries to sound bright.

But thinking of Matt, of my mother being held in custody, my appetite has vanished Taking a small portion, I push it around my plate, before putting my fork down. 'I'm sorry. I'm not really hungry.'

'Have a little.' Cath's voice is sympathetic. 'You need to eat, Jess. Keep your strength up. Your mum's relying on us.'

★

After we've finished eating, Zoe shows me up to one of her guest rooms. 'I've put towels in the bathroom.' She opens the door to a small en suite. 'If there's anything else you need, Jess, you only have to ask. Please make yourself at home.' She pauses for a moment, concern written on her face as she speaks more quietly. 'I really hope tomorrow brings you the answers you want.'

'Thank you. This is so lovely.' And it is, from the pastel patterned bedding to the heavy white curtains, a small set of toiletries thoughtfully laid out on top of the chest of drawers.

The bed is comfortable, the noise coming from outside in the street unfamiliar as I lie there, grateful, but thinking of my own bed at home; where the sky is dark, the only sounds the occasional owl and the wind. But however tired I feel, sleep evades me. Gazing at the ceiling, I try to imagine what my mother's been through these last few weeks, since Matt disappeared. However Matt treated her in the past, she's lost the man she loved and the future she believed lay ahead of her. And now, ridiculously, by the cruellest twist of fate, she's being held in custody by the police.

My mind wanders, as I think about what might have happened to Matt. Then I think of the bouquet of flowers in blood. It sounds as though someone was trying to get at both of them. Suddenly it strikes me, if there's someone with a big enough grudge against my mother, that drove them to kill Matt, then leave the bouquet in blood for my mother to find, what next? Am I in danger, too? Maybe the other woman is behind it all. Maybe she's killed Matt, before setting my mother up as a kind of revenge, out of some form of twisted jealousy.

Eventually I doze, only to wake with a start and a clarity of thought that yesterday escaped me. This has to be connected to the other woman Matt was seeing. I need to find out who she is.

★

After breakfast, Cath and I drive to Steyning. Although my house is off-limits, I want to see what's going on there. The sky is a little brighter, the air dry, the rolling hills comfortingly familiar, until we arrive to find two police cars parked outside. When she sees us, PC Page gets out of one of them. Leaving Cath to park her car, I get out and walk towards her.

There's a frown on her face. 'Morning. I'm sorry. As I explained yesterday, we can't allow anyone to go inside.'

'I know. I just wanted to come here.' This morning, even the air feels different. Then I realise, there are no birds. Instead, there's an eerie silence, and I realise the sense of peace my mother has nurtured is no longer part of the framework of this place; that the intangible serenity she's tried so hard to preserve has gone.

Wrapping my arms around myself, I take in the plastic tape cordoning off the front garden, presumably the extent of what they consider the crime scene, the second police officer sitting inside the other car. Gazing up at the windows, the house looks unfamiliarly cold and bleak. Tears prick my eyes, because when all this is over, life can never go back to how it was.

PC Page's voice breaks into my thoughts. 'How did you sleep?'

'OK.' Still staring at the house, I shrug. 'I was thinking about a lot of stuff.' Turning to look at her, I pause. 'I know my mother's a suspect, but if she's innocent, which I'm a hundred per cent sure she is, I was trying to think who else could be involved in Matt's disappearance. The obvious answer is this other woman he was seeing. Maybe she ran out of patience when he didn't leave Mum. She killed him because she couldn't bear the thought of him being with someone else. The bouquet was to get back at Mum. Or maybe he was as awful to her as he was to Mum.' My voice wavers. 'Either way, she could have a motive.' I hesitate before asking the burning question I need an answer to. 'I need you to tell me what you think my mother has done.'

PC Page is silent for a moment. 'While the investigation is still going on, all I can tell you is that we have sufficient evidence to implicate your mother. I'm afraid I can't tell you any more than that.'

My stomach churns as she speaks, but it still isn't conclusive. 'Have you found his body?'

'Not yet.' She sighs. 'There's no easy way to say this, Jess. But as well as physical evidence, we have accounts of what was going on between Matt and your mother. Enough for us to build a fairly clear picture of what was happening.'

'But you still don't actually have a body.' My voice is fierce as I challenge her.

She doesn't comment. Then she changes the subject. 'I did want to ask you more about what you've discovered about Mr Roche – through Facebook. Is now a good time?'

Nodding, I think of the pictures on my wall at uni. 'I started looking through his friends. There was a woman called Mandy, who he was with before he met my mother. From the comments, I think he treated her quite badly. Before her, there were others, more short-lived – mostly wealthy women who led him to meet the next wealthy woman. It was through Mandy that he met my friend Sasha's mum. And it was through her that he met Mum.'

All the time I'm talking, she listens intently, a frown on her face. 'I think you should show me. And we'll try to contact Mandy. See what she has to say about him. If it was as contrived as you're describing, it suggests there has to be a reason.'

'He's motivated by money – at least, that's what it looks like. I honestly think he was after our house. He was adamant about selling and moving to Brighton. I think that's why he hadn't cancelled the wedding. Once they were married, wouldn't he have been entitled to half the house? Or else . . .' I stop, not knowing what to believe. 'Unless Mum was his key to someone else – someone he's already met. The next woman whose money he wants to get his hands on.'

Quiet for a moment, PC Page gets out a small notebook and starts writing. 'You mentioned your mother met Matt through your friend Sasha's mum – can you give me her name and address?'

Nodding, I tell her, watching her write it down, suddenly realising it's me who needs to talk to Sasha's mum, as soon as possible. 'Are you going to call her?'

'We may well do.' She pauses, frowning. 'Going back to what you said just now, about Matt eyeing up a potential partner . . . Have you found anything to suggest who that might be?'

I shake my head. 'Not yet. It was a hunch. But as far as I can see, there's a pattern. It seems to fit.'

She frowns again. 'I wanted to ask you about your mother's workshop. Do you know what she keeps in there?'

'Mostly her herbs in labelled jars. It's the most potent form, from which she dilutes them. It's very precise.'

'I need to take another look.' Then as we start walking back towards Cath's car, I ask her, 'How much longer will this be cordoned off?' I want the plastic tape gone, my freedom back.

'I can't say, Jess. But I'll let you know as soon as we're done. I'm going to look into the Facebook thing. I'll let you know if I find anything.'

As Cath gets out of her car and walks towards us, her face is anxious. 'Are you OK, Jess?'

I nod. 'Yeah. We're done here.'

'You want to go?'

Nodding, I walk over to her car and get in. After a brief exchange with PC Page, a couple of minutes later, she joins me.

'Did you find out what you wanted to?'

'Not really.' My voice wavers, while a tear snakes its way down my cheek. 'She said they have evidence, but she wouldn't tell me what it was. She also said they have a clear picture of how things were between Mum and Matt. I don't know how, exactly. And after the way Matt's treated her, then met someone else, they probably think she has a motive. It's completely and utterly shit.' My voice is bitter, my brain desperately casting around for other answers – the right answer, because at the moment, the police are missing something.

1996

After. Grief. Sadness. Ripples multiplying. One death leading to another death – the boy you wanted for your own. Not one, but two devastated families, all because of you.

How long before you shrugged it off? Telling yourself it was an accident – how many hundreds of times, until you believed your own lies? I wonder if when you look back now, how you'd tell the story of what happened that day. Who you'd blame. Knowing your mind has distorted it and turned it into something more palatable; because even a heart as twisted as yours has become, somewhere deep inside you must know the truth.

And when it comes out, the whole world will know your game and it will be over. The pretence, the lies, the hiding behind false names. Because I know who you are. I've always known. And I'll make sure you pay for what you did.

Amy

Chapter Thirty-One

Each session of questioning conspires to lower me further. Maintaining my composure in the interview room, it's only when I'm back in my cell that I allow my tears to fall, holding on to the only fact I'm sure of: that I'm innocent. None of this should be happening to me.

When I'm next taken to the interview room, instead of DI Lacey, there's another woman with PC Page.

'Amy, this is Dana. She's a police psychologist. She wants to talk to you about . . .'

My frayed nerves already stretched to breaking point, I snap. 'You think I'm mad, don't you? I'm not. I know I'm not. I won't let you section me. Please.' Agitated, I turn to my solicitor. 'You're supposed to be on my side. Can't you do something?'

But he doesn't respond. For a moment, no-one speaks. 'Amy?' PC Page's voice is calm. 'Please sit down. No-one's accusing you of being mad or trying to section you. We know you've struggled with depression before – we've spoken to your GP. We've also been talking to your daughter and your therapist,

Sonia Richardson. The point is we think Matt's been playing mind games with you.'

My eyes flit between PC Page's and the psychologist's, as I take in what she's saying, frowning as I wonder why they've spoken to Sonia.

Dana looks at me. She's pretty, with reddish hair and pale skin, the kind of looks no doubt Matt would have found attractive. 'Have you heard of gaslighting, Amy?' When I shake my head, she goes on. 'It's when a man – usually it's a man – starts altering the reality of the woman he lives with. It starts in small ways, such as him telling her she's forgotten something he never asked her to get, or reminding her about a conversation they've never had. Gradually it escalates, until she starts to doubt herself. Eventually she thinks she's going mad.'

As I listen, there's an uncomfortable familiarity to what she's saying.

'Your daughter gave me an example.' PC Page speaks slowly. 'She told me how when you were planning your wedding, you were going to get married on a beach. You'd even picked the venue in the Caribbean. Jess said it was the wedding you'd dreamed of. You'd even emailed them and confirmed a date.' She pauses, watching me. 'Then after buying the dresses, Matt reminded you you'd discussed it and changed your plans. You were getting married here, but you'd obviously forgotten. He was kind, but firm. He'd already booked somewhere else. There was no way you were having the beach wedding you'd dreamed of.'

As she speaks, I feel my mouth fall open, then tears fill my eyes, only this time they're tears of release pouring unchecked down my face, as a new feeling comes to me. Relief – that I'm not mad, that I didn't imagine it. God, I remember that night so clearly. How thrilled I'd been to have found fairytale dresses for both Jess and me, picturing a wedding under the Caribbean sun at this gorgeous guesthouse I'd found. I was so sure that Matt had agreed, otherwise I'd never have bought those dresses, but in the end, when he disputed it so confidently, I'd believed him, just as I'd always believed everything he said to me. What PC Page described is exactly what happened, countless times. 'He must have deleted the emails.' I'm dumbfounded. 'I knew I didn't remember having that conversation. I was sure we were planning a beach wedding.' I look at them both in disbelief. 'He did that to me so many times. I can't believe I didn't see it.'

'That's how it works,' Dana says quietly. 'Nothing too aggressive to start with, just a subtle undermining, chipping away at your reality, until before long, you're so under their spell, you believe everything they tell you, to the point you question your own sanity.'

I gasp in surprise at how accurately she describes it, because it's exactly how it was. Even at the end, when Matt told me it was me who was controlling him. That he was was walking on eggshells, when in fact it was the reverse of what was happening. I knew he was wrong, but through sheer force of will, he'd convinced me he wasn't.

Dana continues. 'Very often, there's an abusive background. It's a means of avoiding emotional intimacy.'

Instinctively, I shake my head. 'What if he was doing it intentionally? Trying to wear me down?'

'That's what we need to establish.' PC Page's voice is grim. 'Because that's what it's starting to look like. And if he was, the next question has to be why.'

'I have to ask you something.' My voice is shaky, unsure how much I should tell them. 'The woman Matt was seeing . . .' I watch PC Page exchange glances with the psychologist. 'Have you spoken to her?'

After a pause, PC Page nods. 'We've interviewed her, yes.'

'I imagine she will have said things about me. The way Matt could behave . . . he could have said anything he wanted to about me – true or false – if it served his purpose.' I pause for a moment, looking at them. 'You do realise that, don't you?'

'We do understand he was playing with you.' Dana sounds reasonable. 'Did you have any idea that there were other women?'

Leaning forward, I sigh, for the first time being completely honest – with the police, as well as with myself. 'I suppose, once or twice I did have suspicions, but I told myself I was imagining it. I really couldn't bring myself to believe that Matt would do something like that. When he was the same as he always was towards me, and with the wedding coming up, I was convinced I'd made a mistake.'

Dana's quiet for a moment. 'It must have been so hard for you. I think the fact that he managed to carry off this double life, shows the extent to which he'd been manipulating you.'

Leaning forward, I rest my head in my hands. 'It sounds weak, but I couldn't acknowledge that he was mistreating me. I kept asking myself, was it really so bad? No relationships are easy all the time but I thought he loved me. If I'd challenged him, it would have meant the end of our wedding, of the future we'd planned . . .' My voice is uneven. 'I'd been on my own for so long. When I met him, I was so happy . . . There was a lot that was good in our relationship and that's what I focused on. It's what I do when things are painful. It's a way I've learned to block them out.'

'I can understand why you'd do that.' Dana's voice is kind, but there's an edge to it. 'But this is a police investigation. Right now, it's crucial you tell us everything.'

Chapter Thirty-Two

The following morning, when I'm taken back to the interview room, I ask for a moment with my solicitor.

'I've been here three days. How much longer can they keep me here?'

Andrew Nelson looks uncomfortable. 'If they have reasonable evidence to incriminate you in the case of Mr Roche's disappearance, they can charge you and remand you in custody until the case comes to trial.'

As he speaks, blood drains from my face. 'But they can't do that. I haven't done anything.'

He sighs. 'Unless they've found new evidence, I don't think they will keep you much longer. I will request that you are allowed to leave, but it's impossible to guess what they'll say to that.' As he finishes speaking, footsteps come closer, then the door of the interview room opens.

'Good morning.' PC Page sits opposite me, DI Lacey next to her.

Before either of them can say anything, Andrew Nelson speaks up. 'In the absence of a body being found, and unless you have further evidence to the contrary, my client would like me to voice very strongly on her behalf her objection that she is being held when she is clearly innocent.'

'Noted.' It's all PC Page says, glancing at the notes in front of her before turning to me. 'As it happens, we do have such evidence. Since we've been holding you, we've uncovered a potential murder weapon at the back of the drawer in your workshop table, buried under various garden items – old trowels and secateurs, packets of seeds, brown string, that sort of thing. It's a knife, part of quite a new set in your kitchen that someone had obviously tried to clean but not well enough. As well as finding your fingerprints, there was a microscopic amount of blood on it, of the same type as Mr Roche's. This, added to the fact that Mr Roche is still missing, a person who according to several witness accounts described you as unstable, who was frightened of what you were capable of, a man who tried to help you but whose help you repeatedly refused, I'd say the picture is getting clearer.'

Of course the knife has my fingerprints on it. Everything in my workshop does. But as she speaks, my fear escalates. Suddenly I'm terrified. They really believe they have proof I killed Matt. My body starts to shake. 'Have you found him?'

'Not yet. But I can't imagine it will be much longer. We still have one or two leads to follow up.'

I stare from one to the other. 'How can you accuse me of murder when there's no body?'

'If we have enough evidence, it is possible.' The DI leans back in his chair. 'Unless there's anything you can prove to the contrary?'

'I can't prove anything,' I cry. 'But nor can you.'

PC Page takes over. 'We've been speaking to some of your clients. They speak well of you, but one of them did say that when you delivered her order the morning after Matt disappeared, you did seem unusually agitated.'

I can't believe how she's turning this against me. She's talking about Davina, and I had been anxious. 'It's hardly surprising. I couldn't get hold of Matt. I was worried out of my mind.'

'I see.' Then she moves on to something else. 'Amy, I went to your house today.'

The fact PC Page has been there again doesn't shock me. I've become immune to the repeated invasions of my privacy by the police. The words are out before I can stop them. 'Did you see Jess?'

'I did, only briefly. But while it remains an active crime scene, Jess is staying with friends.'

The mention of Jess is like scraping away a layer of raw skin. Where is she staying? Is Cath still with her?

'By the way, Jess ferociously defends your innocence.' PC Page pauses. 'While I was there, I went to look at your workshop. After, I was looking at your garden.' She pauses. 'It tells quite a story, if you look closely enough. But you don't need me to tell you that.'

My skin flushes hot. 'What do you mean?'

'When you're quite the expert on the meanings of flowers and herbs, you can't tell me you haven't noticed?' There's a slightly scathing tone in her voice.

I look at her, confused. 'I'm really not sure what you're getting at. I grow herbs as you know. And flowers. They have meanings. But there's no story.'

'I'd disagree. It was something your therapist, Sonia Richardson, said to me, about gardens telling stories – apparently she came to see you and found you standing in your neighbour's garden. She overheard you apologising.'

261

'That is out of context,' I contest hotly. 'I was fond of Mrs Guthrie. I was sorry I hadn't been more help to her – that was all.'

'When I asked Ms Richardson why she'd visited you, she said she'd been in Steyning to see a friend. As she was near, she'd gone to check how you were. Apparently, she had concerns about you – you saw her before, some years ago, didn't you? She said you'd had some kind of breakdown when your marriage ended and she was worried you were on the edge of another one. Once she was satisfied you were coping, she said you talked about the plants in your neighbour's garden. Quite a coincidence that she has the same interest in herbs and flowers that you have. She told me she had this theory that a garden could somehow tell the stories of the people who'd lived there.' For a moment, she sounds disbelieving of herself, as beside her DI Lacey looks irritated. 'To be honest, I didn't pay too much attention. But then I went back to your garden. After the conversation with Ms Richardson, I started looking around. One of our officers is a bit of an expert and between us we identified some of the plants, so that I could look them up. And like I said, it's only a theory, but you have mock orange – which means deceit. Anemone, meaning forsaken. Marigolds, which signify pain and grief – they are everywhere. Narcissi – for egotism. Lavender – it isn't in flower at the moment, but its meaning is distrust. The aconites are coming up in your polytunnel – meaning poisonous words. Oh – and down behind your workshop are a clump of yellow hyacinths. Interesting choice of colour, because they're about jealousy, aren't they Amy? Rosemary, for remembrance of whatever it was that's taken place there. I have one question.' She pauses. 'Tell me. Are there snowdrops in your garden?'

I remember Sonia asking the same question, of Mrs Guthrie's

garden. Snowdrops mean hope. And they used to be there, but they stopped flowering a year or so after I moved in. 'There used to be.' I frown. 'Most of the plants you've named were there when we moved in.'

'Maybe your garden is cursed.' Beside her, DI Lacey shifts in his chair.

'Maybe it is.' I swallow, willing her to change the subject, but the questions keep coming.

'Some of the shrubs must have been planted years ago.' Breaking off, she frowns. 'Did you know the previous owner, Amy?'

I shake my head. 'As far as I know, it belonged to an elderly woman who had died. It had been empty quite a while when I moved in.'

'It never seemed an odd choice for a single mother and a young child, to be so far away from community life?' Each word is like a bullet, carefully loaded, aimed at me.

I defend myself. 'It wasn't that far. I love the countryside – and it's a wonderful place to bring up a child. I needed the garden for my work. Steyning is only two miles away. That's nothing. And when Jess was young, Mrs Guthrie used to help out babysitting.'

DI Lacey glances towards her. 'This is the neighbour who died recently?'

'Yes, sir.' Nodding, PC Page falls silent, apparently satisfied by my answers, at least for now.

'It wasn't suspicious, was it?' He sounds thoughtful.

It's the same question I asked PC Page when I met her in Mrs Guthrie's garden that evening. 'It wasn't.' But there's what sounds like a hint of doubt in her voice.

For a moment I'm aware of how fragile my position is. How little it would take, in the eyes of the police, to swing the balance from being a suspect to guilty. But then we're interrupted by a knock on the door. It opens enough for me to see the uniformed officer who completed the paperwork when I was brought in.

'Can I have a word, sir?'

Getting up, the DI follows him out, closing the door behind them. Left with PC Page, I seize my chance. 'How much longer do I have to stay here?'

'Amy, you know I can't answer that.'

After waiting in silence, when the DI comes back in, I ask him the same question. 'It isn't possible to say. At the moment, all our evidence points to you, and you alone being involved in Mr Roche's disappearance.'

'What evidence?' I stare at him. 'There's no body. You have what you say is a potential murder weapon, but it could have been planted by anyone. And snippets of gossip from two women who aren't reliable.'

He frowns slightly. 'We have a bit more than that – the knife that matches a set in your kitchen, more blood, in your workshop, which someone had obviously tried to clean up, and more in the area of your compost heap. Then there's the fact that the night Mr Roche disappeared, you were in Brighton.'

'But I've already told you what happened.' I shake my head, horrified at the thought of where they're going with this. 'I went to deliver an order, then I drove straight back home.' I break off, as all of a sudden, it's making sense. 'That order wasn't genuine – it must have been placed by whoever's trying to set me up. They must have known there's CCTV there. They wanted me to be seen. Can't you see that?'

Ignoring what I've said, he carries on. 'Even if what you say is true, you still knew where Mr Roche had gone. Once you'd seen him, you could have gone home and waited for him. Then when he came back, you were ready for him. You stabbed him

– most likely in your kitchen – or in your workshop, after which he tried to get away from you.'

I gasp in horror. Not a single word he's saying has any truth in it.

The DI goes on. 'He left a lot of blood behind, though, didn't he? It must have been splattered all over the place. The bouquet of flowers in blood was inspired. You knew you couldn't remove every trace of his blood, so you made the huge bouquet of flowers, left it on your doorstep, before taking it inside and purportedly dropping it by accident. The perfect cover for what really happened. As for the van your neighbour saw, that could have been delivering anything.'

'This is insane.' However plausible they think they sound, they're wrong. Backed into a corner, my fear knows another level. 'I keep telling you, none of this is true.'

'We still haven't found his car. Do you have any idea where it is?'

When I don't answer, PC Page looks at me. 'There's too much you haven't told us, Amy. As well as that, almost everything you say is inconsistent.' She sits back. 'Even your friends have described your behaviour as erratic. And I've seen it here. Even at your most plausible, it's impossible to know whether to believe you or not.'

I'm shocked into silence. Where I'd been hoping for a glimmer of light, there is none. Instead, as I look at PC Page and DI Lacey, then at my solicitor sat next to me, within the confines of these dingy walls, I know I'm trapped.

Jess

Even Matt's Facebook page is embedded with lie after flab-bergasting lie, about the fictitious house he's in the process of buying, a photo of a Caribbean beach on a date I happen to know he was in Brighton. So many lies. How difficult it must be keeping up with them.

As I scroll down over older posts, getting a picture of the kind of friends he has, before I message anyone, I find her. Mandy. I note the heavy jewellery, how skinny and tanned she is, how her face wears the same troubled look I've seen on my mother's, as I bring up her Facebook page. Unlike Matt, Mandy's actually in her photos of exclusive hotels and exotic beaches. As I keep scrolling down, about two and a half years ago I find a post about them breaking up, followed by dozens of sympathetic messages that make no attempt to hide what they think of Matt. Unlike him, it seems Mandy has real friends, who see him for the rat he really is.

Having already studied her face, I know I've met her – just the once, at Sasha's house. Clicking on her list of friends, I find that she's still connected to Sasha's mother. Like I tried to explain to PC Page, Mandy had been Matt's way in to the party where he met my mother.

Needing to find out what Mandy knows about Matt, I send her a carefully worded message. Then going back to Matt's page, I scroll back further, looking at posts I've already studied, searching for something I've missed. For a few weeks there's another pretty woman, expensively dressed. Then before her, another. As I go through the posts, there's a clear pattern of eligible women flitting through his life, confirming my suspicions that he's a serial charmer. A liar. A fake, who targets specific women, lures them in then leaves them, but they have one thing in common. Money. And somehow, he knew.

Needing to find out what Sasha's mum knows, I call her.

'Jess, I'm so sorry to hear about your mum. I couldn't believe it when I found out. Are you OK?'

Hearing the warmth in her voice, tears fill my eyes. 'Yes. But I need to ask you something.'

'Go on.' She sounds puzzled.

'That party at your house – when Mum met Matt. How long had you known him?'

'It's hard to say, exactly. I didn't know him that well. I don't know if you know, but he was with Mandy before that. She and I are not particularly close, but I've known her for years. I would certainly have invited her, but they'd broken up long before the party. I wouldn't have invited him on his own.' There's a brief silence. 'I'll have to ask Michael.' Michael's her husband. 'Maybe they might have bumped into each other in the pub or something. But thinking about it, it really is strange.'

'I messaged Mandy but I haven't heard back from her. Do you have her phone number?'

'I think so.' Sounding cautious, she breaks off. 'Don't you think this is best left to the police, Jess?'

'Maybe. But it wouldn't do any harm, would it? If I gave Mandy a call?'

★

With still no response to my Facebook message, when I try Mandy's mobile number, it goes to voicemail. But even talking to Sasha's mum seems to confirm my suspicions. If I'm right, going on the pattern I've observed, Matt would already have been planning his next move.

If the other woman who reported him missing to the police is to be believed, she was the woman he was going to leave my mother for. But in time, he'd have left the other woman, too. Maybe he'd already found the next woman to follow her. Maybe it's her who's set my mother up. Feverishly, I start going through the profiles of every woman he's friends with, staring at their photos for a giveaway sign, that I'm right. But if he's the master of deception he appears to be, he'd have made absolutely sure there were no clues.

My only hope is that somewhere along the line, he's slipped up, leaving damning evidence. I just have to make sure I find it.

Amy

Chapter Thirty-Three

As time inside takes its toll on me, I grow more weary, increasingly dispirited, while my mind tortures me with thoughts of what will happen to Jess if I'm charged with murder. Losing track even of the day of the week, my only reminder is when PC Page starts the tape.

'I have a question for you, Amy. When you bought your house, were you made aware that in 1996, a teenager died there?'

As I look at her, I feel my pulse start to race. 'No.' Shaking my head. Why are they asking about this now, of all times?

Their eyes are glued on me as she goes on. 'Apparently it was a tragic accident. We received an anonymous letter from someone saying that when it happened, the truth was hushed up. The writer gave us the name of a Ms Fiona Rose and her address. Does the name mean anything to you?'

'No.' I frown, genuinely mystified. 'I've never heard of her.'

'The only reason I'm asking is that she couldn't really help. So I wondered if you might be able to.'

Looking from one face to the other, I feel the walls close

in. 'Are you charging me? Because if you're not, haven't I been held long enough?' Deliberately confrontational, but at this moment, I've nothing to lose.

When no-one speaks, DI Lacey leans back in his chair, watching me. 'We've been trying to trace the family of the woman who owned the house before you. Her name was Ruth Preston. So far, we haven't had any luck. Perhaps because of the tragic association, they would prefer not to have anything to do with it. We know she was the teenager's grandmother and that apparently, she made herbal remedies – rather like you, it would seem. Apparently the teenager who died accidentally took something toxic. Either that, or someone intentionally gave it to her.'

There's only one answer as I shake my head. 'It really is the first I've heard of it.'

For a moment, I think that's the end of it. But I should have known PC Page wouldn't let it go. 'It's a coincidence, isn't it? That you buy a house that belonged to a herbalist, then you train as one?'

Trying to hide the racing of my heart, I shrug. 'The garden appealed to me. You've seen what I grow there.'

She nods. 'Maybe it explains why there's such a clear story in the plant meanings. Deceit, pain, distrust, grief. Remembrance . . . It's a memorial garden.' She pauses, her eyes boring into me. 'I think you inherited a memorial to the dead teenager. There's jealousy there, too.' Her eyes narrow slightly. 'Why would that be, I wonder? Was someone jealous of her?'

I try to appeal to their common sense. 'I've no idea. Isn't it possible they were all planted because the old lady liked them? It might not have been anything more than that.'

She's silent for a moment. 'There are so many stories in your home, Amy. A lot of earth that's been newly dug, the rose garden you haven't planted yet. Did Matt help you dig his own grave?' Without waiting for me to speak, she turns towards DI Lacey. 'We need to get a team over there. That new bed. When I was there this morning, it hadn't been touched.'

'Please don't.' My voice is mildly hysterical at the thought of the garden I love being trashed more than it already has been. 'You won't find anything. You're wasting your time, I promise you.'

As the DI nods towards her, he gathers his papers together. 'Let's leave it there, shall we? We need to check this out.'

'But I can't stay another night. Haven't you held me long enough?' My voice rises with each word, even though I know it's futile.

'For a serious crime, we can hold you for up to ninety-six hours without bringing charges. That gives us until tomorrow morning.'

★

I doze briefly that night, waking in the early hours, my mind racing. In a few hours, I'll know if the police are charging me or not. What might follow, I can't bear to think about. So little has been said about this other woman in Matt's life, it's as though somehow she's above suspicion. Yet she has the strongest motivation of anyone for framing me.

★

The following morning, as I wait to be led back to the interview room, I'm filled with trepidation, knowing I've been set up, by someone who wants me to suffer. By the time I hear footsteps coming towards my door, I'm dreading the worst.

Trying to maintain a semblance of composure, as I walk into the interview room, DI Lacey and PC Page are already there, talking in low voices. When they see me, they look up. 'Good morning.'

Both of them watch me pull out a chair, trying to still the flutter of nerves. 'Morning.' I look at their faces, trying to read them, but as always, they give nothing away. 'Can I say something?'

The DI looks at me. 'Go on.'

'I was thinking.' Nerves mean my voice is husky. 'I know I've been set up. The question is, by who?' As I look from one to the other, their faces are blank. 'It could easily have been the other woman. She has a strong motive. It could have been her who killed Matt, in a fit of jealousy that got out of control. She could have taken a knife from my kitchen – she would have had his key – then hidden it without me knowing. She could even have sent the flowers.'

'It sounds a little far-fetched.' DI Lacey clears his throat. 'Where are her fingerprints? For your information, Mr Roche's car has turned up – burned out next to some derelict farm buildings near Beachy Head. It could have been there for some time. You must have dumped the body before setting fire to it, Ms Reid. The chassis number was found, and the vehicle traced to Mr Roche, but it seems it was registered to his old address, so even though it was in our system, it's only recently been connected to this case. We haven't found his body yet. It would seem it's only a matter of time – and the tides – before we do. There was something in the car.' As he pushes a plastic bag towards me, with horror, I recognise the bracelet sealed inside. 'Yours?' He pauses for a moment, studying my face. 'I take it that's a yes?'

Slowly I shake my head. 'It could have come undone at any time. The fact that it was in Matt's car doesn't prove anything.'

He doesn't comment. 'Ms Reid, as you are aware, we've been

back to your house – more specifically to the area of your garden you've recently dug up.'

I wait with bated breath for him to tell me that they've found nothing, which means I'm free to leave here, but what he says next mystifies me.

'Despite your conviction that there was nothing to find, we did find something. A hardback book.'

Until now, I haven't noticed there's another bag on the end of the table. As he opens it, then slides out my notebook, I'm confused. 'That doesn't make sense. It's only a collection of garden ideas – a kind of scrapbook. Why would someone have buried it?'

He frowns. 'Oh, it's some scrapbook alright. We've had a close look – there's more than at first meets the eye. What was it? Did you cast one of your spells as you buried your secrets, hoping no-one would ever find them?'

A chill runs through me. 'I don't know what you're talking about.'

'Where to start . . .' Pausing, the DI opens it, then turns the first couple of pages. 'The first item of note here is a list of plants – or perhaps I should say herbs – and their effects on the human brain, ranging from nervousness and tremors, to suppression of the nervous system, then to respiratory and cardiac arrest. Quite a comprehensive list it is, too. It mentions hemlock, digitalis, deadly nightshade . . .'

Nausea rises in me. 'Someone's added it. I'm a herbalist. I abide by a healer's code. I've only ever used remedies for good.' I look at him, willing him to believe me, knowing how futile it is to convince him he's wrong when he's so sure he isn't. 'Where was this list?'

'Hidden behind a magazine cutting you've glued in – about rose gardens.'

Remembering the cutting, I frown. But my stomach is turning

over. I glance at PC Page, then back at the DI. 'The magazine cutting is mine, but I honestly didn't put anything else there. You have to believe me. I don't know who or why, but someone else has done this. Not me,' I repeat, taking a shaky breath. 'I want a new lawyer.' I glance sideways at Andrew Nelson. 'Someone who can actually help me.'

DI Lacey glances at PC Page. 'It's a bit late for that.'

Starting to panic, I raise my voice. 'I have the right. I just need you to arrange it.'

'That's slightly ridiculous in the circumstances.' The DI's voice is dry. 'For now, I'd like to get back to your book. There's another cutting we found.' He picks up a torn-out newspaper article that's vaguely familiar. 'It relates to the case of the teenage girl who was murdered at your house before you bought it. Her name was Kimberley Preston. But we've been doing our own research. It was her grandmother you bought your house from. Only you didn't buy your house, did you, Ms Reid? She was your grandmother, too. She left you the house on the understanding that you would live there for the rest of your life. We have the records of ownership and we've contacted the solicitors who handled the transfer of the deeds. We know about the letter your grandmother left detailing exactly what happened to Kimberley Preston. It clearly states that if you didn't fulfil her request, it would find its way to the police. You weren't prepared to put it to the test, were you? Amy isn't the name you were born with, is it Ms Reid? It was Emily.'

I stare at the table, blood rushing in my ears, unable to speak, as all the memories I've blocked out flood back. The long summer days in my grandmother's garden, of friendship, heat, freedom. The day my sister died, her death causing ripples into so many lives. The stupid pact with Allie that meant we'd kept our silence.

Suddenly I think of her phone call, how I blocked her number. It had been just before I was arrested. After all the years we haven't seen each other, is it possible Allie is behind this?

'Why have you lied, Ms Reid? What are you hiding?' The pause is ominous. 'We've found your friend. Allie Macklin.' There's another pause, in which my brain seems to become paralysed. 'These days, known as Fiona Rose. I find it very hard to believe that when your pasts are so entwined, you honestly didn't know about her and Mr Roche.'

'*What?*' I stare at him, utterly shocked.

The DI leans forward. When he speaks, his voice is disbelieving. 'Surely you must have known that it was Ms Rose that Mr Roche was planning to leave you for?'

As he speaks, it's as though I have no breath in my lungs. 'I didn't know.' I stare at him, my heart racing. Imagining them together, an image fills my mind, expanding until I can't think of anything else. 'It can't be her.' It's too far-fetched to believe it was *her* he was having an affair with – of all people. She must have known, all along.

The DI looks disbelieving. 'Surely you're not expecting us to believe that you didn't know about Ms Rose or where she lived? She's a lawyer, by the way – with a firm in Brighton. She was on her way home from work when she saw you.'

Dazed, I'm still reeling. So Allie – or Fiona – was the witness. As it sinks in she's now a lawyer, I realise she's given herself the credibility she always said she would. 'You said the anonymous letter was addressed to her?' Frantic, I seize the last chance to make them see reason. 'It makes even more sense now. She would have known where we lived, wouldn't she? Even as a teenager, she was selfish and reckless. Don't you see how easy it would have been, for her to kill Matt and frame me?' I'm pleading with them, desperate for them to see what to me is obvious. But they don't know what Allie is like. How furious she was with me. How she'd say anything to anyone, just to get to me.

The DI doesn't respond. 'There's one thing I don't understand. It's why you've lied about your house.'

Still stunned by the revelation that it was Allie Matt had been seeing, I shake my head. 'But you didn't ask about my house.'

'You lied by omission, Ms Reid. You let us assume facts which weren't correct. And the house is only part of it, as you know. Can we continue talking about the day your sister died? Ms Rose has already told us her version of events. We know something happened there, that until now, the two of you have kept secret. What was it?'

This is the moment I've dreaded. The moment I thought would never come, knowing that after the lies I've told, when I tell them the truth, they won't believe me. 'Kimberley drank a herbal remedy. Only it wasn't one of my gran's. Allie — Fiona — and I made it.' As I pause, silence falls. 'She was jealous of Kimberley. She had a crush on Kimberley's boyfriend, Charlie. She wanted him for herself, it was as simple as that. When Allie got something into her head, she could be ruthless. One night, when she saw them together, something snapped inside her. The next day, she persuaded me that we could prepare a potion to make Kimberley fall out of love with Charlie.'

'You went along with it?' The DI sounds disbelieving.

I nod. 'It was honestly intended to be innocuous. Kimberley was my sister. I would never have wished her any harm. Allie and I climbed into the walled corner of the garden where my gran worked. There was a door which she always kept locked, but part of the wall was crumbling – it had completely collapsed by the time I moved there. We found her notebook.' In the small room, my voice seems to echo. 'It listed what each plant symbolised. I don't remember exactly what we used, but it was probably something like cyclamen, which means goodbye. Yellow rose for infidelity – Allie thought if Kimberley was unfaithful to him, Charlie would break up with her. Five-leaf clover for bad luck. Then . . .' Remembering, I shake my head. 'Allie added something from a bottle she found. I didn't see her do it. I found out later, it was labelled darkness. She didn't tell me until after Kimberley had drunk it – we'd poured the potion into her orange juice. We were always making potions – harmless ones, from lemon balm and mint or other such plants. Kimberley had no reason to believe this was any different. She went outside.' I break off, struggling with my emotions. 'That was when Allie told me what she'd done. I rushed after her. Kimberley was in front of the house. Her boyfriend had just turned up. She was already unsteady on her feet. Then she seemed to lose her balance . . .' There's anguish in my voice, the memory as clear as if it happened yesterday. 'It was bad luck a delivery van was driving past. She was clearly disorientated. Somehow she lurched in front of the van. He hit her.'

The DI's frown deepens. 'You're saying Ms Macklin did this? Without your knowledge?'

I nod. 'I could never have done anything like that. I never wanted to hurt my sister. And I knew my gran's philosophy, about the power of intention.' I stare at him, imploring him to believe me. It's like reliving a nightmare as I remember Allie's recklessness, her obsessive jealousy. Her determination that she was going to have Charlie, no matter what it took.

'Did you tell anyone what Allie had done?'

'No. After the ambulance arrived, Allie and I hid. She told me it was my fault too and we were in it together. Then she said we had to make a vow, to protect ourselves. We cut our fingers and held them together, so that our blood blended. It meant we had to keep our secret. From there on, we were blood sisters.'

'And all this time, no-one knew?' PC Page sounds incredulous.

'My gran found the potion we'd made.' I stare at my hands, clasped in front of me on the table. 'Then she found the bottle labelled DARKNESS in one of Allie's pockets. She didn't tell the police what we'd done, but she spoke to our parents. She told them that we'd meant no harm, but the fact that it happened at all was her fault, because she should have been more careful about locking everything away. Of course, it wasn't her fault. They were behind a locked door.' I remember, because we hadn't been able to open it.

'What happened next?'

Oh God. My parents. I remember their shocked, stricken faces, their inconsolable grief as their lives were devastated. Kimberley's death killed something in them, too. It's a memory that haunts me to this day, as does guilt, because I should have seen what Allie was doing. Even now, it's too painful to think about. 'My parents were devastated. They never got over it. How could they have? As soon as I was old enough, I left home. My father died shortly after and my mother sold the house and moved away. We kept in touch, but then I found out she'd had a heart attack and died. That was when I changed my name to Amy, before I met Dominic. I was desperate to leave that part of my life behind.' It's a part of my life I've hidden from Jess, too, hating how I haven't been honest with her.

'But even after changing your name, your grandmother still knew where to find you.'

'She left me the house. But if I ever sold it, there was a letter that would go to the police, giving an account of what happened to Kimberley.' I shake my head, defeated. 'It was her way of punishing me.'

'It's hardly surprising you and Ms Macklin lost contact.' The DI leans back in his chair. 'You were each other's worst reminder of what happened to your sister.'

It's true. I couldn't think of Allie, still can't, without thinking of my sister. 'After we lost touch, I found out that her parents had sent her away. Later, she told me they'd disowned her.'

DI Lacey taps his fingers on the table. 'Which they clearly considered to be her punishment. While your grandmother didn't consider the punishment you'd received severe enough, she left you a living memento of what you'd done, didn't she? A house you could never sell, and a garden she'd planted so you'd never forget.'

Tears stream down my cheeks as I nod. Because it's true. Each day I've lived there I've seen Kimberley's face, lived with the echo of my grandmother's anger, heard her words in my head, about the alchemist's curse. Waited all these years for the balance to be redressed, knowing at some point, it would be. And now it has. Then I look up at him. 'It's true that I should have said something about what Allie did. It doesn't excuse anything, but she was formidable – and I suppose I was under her spell. You have to believe I had nothing to do with the poison she gave Kimberley.'

'Can anyone corroborate what you've told us?' PC Page's voice is sharp.

'Only Allie.' I pause. 'But she won't. She's convinced herself that it was me who did it, to the point that she believes her own lie.'

'What about the boyfriend? Maybe he saw something.'

Shaking my head, more tears roll down my cheeks. 'He may have found out from my grandmother. They spent a lot of time together in the weeks after Kimberley died.'

DI Lacey glances at PC Page. 'I think we need to find him and bring him in for questioning.'

'Oh no . . .' Wiping my tears away, I stare at them. 'Oh, God. You don't know, do you? After Kimberley died, Charlie killed himself.'

Chapter Thirty-Four

'When did this happen?' PC Page's voice is sharp.

'I'm not exactly sure.' My memories are sharp, but not the timing. 'But Charlie hung himself. In my gran's garden . . . My garden. From the apple tree – it's still there.' I wasn't there when it happened, but every day, when I look at the tree, it's impossible not to think of him. 'It happened about a couple of months after Kimberley died. He didn't want to live without her.'

The DI is silent for a moment. 'You'd have saved us all a lot of time if you'd been honest.' Glancing at PC Page, he speaks under his breath. 'We need to find Ms Rose and bring her in for further questioning. We may well have enough evidence to reopen the investigation into Kimberley Preston's murder.' He turns back to me. 'We will get to the bottom of this, no matter how long it takes.'

'So what happens now?' I'm still clinging on to the most fragile of hopes. 'I've been held for ninety-six hours. Surely I can leave?' But my words fade. Knowing they think I'm involved in the death of my own sister, that whatever I say I can't be trusted, the churning feeling in my stomach grows. It's the look on their faces, in their eyes, telling me they think I'm the ultimate unreliable witness.

'Apologies.' The DI fidgets in his chair. 'I got somewhat sidetracked. We were talking about your house. And actually, there is one more thing, Ms Reid.' Under his scrutiny, I feel myself shrink. 'When we found your notebook, there was a carrier bag buried in the ground next to it. Inside, were some of your clothes – an orange sweatshirt with a flower print on the front, a pair of faded jeans, patterned socks . . . We'll need you to identify them, but I'm fairly sure they're yours?'

As he describes the familiar clothes, I'm speechless.

'All of them stained with blood, Ms Reid.' Sitting back, he looks smug. 'Obviously we're testing it, but I imagine it's of the same type we've found everywhere else. There was a wallet, too, containing bank cards in the name of Matthew Roche.'

Silent, I stare at him in disbelief as he goes on. 'We've been making enquiries into local taxi companies near Beachy Head, to see if anyone picked up a woman and took her to Steyning that night. We spoke to a John Angel. Does that ring any bells?' Seeing my frown, he goes on. 'He remembered that night very well, as he received a call from a woman looking for a taxi from Beachy Head. It was in the early hours and he was about to turn in, but she sounded distraught. Being the good sort he is, he went to pick her up. When he got there, he said she was freezing cold and clearly upset. He couldn't get out of her why – she didn't want to talk. Once he got her into the taxi, she asked him to take her home. When he asked where that was, she said Steyning.'

As he pauses, I'm terrified of what's coming next.

'The woman was wearing a silver jacket.'

I gasp out loud. I'd looked for that jacket only recently, but it hadn't been hanging where I usually left it, with my other jackets.

He goes on. 'The only other item of note he could remember, was the orange sweatshirt she was wearing underneath. It had a flower print on it – he noticed as she got into his car. He gave us quite a clear description of her – in her late thirties, with fair hair. Most interestingly, he noticed her ring, because it was unusual. He said it reminded him of one his wife bought, in Morocco – dull gold, with a green stone. He saw it clearly while the lights were on inside the taxi when she came to pay him. When she'd called him initially, she'd given her name as Amy. He dropped her just off the High Street.'

In shock, I stare at him, trying to imagine a woman who looks like me, wearing my silver jacket, my orange sweatshirt that was later found buried in my garden, stained with blood. A woman who wasn't me. 'She may have looked like me, but I swear it wasn't me. I've told you, so many times, I was at home.' But as piece after piece of false evidence stacks up, I know I'm sinking. Going down for a crime I didn't commit.

'There's also the fact that you and Fiona Rose claimed not to know each other, when the truth is, you go back a very long way, a fact both of you have avoided talking about.' He pauses for a moment. 'Strange too, that both of you hook up with the same man.'

I look at him, utterly aghast. 'That both of us know Matt was a coincidence. You have to believe that.'

'It's a little unlikely, even by your standards.' The DI leans back in his chair. 'You both had very good reason to be angry with Mr Roche. Maybe angry enough to push you to the point where you cooked up some plan between you to get rid of him, using the wedding as a smokescreen to make people think he'd simply taken off. But even without her . . .' He breaks off for a moment. 'There are consistent accounts of your mental instability. Your therapist, Sonia Richardson, backs them up. Didn't you stop to think why she came to your house? It was because you'd been suicidal in the past, she was concerned enough to call round to check on you.'

My mind races. Sonia would never have told them that, not in so many words. And I could never have gone through with it, because of Jess. 'It isn't true. I was low at that time, yes. But nothing more.'

'According to Ms Richardson, at the time, you admitted as much to her. Are we supposed to believe you over a mental health professional?' His eyes bore into me.

It's an impossible question – one that I either answer truthfully, risking adding to the damaging picture they have of me, or else lie. But there have been too many lies. 'When I was at my lowest, I thought about it. But I could never have done that to my daughter.'

He goes on, each new statement filling me with fear. 'Like I said, there are other accounts. Whether or not you had an accomplice, Ms Reid, I don't think there's any question that you are guilty of the murder of Matthew Roche. You will be remanded in custody until we can arrange a court hearing. I'm not sure what your role was in the death of your sister, Kimberley Preston, but the truth will come out. It always does.' Sounding matter of fact, he pauses for a moment. 'Ms Reid, I am charging you with the murder of Matthew Roche. You do not have to say anything . . .'

But as he goes on, his words go over my head. Then I'm thinking of Matt with Allie again, suddenly dizzy, unable to think, to take any more in, feeling my mind close down.

1996

Kimberley's grandmother knew what you'd done. She found your potion, found out what you'd put in it. Suspected who was guilty – how could she have missed the jealousy in your eyes? But she didn't tell the police. It was that belief she had – about nature's way of finding balance; in the alchemist's curse. The circle of life – and death. At some point, what you'd done would come back to haunt you.

But your actions stretched further; had consequences you couldn't have foreseen. A boy who never got over losing the only girl in the world for him, who could only follow her to her grave. Two devastated families. A friendship tainted forever, by the shared knowledge of what you'd done. The guilty secret that would stay with you, every waking day, until your last.

So many wrongs you could never right. So much grief you left so many people with. Grief that will never fade – grief for the young never does. When a life is wasted, how can it?

Fiona

Chapter Thirty-Five

A hint of early spring brings Brighton to life. As I walk to work, I notice more people running or cycling along the seafront, under clear skies, the sea becoming a chalky blue. When I hear no more from the police, I begin to believe that justice will at last be served and my life can go on as planned.

When I think about the letter that deliberately implicated me, there's no way of knowing whether it was inspired by a desire to tell the truth or by some other motive. Why name me and not Amy? Or maybe it doesn't matter. Maybe in their twisted mind, the writer wants the police to question both of us. My stomach turns over as I think about how they already have Amy. How long before they want to question me again?

I try not to dwell on it. After weeks of angst, peace of mind no longer exists. Every street corner, the people I work with, even my flat, are a constant reminder of what I've lost. I imagine going away, picture somewhere quiet, where the sun is hot, a place where no-one knows who I am, while I come to terms with losing Matt.

When I hear through the legal grapevine again that Amy's

been charged with Matt's murder, hatred fills me, then sadness, as I allow myself to grieve for the man I loved. But with clarity comes the sense of a weight starting to lift. That morning, as I walk to work, my mood is brighter, my step lighter than it's been in months. Thinking about booking a couple of weeks off while I work out a long term plan, my sense of optimism builds. There are times it's good to step away from what you know. There's no doubt in my mind that this is one of those moments.

At work, instead of waiting for the lift, I take the stairs to the first floor, but when I pass through the swing doors into the reception area, I'm stopped in my tracks.

'Ms Rose.' It's PC Page, with another uniformed officer I don't recognise. 'We'd like you to come with us, please.'

A feeling of foreboding fills me. Then as I stand there, I feel my plans disintegrate, falling like rain. Staying calm, in an attempt to mask it, I smile at her. 'PC Page. I don't understand. Surely whatever it is, we can talk about it here? Would you like to come through to my office?' As I speak, I'm aware of people around us, watching, as a horrifying thought occurs to me. Surely they're not about to arrest me?

As PC Page frowns, then opens her mouth to speak, I nod. 'Yes, of course.' I turn briefly to the receptionist, Sheila. 'Could you cancel my meetings for today?'

A look of astonishment on her face, she nods, as I turn back to PC Page, summoning as much dignity as I can muster. 'Right. I'm ready. Shall we go?'

We walk to the lift in silence, PC Page beside me, the younger officer slightly ahead, silence that's maintained as the doors open and close. Even when we reach the ground floor and walk to the car, I don't speak. Around me, the Brighton I walked through just minutes ago, where the future felt filled with hope, doesn't exist any more. If I'd objected to their request, they would have

290

arrested me in front of my colleagues. Of that, I'm in no doubt. That I've avoided it by the skin of my teeth is of little comfort.

At the police station, I'm led into a small interview room. The younger officer stays with me, while PC Page disappears for a few minutes. When she comes back, she nods towards him. 'That'll be all. The DI's on his way. When he gets here, can you show him in?'

At the mention of the DI, my heart sinks further. 'Can I ask what this is about?'

Her voice is short. 'You'll find out in a few minutes, Ms Rose.'

As she finishes speaking, the door opens and DI Lacey comes in. Looking directly at me, he pulls out a chair and sits down.

'I still don't know why you've brought me in, Detective Inspector.'

'Before we go any further, we have one or two more questions about Mr Roche.' He pauses. 'From what we've learned, it looks as though he subjected Ms Reid to a form of emotional abuse known as gaslighting. Are you aware of what that is?'

I nod. 'Yes. I've had clients who've been exposed to it.'

'So you would recognise it if someone tried it on you? Even though it begins in ways so subtle they're barely detectable?'

'I think I would.' When it comes to relationships, at the first sign of any sociopathic tendencies, I walk away. And usually I spot them a mile off. 'But I take your point.'

'You weren't aware of Mr Roche behaving in this way towards you?'

I frown. 'I don't think so. I often felt he had the upper hand – but that was because of the situation. My understanding of emotional abuse is that for all kinds of reasons, some people are more susceptible than others.'

Until now there's been a kind of mutual respect. But this

time, as DI Lacey speaks, I know I have every reason to be very worried. 'If you require a solicitor, Ms Rose, now might be that time.'

Suddenly I'm rigid, playing for time as he glances at PC Page. 'We need to question you about the murder of Kimberley Preston. The matter of the herbal potion designed to make her fall out of love with her boyfriend. The boyfriend you wanted for yourself. Except at the last minute, you added a substance that killed her.'

It's as though every last drop of blood has drained out of me, leaving me lightheaded. 'I . . . I'd like to call Bill Merton.' Even my voice sounds different. 'I used to work for him. He's a partner at Dentons – in their Cobham branch.' Bill's hardcore, used to defending serious criminals. Once upon a time, he and I had a brief dalliance, one I've no wish to resurrect, but right now, he's my best hope.

Clearly his reputation precedes him. 'You haven't been arrested, Ms Rose.' DI Lacey looks surprised.

Folding my arms, I stand my ground. 'I have the right.'

'I'll see to it.' Glancing at the DI, PC Page gets up and heads for the door, leaving me alone with him.

'As I told Ms Reid, the truth always comes out.' Speaking quietly, he sits back, his eyes resting on my face, as if waiting for me to speak.

I refuse to be drawn. Then I'm thinking of the anonymous letter again – how the police now have both Amy and me. Is this what the writer of the letter wanted? Staring back at DI Lacey, we're adversaries, our accounts conflicting; suspended in the air between us, the truth.

Chapter Thirty-Six

Two hours pass before Bill arrives, the small room growing stuffier with each passing minute, DI Lacey long replaced by a junior officer. My eyes scan my surroundings, observe every mark on the wall, imagine the conversations that have taken place here. 'Could I have a glass of water?'

When he goes out, I lean forward, resting my head in my hands. Amy's cracked. How else could they know about the potion Kimberley took? But I know she'll have told them her version of events, saying whatever it takes to save her own neck, not caring for a second what will happen to me.

A wave of rage floods over me as I think how her life has been. No-one's ever disowned Amy, or washed their hands of her. Compared to what I've been through, she got off scot-free. If I'm not careful, it will happen again. I'm the only person who can make sure justice is served. Amy deserves to suffer.

When Bill eventually walks in, he looks fraught. 'Sorry I couldn't get here earlier. I got caught in terrible traffic. What's going on?'

As he sits down, I start talking. 'It's unbelievable, Bill. It's to do with something that happened twenty-three years ago. It's a long story. I was at my friend's grandmother's house in the summer holidays, with her older sister. My friend's name was Emily. She changed it to Amy subsequently, for reasons which become apparent.' I go on, telling him what happened and how Emily and I played this prank which went horribly wrong. 'We were kids, Bill. Emily was hopelessly jealous of her sister. Kimberley was beautiful and had everything Emily wanted – especially her boyfriend. We cooked up an idea to create a love potion, so that Kimberley's boyfriend might fancy Emily. Childhood games. Her gran had all these bottles and a book of recipes – she dabbled as a herbalist. We cooked up something to make Kimberley fall out of love with her boyfriend. It was supposed to be completely harmless, more of a joke rather than anything serious. But at the last minute, Emily added something extra when my back was turned. It had hemlock in it, I think. Possibly digitalis, too. It killed Kimberley. Bill, it was the most terrible time.' I break off, as a look of shock crosses Bill's face. Shaking my head, remembering the events that day, I go on. 'The police have been talking to Emily about it – or Amy as she is now. She's told them this cock and bull story about how it was me who added the poison. I'm really worried they believe her.' Pausing for a moment, I stare at Bill – it's imperative he believes me. 'She's already in a lot of trouble. She was recently charged with the murder of a man.' I hesitate again, knowing how implausible this is going to sound. 'The man's name is Matthew Roche. She was living with him. They were about to get married.' I look at Bill. 'The thing is . . . You couldn't make this up, Bill. A few months ago, I met Matt in a bar. He told me his relationship with Amy was over and we started seeing each other. The night he disappeared, he was about to tell her he was leaving her – for me.'

Bill listens without saying a word, a look on his face I can't read. None of this is what I wanted. I never set out to reveal what Amy did all those years ago. But I'm left with no choice but to defend my position. Amy is guilty, weak, selfish. The police should be able to see that now. But for all their razor-sharp insight and knowledge of the criminal profile, they've clearly missed something. I go on. 'I know. What are the chances. Even to me, it sounds implausible. But the problem is, what if they believe her?' My voice drops to a whisper as I clutch his arm. 'I didn't do it, Bill. Even though I've no way of proving it. You have to believe me.'

'Of course I do.' His face is grim. 'We'll see what they have to say. If you're sure there's nothing else I should know, let's get this started.'

I shake my head. 'Thanks for coming.' I'm genuinely grateful, my words heartfelt but I'm nervous. Not only is he my best hope, he's my only hope. If Bill can't help me, then no-one can.

★

In all the years as a solicitor, for the first time I'm on the other side, with someone else acting on my behalf. When PC Page and DI Lacey return, Bill is straight onto it.

'I'd like to know exactly why you're holding my client.' Bill speaks with an authority that comes from years of experience, that so many solicitors lack.

'Then let us tell you.' The DI is unruffled. 'In 1996, a teenage girl tragically died. At first, her death was thought to be an accident. But a post-mortem revealed she'd ingested enough digitalis and hemlock to cause respiratory and cardiac arrest. Her grandmother was a herbalist and had a collection of dried herbs and extracts, which she kept in labelled jars. There was, however, one jar that was kept separately. A jar that someone found and that day, deliberately added to her drink, so that she ingested enough poison to kill her.'

'What does this have to do with my client?' Bill's voice is calm.

'The teenager's name was Kimberley Preston. She had a sister, Emily, who was close friends with Ms Rose. In fact, it's fair to say you were very close, weren't you, Ms Rose?'

'You don't have to answer that.' Bill interrupts. 'Go on.'

'Ms Rose had a crush on Kimberley's boyfriend, Charlie. Between them, Ms Rose and Emily Preston cooked up a herbal concoction to make Kimberley fall out of love with Charlie. It was concocted from fairly benign substances – but at the last minute, somebody added something else, primarily the digitalis and hemlock that killed Kimberley. According to our witness, that was you, Ms Rose.'

It's what I'd known Amy would tell them. By getting in first, she's ahead of me, her story already lodged in their minds. Bill's quiet for a moment. 'And apart from this so-called witness, what proof do you have of this?'

The DI sits back. 'I'd like to hear Ms Rose's version of events. Ms Rose?'

The moment of truth, when I explain why she's told them this. 'It's true. We made up this herbal potion. We got a bit carried away. But I never expected Amy to add the poison.'

The DI interrupts. 'She told us about the small bottle labelled darkness.'

Silence fills the room, as I nod, my stomach turning over. 'Amy was jealous of her sister. She was obsessed with her boyfriend. She wanted Kimberley to dump him, but at the last minute, I think she saw her chance and got carried away.'

DI Lacey shakes his head. 'And the pair of you told no-one.'

Ashamed, I nod. 'But in actual fact, Kimberley was hit by a car.'

'Which would never have happened if the poison wasn't taking effect,' the DI points out. 'In any case, the post-mortem showed she'd ingested enough of it to kill her.'

'I don't remember the details.' My voice is low.

'Tell us the reason you and Emily kept your secret all this time, Ms Rose.' The DI's voice is harsh.

I shake my head. 'I think we both wanted to forget. Nothing we did was ever going to bring Kimberley back. My parents moved me to another school. After that, we lost touch.'

'Let's go back a bit.' The DI pauses. 'To right after Kimberley was hit by the car. What did you and Emily do next?'

'I don't know. We were too shocked to do anything. It was horrific.' My shoulders tense as I remember.

'Not too shocked to steal away and cut your fingers, then press them together in some sort of twisted little ritual while you swore a vow of secrecy? Minutes after your friend's sister had died?'

'That isn't what happened.' My teeth are gritted. The only reason he knows this is because Amy's told him.

'That's not what we've been told. And you still haven't really answered my question. Why have you never told anyone?'

I sigh. 'Emily's grandmother took the blame – she felt it was her responsibility to ensure the jars weren't accessible. They didn't prosecute her, because it wasn't her fault. But you don't forget something like that. The reality stays with you. Forever.'

'Is it true she found the bottle labelled DARKNESS in your pocket?'

Startled that he knows about the bottle, I shake my head. 'I don't remember. But if she did, it doesn't mean I put it there.'

Clearing his throat, DI Lacey looks at the papers on the table in front of him. 'Emily was punished for her part – eventually, after her grandmother's death. She left Emily the house, but in the intervening years, she'd planted a memorial garden to Kimberley, so that each day Emily lived there, she would always be reminded of what she'd done.' He pauses. 'There was another proviso in her will, that Emily could never sell. If she did, your secret would have been out. Her grandmother had left a letter with her solicitor, addressed to the police, explaining Emily's involvement in Kimberley's death.' He leans towards me. 'My question to you, Ms Rose, is what punishment did she mete out to you?'

My first instinct is to say none, because I wasn't guilty. 'She didn't need to. She told my parents what happened to Kimberley. They sent me away to a vile school where I was bullied. Then they cut me off. I never went back home again. From the moment she told them, I was on my own.'

'But at least you were alive.' This time, the DI speaks quietly. Then he shakes his head. 'While Kimberley wasn't. And when you met Mr Roche, you had no idea it was Amy who he was living with?'

'None whatsoever.' This time, I'm completely straight. Glancing at my watch, I'm unable to believe how much time has passed. It's early afternoon already.

DI Lacey notices. 'We'll take a break. Twenty minutes. There's still something I don't understand.'

★

Outside the police station, I have a cigarette for the first time in years.

'I'll go and get us sandwiches.' Bill looks up and down the street for a shop.

I shake my head. 'Don't worry on my account. I won't be able to eat anything.'

'This is a mess, Fiona.' Bill's voice is quiet, urgent. 'Your word against Amy's, no proof on either part . . .'

'I know.' I exhale slowly. 'There is one factor in this. Emily – Amy – is completely unstable. I wish I knew what she'd said to the police. She's probably sent them all around the houses before finally coming up with her version of events – a version she believes, even though it's wrong, because she can convince herself of anything.' There's a bitterness in my words that comes from knowing the way she works, her ability to play the innocent victim. 'We've both come across those types of people, Bill. They're completely unreliable – a nightmare. You can't believe anything they say. I wouldn't mind betting Amy's pushed the police to that point. She's been charged with Matt's murder, so they already know what she's capable of. That has to strengthen my case?'

Bill's silent for a moment. 'Let's hope you're right.'

★

As we return to the interview room, Bill nudges my elbow. 'Don't worry. If all they have is an unreliable witness, it isn't going to be enough.'

'I hope you're right,' I mutter as we walk inside. After standing outside, the staleness of the air in this room is suffocating. 'I need to open the window.' But when I go over and try to, it's firmly locked.

'I'll see if I can get someone to sort that.' Bill heads for the door, but before he reaches it, it's opened from the outside as DI Lacey and PC Page come in.

'Could we open the window?'

DI Lacey glances towards me. 'Someone was looking for the

key the other day. They 'didn't find it.' Pulling out a chair he sits down. 'Shall we continue?'

Irritated, I sit down next to Bill, but this time, it's PC Page who speaks. 'All evidence so far points to your involvement in Kimberley's death. You've even admitted it.'

As she says that, Bill interrupts. 'My client has admitted to no such thing. She had no knowledge of the poison, nor of Emily's intention.'

PC Page is silent for a moment. 'As I was saying, until we have conclusive evidence that proves that either you did or didn't administer the poison to Kimberley, we have no choice but to hold you in custody. Ms Rose, I am arresting you on suspicion of the murder of Kimberley Preston. You do not have to say anything, but it may harm your defence if you do not mention when questioned something you later rely on in court. Anything you do say may be given in evidence.'

Speechless, I turn to Bill. They can't do this. But he's ahead of me.

'Just a moment.' Bill sounds angry. 'You can't hold my client. You already have another suspect in Kimberley's death.'

'That's correct, Mr Merton. But in this case, potentially, we have two.'

Chapter Thirty-Seven

After the paperwork is completed, my fingerprints and DNA sample are taken. Before Bill leaves, he assures me we can work out how we're going to tackle this.

'This shouldn't be happening.' He looked grim. 'I'll do my best to find someone or something to back up your story.'

But as I suffer the indignity of being escorted by a uniformed officer to a cell, Bill's determination doesn't stop the feeling of claustrophobia that consumes me. As I step inside, the door is closed behind me. It's hours until tomorrow. I wonder if Amy is still here or since being charged, she's been moved somewhere else, as I curse her and her ability to ruin everything for me. Feeling my anger return, I get a hold of myself. I have to believe in Bill, make full use of each one of these hours I'm in here, to think.

Sitting on the narrow bed, closing my eyes, I breathe deeply, trying to centre myself. Shaking off my anger, I tell myself that by tomorrow this will be over; that I'll load up my car, leave this county and never come back here – not even for my job. It has the desired effect and when I open my eyes again, I'm slightly calmer. Looking around, I study the room, its white painted walls, cheap carpet, the most basic bathroom facilities, aware of how completely closed off from the world I am. Lying back on the bed, I stretch my hands behind my head. Only this morning I was thinking of the future. I never imagined that by this evening, I'd end up here.

*

I sleep fitfully, waking early. The custody process itself wears you down, making you more vulnerable. I'm brought insipid tea and white toast, which I nibble at, only because I know I must fortify myself for what lies ahead. Then I wait, for the sound of approaching footsteps, of other doors being unlocked until at last it's my turn. This morning, a PC I haven't met before waits outside the open door. 'Ms Rose? Would you come with me?'

*

In the interview room, Bill is already there waiting for me. He looks stressed. 'I'm sorry, Fiona. I didn't get very far. It isn't good.' As he shakes his head, I'm filled with a feeling of foreboding. 'I don't know what they have, but . . .' As the door opens, he breaks off, then lowers his voice. 'I think we're about to find out.'

There's the usual preamble as PC Page starts the tape, before the DI starts. 'Ms Rose.' He settles heavily down in his chair. 'We've been back to Ms Reid's house – or to clarify for the tape, maybe I should say, the house left to her by her grandmother, Ruth Preston. More specifically, we went to Ms Reid's workshop. I was interested to know what was in there. You're probably aware, like her grandmother was, she's a herbalist. In light of what both you and Ms Reid have said about the potion the two of

302

you concocted all those years ago, I needed to see it for myself.' His pause is for dramatic effect, keeping me in suspense when all I want is to know what he's going to say. 'Of course, we'd already examined the workshop, but that was in relation to Mr Roche's murder. This time was about Kimberley. Do you remember Amy's grandmother's notebook?'

As he stares at me, my skin prickles as a memory surfaces, of small pages scrawled in lines of her grandmother's handwriting. Entitled with joy, health or similar, all cloyingly benign and well-meaning. 'Yes.' I'm silent for a moment. 'It had her recipes in, if that's what you call them. She used to go on about intention – and something she called the alchemist's curse. Some hippy-dippy nonsense about natural forces restoring balance – a bit like karma, I suppose. None of it true, obviously.' But I'm not as confident as I sound.

PC Page is silent for a moment. 'I've been looking into it. I have a quote taken from her notebook, about how *nature perseveres, quite markedly, until balance is restored.* Maybe that's what's going on now.'

'I strongly object to this line of questioning.' Bill sounds adamant. 'It's pure speculation. There is no proof that any such thing exists.'

'I think you'll find there are plenty of people who'd disagree with you, Mr Merton.' PC Page shakes her head. 'And whatever you think, you have to consider the train of events that have led to Ms Rose being here.' She pauses briefly. 'If you'll let me finish . . . The notebook that belonged to Amy's grandmother had been added to. In the last pages, she created two more remedies for two specific people. You, Ms Rose, and Amy. I've been examining the constituents of each and while they're similar, there are significant differences. I've taken copies of the relevant pages.'

As she hands me two sheets of paper, I stare at the titles: *For Emily*. Then, *For Allie*. Then at the lists carefully written beneath in the same handwriting.

PC Page's voice cuts through my thoughts. 'I can take you through them, but basically Amy's is designed to remind her of what happened, to protect her against evil and make sure justice is done – perhaps in the form of the living punishment that her house is. The one for you, however, is different. It's about hatred, jealousy, recklessness, danger – and justice again. It's easy enough to read her hidden message. It was you, not Amy, who was the dangerous one. Her only crime was allowing you to sweep her along.'

Beside me, Bill stiffens. 'That's outrageous. This is supposition. You can't possibly use this as proof.'

'Along with the statements we have from both Ms Rose and Ms Reid, it tells a story,' DI Lacey talks over him. 'In the absence of being able to believe what anyone says, we look for clues. This, no question, is one.'

'There is another remedy.' PC Page's voice is quiet. 'It's for Kimberley. The meanings are innocence, sorrow, regret, sweetness and purity. Kimberley's death affected so many lives, and all because of a single act of foolish recklessness.'

It takes every ounce of self-control I can muster to stop myself contradicting her, to tell her not to judge, to walk a hundred miles in someone else's shoes, until she knows what it's like.

'Can I ask what you've done in the years since leaving school, Ms Rose?'

I stare back at her. 'I've had various jobs over the years. I wasn't well qualified when I left school and I had nowhere to go. I had to earn enough to keep a roof over my head.'

'And you started training as a lawyer when?' PC Page seems overly interested all of a sudden.

'Six years ago,' I say shortly. 'I wanted to change my life.'

'You're successful. You work for a good firm. Life must be very different.'

'It is.' I frown, wondering what they're driving at, but then I find out.

'I would imagine you have far more credibility these days. Wouldn't you agree?' DI Lacey's eyes bore into me. 'Rather than your flitting around days, going from job to job, struggling to pay the bills.'

'I didn't flit around and it wasn't a struggle.' I try to sound dignified. 'I just wanted to prove something to myself. It was about self-respect. And money, too – I won't lie.'

'But somewhere at the back of your mind, you must always have known, that as a lawyer, you would have far more credibility than Amy would. Did you always suspect this moment might come? That pitched against each other, each of you with your own version of what really happened, the police would have to decide which one of you was plausible?'

His incisiveness flabbergasts me. This was never supposed to happen. Between me and Amy, there's no question which of us is most credible. Under the table, I clasp my hands together to stop them shaking, feeling the arguments stacking up against me. 'That's hardly the reason to embark on a law degree. It was a major undertaking fitting it around a full-time job.'

As he goes on, his voice is smooth. 'Perhaps that suggests just how desperate you were, to change the way others perceived you. It was a driving force, wasn't it? Your hatred of Amy?'

'This is pure conjecture.' Bill interrupts. 'What you're suggesting has absolutely no basis in fact.'

'But in the context, it's perfectly believable.' DI Lacey looks at him, then back at me. 'And facts are somewhat lacking. You're economical with words, Ms Rose, when it suits you, while Ms Reid, however, omits entire chapters. Neither of you seem to comprehend the gravity of the situation.' He pauses. 'As well as prospectively facing charges for perverting the course of justice, both of you potentially face a murder charge.'

Jess

After speaking to the custody centre, I go to find Cath. 'They're charging Mum.' As I try to speak, suddenly my legs feel weak. I try to go on, but the emotions I've kept at bay catch up with me. Struggling, I get a hold of myself. 'What happens now?' Wiping away tears, I look at Cath. 'Will they make her go to court? What am I going to do?' All along I've believed the police would realise the mistake they've made. But if she's sentenced . . . Where does that leave me? What happens to our home?

Cath's arm goes around me. 'Nothing's decided yet, Jess. You mustn't give up.' She pauses. 'We should talk to your dad. If the press get hold of this, he's going to find out. Far better he hears from us.'

I shake my head. 'He won't be any help. He never has been. And he doesn't really care.' Looking ahead, I see myself becoming one of those students who has no home to go to during uni breaks, one of a handful left on a deserted campus, instead of catching the train back home.

'It isn't over yet.' Cath's voice is firm. 'Let's take each step at a time. First thing, call your dad. There's no need to commit to anything. And we can stay at Zoe's for a while. She's in no hurry for us to leave.'

'What about you?' I look at her. 'You have your own life, in Bristol. You've only just moved. The last thing you want to do is stay here with me.'

Cath comes over and hugs me. 'Your mother's one of my oldest friends. She was there when I needed her.' Her voice is muffled in my hair. 'Let's just say I owe her.'

★

With my entire life on hold, I'm humbled by Zoe's kindness. Then while I'm alone at Zoe's, I receive a phone call from PC Page.

'Jess? I thought you'd want to know, your mother's been moved to Bronzefield prison, in Surrey. She's being held on remand, but if you contact the prison, you can arrange a visit.'

Clutching the phone, it strikes me how much more sinister remand sounds than custody. 'How long will she be there?' My voice is small.

'Until the case goes to court. We don't have a date yet.'

I'm silent for a moment, thinking. 'What if someone finds something to prove her innocence?'

'Jess, the police investigation has been thorough. You have to trust us on that one.' She pauses. 'But if someone did find something, of course it would be taken into consideration.' Then she adds, 'We've finished at your house. You're free to go back any time you want to.'

Out of habit, I start to say thank you, but stop myself. I'm not grateful to the police for anything. They've devastated my mother's life, mine too. And whatever evidence they think they have, they've got this wrong.

★

In Zoe's kitchen, sitting at the large table, I'm trying to work out what to do as Cath comes back in.

'The police called a little while ago. They've moved Mum to Bronzefield prison. They're holding her on remand. But I can visit.'

Cath drops her shopping. 'We need to contact them. I've no idea what the procedure is. I'll get my laptop and find a number for them.'

I watch her hurry upstairs to fetch it. Then when she comes back, I apologise. 'Sorry. I should have asked the police. I was so thrown I didn't think.'

'Don't worry about it. You have far too much on your mind.' Pausing as she turns on her laptop, waiting a couple of minutes, before typing into the search bar. 'Did you say Bronzefield?' When I nod, she goes on. 'Right. I've found their website. Everything we need to know is here, including the number to call. When do you want to go?'

'Any time?' I stare at her. 'If you're sure? Soon? Whenever you're free?'

'Let's see what they say.' Getting her phone, she calls the number.

I let her make the call, overwhelmed with gratitude that she cares enough to help me. After she finishes talking on the phone, she looks at me. 'We need to take ID but it's fixed for tomorrow morning at half-past ten. Is that OK with you?'

I nod, both terrified and overcome by the most profound relief.

★

The following morning, Zoe makes me breakfast and fusses around me. 'Jess? Please let your mum know we're all thinking of her and hoping she's soon home. OK?'

As I nod, she goes on. 'And I know you're free to go home now, but if you'd rather, you're still welcome to stay here as long as you want to.'

'Thank you.' There's a lump in my throat. In a world that feels against me, there seems no end to Zoe's kindness.

★

It isn't long before Cath and I set off for Ashford, in Surrey, where Bronzefield is; the thought of seeing my mother a deceptive ray of brightness in looming clouds that haven't quite reached us. But I don't allow myself to think of the court case that lies ahead, only of the time I have left, in which to prove her innocence.

The roads are busy, the closer we get to London, the heavier the traffic, but at last we turn off the motorway and it isn't long before the imposing exterior of the prison looms into view. Suddenly my nerves are back.

It's as if Cath reads my mind. 'Would you like me to come in with you? There must be somewhere I can wait while you go and talk to her.'

'Thanks. If you don't mind.'

Turning into the car park, she reverses into a parking space. 'Of course I don't.' Switching off the engine, she turns to look at me, then says more quietly, 'It will be OK, Jess.'

I'm silent. Right now, it's hard to believe anything will ever be OK.

She gets out. 'Shall we do this?'

As we walk across the car park, I don't know what I'm expecting. I'm visiting a woman charged with murder, after all,

310

but when we reach the visitors' reception, we're treated courteously as they check our ID, then go into a waiting area, but not for long. Only a short while later, I'm asked to make my way to the main building.

Leaving Cath where she is, I go outside, and round to the main entrance. After presenting photo ID, my biometrics are recorded, then I go through airport-like security, before I'm allowed through an electric door into the visitors' hall.

Inside, I'm taken by surprise. It's far more comfortable than I thought it would be, with soft chairs and a children's play area. With only two or three other people in there, I find a couple of seats away from them, where I wait for my mother.

When she comes in, I almost don't recognise her. As she walks towards me, her hair is lank, her skin dull, her eyes as though she's closed herself up. But they light up the moment she sees me. 'Mum . . .' Jumping up, I want to run towards her but unsure what the protocol is, I force myself not to. She hurries towards me, then her arms are around me.

'Are we allowed to hug?' My eyes are filled with tears.

'I don't care.' But keeping hold of my hand, she pulls away slightly. 'Just in case. Sit down, Jess. Tell me how you are.'

'I'm fine.' Watching her soak up my presence, hanging on my every word, tears pour down my cheeks. 'Really I am. I don't know how long we have. I need you to fill me in about all the stuff I don't know. I know you didn't kill Matt. I'm not giving up until I find out who did.'

Her hand touches my cheek. 'Sweet Jess.' She's silent.

'*Mum.*' My voice is urgent, insistent, the loudest whisper I can manage. 'I'm your only hope. Please. Whatever it is you're not saying. You have to tell me.'

A shadow crosses her face. 'Please tell me the police are still searching for Matt?'

'They have to be.' Her words shock me. I hadn't considered they might not be.

When she glances away, I know my hunch was right. There is something she's been keeping from me. She meets my gaze. 'I never wanted you to know any of this.' When she hesitates, I'm filled with trepidation at what she's about to say. 'It's all going to come out at some point. This is about far more than Matt.' She looks stricken. 'It goes back to what happened to your aunt. Kimberley.'

Looking at her, I frown. I'd always known that Kimberley had died tragically, at seventeen. But as she proceeds to tell me what really happened that day, and about Allie's obsession with Kimberley's boyfriend, Charlie, my jaw drops open. It's the first I've heard of my aunt being poisoned. 'The police thought Kimberley accidentally got hold of one of our grandmother's remedies. It was described as a tragic accident. But it wasn't. Only my grandmother knew what had really happened.'

I stare at her, shocked. 'But you didn't do it. Allie did. Surely the police must believe that?'

'I think they do now.' She pauses. 'But I told too many lies, Jess. I was trying to hide the truth about what really happened to Kimberley, terrified that Allie would convince the police it was my fault. The last time I saw her, she swore that one day she'd be the one people would listen to – not me. And she is – she's a lawyer now. There's another thing . . .' Breaking off again, she's silent. 'I couldn't believe it when I found this out, but it turns out Allie was Matt's other woman. The woman he was allegedly leaving me for.'

'No way.' Shocked, I'm thinking quickly. 'That's too weird to be a coincidence. Could she have made it all up?'

'I don't know what to think.' My mother looks defeated.

'Jess, all I can imagine is that someone's trying to avenge something from the past. Probably Kimberley's death – only because I can't think of anything else. Presumably someone who holds me responsible, so they killed Matt first, before setting me up. I've told the police what I've told you about Kimberley. I've no idea whether they've questioned Allie, and if they have, whether they've arrested her. For all I know, she could have convinced them of her innocence, so they let her go.'

'What's Allie's full name?' I'm desperately trying to memorise every word she says, knowing I need to take it away with me.

'Allie Macklin. Except she changed her name.' She's silent for a moment. 'She's Fiona Rose now. Fiona was her middle name.' Then she looks ashamed. 'I changed mine, too, Jess. My name was Emily Preston. I thought Amy was close enough to Emily that if I slipped up, no-one would notice.'

'I don't blame you for changing your name.' But as it sinks in, I wish she'd told me before. It would have helped me understand so much more, about my mother, her parents, my family. 'Most people would have done exactly the same.' I pause, curious. 'When did you last see her?'

'Years ago.' My mother sighs. 'She came to the house we were living in at the time – in Eastbourne. You were a baby. After Kimberley died, Allie and I lost touch. But that day she came round, she was venomous. She told me how her parents had sent her away, then disowned her, all of which she blames me for. When she came and found me, I was still with your dad. After I opened the door, she just barged in and started throwing her weight around. She was clearly erratic, to the point you couldn't imagine anyone would take her seriously, but she was determined she was going to change that.' As she speaks, my mother's eyes are filled with anxiety. 'It was a kind of threat. She wanted to make herself more credible than I was, almost as if she knew this was going to happen so that one day, it would be her who was believed, not me.'

'Do you think the police will believe her?' I look at her, alarmed.

'I've no idea.' My mother looks helpless. 'But it's important that you do, Jess. I didn't kill Matt and I didn't kill Kimberley. I couldn't have – I'm not made that way. It was Allie. She was jealous. She wanted Charlie for herself. We made a potion together to make Kimberley fall out of love with Charlie, but it was never meant to be anything more than harmless.'

'I do believe you.' I'm still stunned, but it explains the feeling I've had, that she's been keeping something from me.

'My grandmother took responsibility.' My mother's eyes are haunted. 'She told the police that it was her fault that the herbs were accessible to anyone else. But she knew full well it wasn't.'

Staring blankly ahead, realising how long my mother's kept this hidden, I try to think what to do. Then I look at her again. 'There must be something else you can tell me – about that time. Who else was there? Your grandmother? Or Kimberley's boyfriend?'

My mother's eyes cloud over, as she remembers. 'My grand-mother was. Our house was hers, Jess. She left it to me, so that I'd forever be reminded of Kimberley's death. It was her way of punishing me. And poor Charlie Brooks . . . I'll never forget him. The irony is, Allie never had a chance with Charlie. After Kimberley died, he killed himself.' She glances away, but not before I notice her eyes are filled with tears. 'So many deaths, Jess. Kimberley, Charlie, my parents . . . It was devastating. All because of one reckless act of stupidity, by one selfish person, who until now, has got away with it.'

*

314

As Cath drives us back to Brighton, I'm deep in thought, oblivious to everything around me, in my mind going over and over what my mother told me, searching for a link between her, Allie and Matt. There has to be a clue, somewhere, to what the police are missing.

Halfway back to Brighton, I turn to Cath. 'Would you mind if we called in at home? Not to stay. I just want to look for something.'

She nods. 'OK. Anything in particular?'

I pause, then I tell her what my mother said, using her words, because if the court case goes ahead, it's only a matter of time before everyone will know. 'I found out something today. Mum's real name isn't Amy Reid. It's Emily Preston.' I take a deep breath. 'Her sister died when she was fifteen. Everyone thought it was an accident, but it wasn't. Mum's friend, Allie, caused her death. It was hushed up at the time, but suddenly the police have found out about it. It happened in our garden – our house used to belong to her grandmother. Before she died, she left it to Mum.' I pause, because I'm not sure about how much Cath knows. 'It's the weirdest thing about Allie – or Fiona, as she's called now . . .' I stop; it really is strange. 'She's the same woman Matt was going to leave Mum for.'

'You are joking.' Cath's flabbergasted. 'God.' There's another silence. 'That's too weird to be a coincidence, surely?'

'It's why I want to go back to the house. I know the police have searched it, but I need to look around myself. There might be a clue of some kind, as to what's really happened.' I pause, frowning. 'Could Matt have found out that they used to know each other?'

'Even if he had, it still doesn't make sense.' She changes the subject. 'Oh, look . . .'

Hearing a roaring sound, I follow her gaze to the low-flying jet above us, that's just taken off from Gatwick. What I wouldn't give to be on that right now, with my mother, headed away from all this madness somewhere far away, towards the sun.

It's a relief when we finally turn off the busy motorway and take the country roads that thread along the foot of the Downs, through Fulking. Gazing out of the passenger window, I take in the peaceful rolling hills, the fields of sheep, suddenly home-sick for the views from my own home.

'You know, I'd better let Zoe know what we're doing. She's probably wondering where we are.' Pulling over, obviously through to Zoe's voicemail, she leaves a message. 'Hi, just in case you're wondering, we're calling by Amy's house. Jess wants to fetch a few things. Let me know if you want us to pick anything up on our way home?'

Then we're almost there, driving up another section of the Downs, before we turn into the lane. Slowing down, Cath parks outside our house, then sits there for a moment. 'I don't mind waiting out here – unless there's anything you'd like me to do?'

I look at her. 'I don't really know what I'm looking for – but if we both look, maybe we've a better chance of finding something.'

As I get out of her car, I fish in my pocket for my keys, my resolve strengthening, knowing for my mother's sake, we have to find something. Unlocking the door, when I push it open, a cold, alien feeling overcomes me. It feels like forever since I was last here. Picking up the post lying on the doormat, I push the door further open and go inside, Cath following me towards the kitchen. It's untidy, the floor needs sweeping, with plates and mugs left all over the place. Glancing through the post, apart from one letter addressed to Matt, most of it's for

316

my mother. Leaving the letters on the table, I make a mental note to pick them up later.

Torn between clearing up and searching the house, I turn to Cath. 'Is there any chance you could help me tidy – just a bit? Even if we put the dishwasher on, it would be a start.'

But as I start clearing the table, Cath turns around. 'Leave the kitchen to me, Jess. Why don't you look upstairs?'

While she makes a start, I walk out of the kitchen, glancing into the living room where the vile painting of Matt's is still in place on the wall. Silently I make my way upstairs, but halfway up, I'm struck inexplicably with unease. At the top, I head for my mother's room, taking in the clothes and shoes strewn across the bed and carpet, all of it Matt's stuff. Maybe she was about to get rid of it or perhaps the police have gone through everything? Anger rises in me. Suddenly I want every trace of him out of here. When I hurry downstairs, Cath looks up in surprise.

My voice is tight. 'I need some plastic bags. I'm getting rid of Matt's clothes.'

★

Knowing the police will have gone through Matt's pockets, as my mother will have before them, even so, I check again, then roughly fold each item, filling the first bag, then another, until the bed is clear, then the floor. Then I go to the wardrobe. As I open the door, something falls out, startling me so that I cry out, as I realise how on edge I am. Picking up the coat that must have fallen off its hanger, all that's left is a holdall that's on a shelf. Pulling it out and finding it empty, I shove it into another bag, trying to think. If anything was hidden in this house, where would it be?

Methodically I check my mother's chest of drawers, but other than clothes and the trace of her lingering scent, there's nothing to find. Then slowly I go to my own room. If someone's still trying to hurt my mother, the next obvious target is me.

★

It's late by the time we get back to Zoe's. Upstairs in my room, I shower, wanting to wash away any trace of today, then pull on a t-shirt and jogging bottoms. Sitting cross-legged on my bed, I reach for my bag and search inside for my mother's post.

There's a load of junk mail and what looks like a couple of bills. But then I frown. The letter for Matt isn't there. In all the upset of calling the police, I must have left it behind in the kitchen. Then my mind is racing again. I've been so caught up in searching the house, I've completely forgotten about Allie – or Fiona, as she now calls herself.

'Jess?'

Hearing Zoe's voice call from downstairs, I jump up, fetching my laptop and taking it with me. In the kitchen, she's already serving up bowls of curry and rice, and a plate of warm naan bread.

'This looks amazing.' As Cath joins us, she glances at my laptop. 'You're still busy, Jess?'

'I need to see what I can find out about Fiona.' But there's more. I need to look for anything about Kimberley, if there are any news cuttings from that time; any links between my mother, Fiona, Matt. Frowning, I look up. 'Where can you look up old newspaper reports?'

'You could try online?' Zoe suggests. 'There are archives, too. But that's where I'd start. About Fiona . . . do you know anything about her?'

When I shake my head, she goes on. 'It's just that one of

Nick's golfing friends is a lawyer – in Brighton. I'm sure he'd do some digging if you wanted him to.'

At the prospect of more help, relief fills me. 'That would be amazing.'

'I tell you what.' Zoe sits down opposite me with her phone. 'I'll text Nick now. I think James is with him in the Algarve. What did you say her name was?'

'Fiona Rose. She used to be known as Allie Macklin. The name of the girl who died is Kimberley Preston, in case he needs that.' Hardly able to believe she's doing this, I take a mouthful of curry. 'Thanks.'

★

After we've eaten, I take myself off to one of the armchairs in the sitting room. Opening my laptop, I google Allie Macklin. Then out of curiosity, I google Matthew Roche and a list of headlines come up. 'Local man missing,' and 'Missing man suspected murdered.'

Sitting there, I try to think. Then slowly I start to type into the search bar. *Kimberley Preston 1996 teenager death.*

Even though it happened over twenty years ago, there are links to news articles and screenshots of newspaper front pages, but it's no surprise that the death of a teenager would have been headline news. As I read about the parents of Kimberley Preston, instead of dissociated names, they become my family: Kimberley my aunt, her parents my grandparents. People I've never met, a chapter of her life my mother rarely talks about. And at last, after all this time, I understand why. In the aftermath of Kimberley's death, their lives must have been devastated.

I focus on a photo of an elderly woman, grief clearly written in her eyes, in the lines of her skin. Kimberley's grandmother

– my mother's grandmother, more family I've never known about. Then I find another photo of happier times, of my mother and Kimberley, with their parents.

As I continue searching, another story comes up. This time it isn't a headline, but mentions Charlie Brooks, who after losing his girlfriend, Kimberley Preston, hung himself from a tree in the garden where she'd died. Realising it must have happened in our garden, shock hits me. It's as my mother said, one reckless action from which waves of heartbreak rippled; are still rippling, even today.

While I'm searching, Rik texts me from Falmouth. *Miss you.* It's followed by a line of red hearts. I text him back. *Miss you too xx Will fill you in on everything xxx*.

Zoe comes back into the kitchen. 'Jess? I just heard from Nick. When James gets a chance, he's happy to look into this. He couldn't say when, but he'll be in touch with you when he's back.'

'That's so brilliant. Thank you so much . . .' I glance down as another text from Rik flashes up on my phone. *Can I help?* I think quickly. Rik is a geek. I should have thought about it before. Quickly I start typing. *Any dirt on Fiona Rose, a Brighton lawyer, or info on what really happened to Kimberley Preston. xxx*. Then as an afterthought adding, *any dirt on Matthew Roche would be a bonus*.

Pressing send, a bubble of hearts float up the screen of my phone, then I turn back to my laptop.

*

I spend the following day finding out everything I can about Fiona Rose, when I google her, finding out there are many. But as I whittle them down by location, I find one listed as a partner at Hollis and James, a law firm, which fits with her ambition to become respected and credible. It mentions her previous position at a firm in Cobham, Surrey, called Dentons. But not a whole lot more than that. Studying the headshot of her, estimating her at around my mother's age, I take in coolly appraising eyes, a posture that suggests confidence, feeling my heart sink. Pitched against my mother, it's easy to imagine who the police would find more plausible.

Scrutinising her social media, I search for her parents, but in every visible aspect of her life, there is no sign of them or any other family members, as my mother's words come back to me. *Allie's parents sent her away, then they disowned her.*

Sighing, I try to imagine what that must have felt like. When her parents found out she'd been involved in Kimberley's death, I wonder if they ever forgave her. And if they didn't, what that could do to a person. As a teenager – then later, as an adult, carrying all that unresolved anger and bitterness. It would seriously screw someone up, to the point that if you were bitter and twisted enough, you'd stoop to anything to get revenge.

Maybe that's what this is about. Revenge.

At last, I receive a message from Mandy. *Thank you for your message, Jess. All I can tell you about Matt is to never believe a single word he says about anything. He's the worst kind of liar – insidious, yet utterly believable. Nothing he does is without a self-serving motive. To be honest, I wouldn't be surprised if someone had tried to kill him. There isn't much more I can add. But I do hope you find the evidence you're looking for.*

After I read the message, I keep it to forward to PC Page. And Mandy's right about needing to find evidence. Turning back to my laptop, I think about what I definitely know. I have my mother's account of Kimberley's death, and about what happened to her and Allie/Fiona after. Then Charlie. Then I remember my mother's words. *So many deaths . . . Kimberley, Charlie, my parents . . .* Then *poor Charlie Brooks . . .*

Suddenly my heart is racing. What about Charlie's parents? Might they have been seeking some kind of retribution for their son's death, even this many years on? I know enough about revenge to understand that it's one of our deepest instincts. I try to imagine how it must have felt, seeing their son's body hanging from our apple tree, as powerful emotions take over. The sorrow, empathy, regret, my mother must have felt. Not only had she lost Kimberley, she'd been faced with another death.

Frowning at my screen, I wonder where Charlie's parents live now. *Charlie Brooks. Death. 1996. Steyning.* I type the words into the search bar, then start scrolling down the list of links. A couple of news items I haven't seen before have come up, one of them mentioning Charlie's father, Harold Brooks, a well-known local businessman.

After typing *Harold Brooks Steyning* into the search bar, a photo comes up. It's black and white, grainy, alongside a piece about the growing success of his health foods business.

Clicking on the next link, there's a photo of the shopfront, on Steyning High Street. It's no longer there, but when I read the following link dated 1997, it describes how the business was sold after a family tragedy.

Which can only have been Charlie's death. Absorbed, I keep reading article after article, then I stumble across another photo. But this one isn't just of Harold. Instead, he's with his family – his glamorous wife, their two teenage boys standing in front of them. I study the taller one, recognising him as Charlie, then my eyes turn to the younger boy. Until now, there'd been no mention that Charlie had a brother. Zooming in on him, I stare, as shock hits me.

*

After telling Cath what I've found out, I call the police. When they arrive, I show PC Page what I've found. 'I think Matt is Charlie's younger brother. I was looking online into Charlie's family and I found a photo of the family together. I know he was much younger, but it would explain everything wouldn't it? If Matt held my mother responsible for his brother's death – and why he'd want revenge.' I show her the photo. 'Look at his father. There's a real likeness.'

She studies it carefully. 'So you think Matthew Roche is really Matthew Brooks? If it is and he's changed his name, there will be records. We need to look more into this, but if you're right, it does suggest a motive.' She pauses. 'But it doesn't explain why he would have waited for so long. And it still doesn't tell us what's happened to him.'

When I'd been hoping for so much more, her response disappoints me. 'It's him alright. And if I know Matt, he'll be hiding out, enjoying every minute of this,' I say bitterly.

PC Page glances at me. 'We'll definitely look into this, Jess. If you're right, I'll let you know.'

'Oh.' I've almost forgotten to tell her. 'There's something else. I had a reply from Mandy. I think you should read it.' Getting my phone, I bring up the message to show her, passing her my phone.

Her face is grave as she reads it. 'Can you forward it to me?'

*

When she leaves, I'm filled with frustration that what I've found isn't enough to clear my mother. Still needing to find concrete evidence of her innocence, by mid-afternoon, it seems like my only option is to go back to the house. Not wanting to go alone, I try to find Cath. But I only see Zoe, in the kitchen, sitting at her laptop. 'I was hoping to go back to the house. Do you know where Cath is?'

Zoe's eyes search my face. 'She popped out a little while ago. She didn't say when she'd be back. Why don't you call her?'

I shake my head. 'Don't worry.' I don't want to put her out any more than I already have. 'I'll get a bus.'

Zoe hesitates. 'Are you sure this is a good idea? I really don't mind driving you.'

Not wanting to feel pressured by time, I turn her down. 'Thanks. But I'll get the bus. I'm not sure how long I'm going to be.'

'OK . . .' Zoe sounds reluctant. 'If you're sure? But I'll tell Cath what you're doing. I expect she'll want to come and join you.'

Pulling on my jacket, as I step outside, under the shade of the trees that line the road, the air is cool. Pausing for a moment, I zip my phone into a pocket, before I turn and start walking in the direction of the seafront. It's a typical February day − grey, the breeze cold where it catches me, clouds scudding across the sky. As I walk, I try to think what the missing pieces of this jigsaw are, knowing the person I need to talk to is Fiona.

Reaching the seafront, I cross over and stand there, gazing at the green-grey waves rolling towards the shore, turning to white foam as they crash onto the shingle. On impulse, I get out my phone and search for a number for Hollis and James, the firm Fiona works for. When I call them, someone answers straight away.

'Can I speak to Fiona Rose?'

The voice sounds surprised. 'Ms Rose has been called away unexpectedly, but perhaps I can transfer you to one of our other partners. Can I take . . .'

I hang up before she finishes. *Called away unexpectedly . . .* by the police? Deep in thought, I carry on walking along the seafront, breathing in the clean salt air, feeling the breeze buffeting my face, until I reach a bus stop.

After checking the timetable, I don't have to wait long. As I find a seat, the bus is half-empty, and as it sets off along the coast road, through the window, I watch a couple of kite surfers. Since moving to Cornwall, I've developed a fascination for the power of the wind, the might of the waves and I watch in awe as one of the kite surfers is lifted airborne, before speeding away along the coast. Suddenly homesick for Falmouth, I take a photo, texting it to Rik. *Miss you xxxx*.

While the bus makes its way towards Steyning, I lean my head against the window, watching the landscape change from busy streets to empty fields, the river meandering through them, trying to think hard. If I wanted to hide something where no-one would find it, where would I put it?

★

As I walk from Steyning up the lane to our house, on edge, I check my phone is in my pocket. When I reach the house, I stand there for a moment, looking up at the windows. I've always felt so safe here, but today, for some inexplicable reason, the idea of walking in there alone unnerves me. But for my mother's sake, I have to do this. Inside, I lock the door behind me, then turn on lights. Like last time, the house is cold and unwelcoming, a feeling that grows stronger as I go upstairs.

In the small study, my mother's old course notes and my school books are piled inside an old chest, a bookcase holding her collection of books, most of which I've read. Running my finger across their spines, I take in the titles that are so familiar to me. But on the desk or in the small drawer underneath, nothing is out of place.

In my mother's bedroom, I turn all the lights on. The bags of clothes I filled are where I left them, piled in one corner, everything exactly as it was when I was here last. But now I'm here, not knowing where to start, I sit on the bed, disheartened. On my mother's dressing table, her perfume bottle and hairspray are next to the make-up bag I gave her several Christmases ago. There's the photo of me as a child, the small china horse I bought her. The print of sunlight through trees, on the wall. All symbolic in some way; personal to her. Frowning, it hits me how unnatural it is, that in all the time Matt lived here, though he changed the sofas and the colour of the walls, apart from his clothes and the hideous painting downstairs, there's nothing else here that's personal to him.

Knowing the police have already searched thoroughly, it dawns on me that it's pointless to search again. Getting up, I head downstairs. As I pass the sitting room, Matt's horrible painting stares at me from its place on the wall above the fireplace. Suddenly wanting it out of the house, anger fills me as I go and wrench it from the wall. Taking it through to the kitchen, I slide open the doors and drop it heavily outside, not caring as I hear the glass shatter.

Then the sound of someone trying to open the front door makes me leap out of my skin. It's followed by the sound of the doorbell ringing, before I hear Cath's voice call out. 'Jess? Can you let me in?'

*

After Cath comes in, I go outside to clear up the glass that broke when I dropped Matt's painting. Picking everything up, as I take it inside, for the first time I notice two initials in the bottom right-hand corner, in Mondrian-esque blocky letters, CB. *Charlie Brooks*. At last I know the reason Matt was so obsessed with the painting. It's the one remaining link to his dead brother.

'You need to tell the police.' Cath stares at the painting. 'I mean, it could be proof, couldn't it, that Matt is Charlie's brother?'

'I really hope so.' I pull my mobile out of my pocket. My call is answered immediately. 'Hello? It's Jess Reid. Can I speak to PC Page?'

But as I'm put through to her, it goes to voicemail. I leave a message. 'It's Jess Reid. I've found something I think you should see.'

★

With the painting in the back of Cath's car, we set off for Brighton. As we get closer to the city, I wonder if things will ever go back to how they were. 'This has to be enough,' I say to Cath, terrified that even the painting isn't going to be enough for the police. 'If not, what's it going to take? I was going to search the house again but the police have already been through everything. I'd really hoped that the photo of Charlie Brooks' family was enough proof.'

'Well, maybe this painting is what they need. You have to hang in there, Jess.' Cath tries to reassure me. 'Wait until you've spoken to them. Who knows what else they've found out.'

Dispirited, I shake my head. 'If there was anything, PC Page would have called me.'

'She still might. And surely she's going to want to see the painting.'

As Cath turns into Zoe's road, I'm silent as I check my phone for any calls. As she pulls in near Zoe's house, I get out and go to get Matt's painting. Taking it inside, I lean it up against the wall just inside the front door, then go through to the kitchen where I watch Zoe put the kettle on. Leaning against one of the work surfaces, I'm still preoccupied as the sound from my mobile distracts me. Glancing at the screen, seeing an unknown number, hoping it's the police, my insides lurch. 'Hello. Yes, it's me.'

PC Page sounds in a hurry. 'It looks like you may be right about Matt being Charlie's brother. We've found records of him changing his name by deed poll. It's all there, in black and white.'

Filled with relief, for a moment, I can't speak. 'So . . . my mother? She's no longer a suspect?'

'It isn't quite that simple.' PC Page sounds reluctant. 'While it's proof of Matt's real name, it doesn't actually prove anything as far as your mother's concerned. And Brooks is a common enough name.'

'But you have the photo. And it gives him a motive,' I interrupt her, angrily. 'Don't you realise? He's set this up?' I pause briefly. 'There was a painting in the house – it was Matt's. He was obsessive about it. Earlier today I took it down, but when I put it outside, the glass smashed. The painting itself came loose. Anyway, there are initials on it that weren't visible before. The artist's. CB. Charlie Brooks.'

'You're quite sure?' Her voice is sharp.

'Yes. I brought the painting back with me. I thought you'd want to see it.'

'If anything like this happens again, please call me.'

'I did.' There's surprise in my voice. 'I got put through to your phone and I left a message.'

'It must have been the office phone. It certainly didn't come through to my mobile.' She sounds irritated. 'I'll come over. We need to see that painting. Are you there if we call over this evening?'

Hope rises in me. 'I'll be here.'

'And Jess, we still don't know where Matt is – or even if

he's still alive.' She hesitates. 'But you do realise, don't you, that if there's any chance he is out there, you need to be careful.'

From her words, I know she hasn't ruled the possibility out. She goes on. 'I'm going to text you my mobile number. If you see anything suspicious, I want you to call me.'

After she ends the call, I turn to Cath and Zoe, who must have heard most of the call. 'They have proof that Matt changed his name by deed poll. But they're still holding Mum.' Tears prick my eyes as I pause. 'She said I need to be careful – in case he's still out there.'

'She's right.' Zoe shakes her head. 'You must be. It's unbelievable isn't it, the lengths he's gone to already. Who knows what else he's capable of?'

'He's a vile, twisted human being.' I shake my head. 'I hope the police find him and lock him away for good.'

'Hopefully they will.' Cath goes to the kitchen windows and closes the curtains. 'I'll do the rest, shall I?'

Zoe nods. 'Thanks. Now, Jess. How about I make us something to eat?'

★

Half an hour later, when PC Page arrives, I show her the painting. 'Thanks, Jess. We'll take it with us.'

'It's proof, isn't it?' I insist. 'That Matt is Charlie's brother?'

'It's certainly possible.' She pauses. 'I'll be in touch.'

★

That night, I try to think where Matt could have been since he disappeared or where he could have hidden. Then as I think of the painting again, my heart starts to thump. If all this has been about Matt losing Charlie, he's going to go back to the house, I'd put money on it. He's going to want to pick up his brother's painting, I know Matt and the twisted way his mind works. Then it's like a light switches on in my brain. Even though it's late, I call PC Page.

'It's another hunch, but I think I know where Matt may have been hiding.'

'Where?'

'I honestly think he's playing a cat and mouse game. It's somewhere close enough to watch my mother, but the last place anyone would guess at.' I pause. 'Mrs Guthrie's house.'

She's silent for a moment. Then all she says is, 'I'll get a car up there straight away.'

'There's something else.' I hesitate. 'I think he'll go back to our house. He was obsessed with that painting. It's his only remaining link to his brother.'

Outside my bedroom door, I hear a floorboard creak. Then there's a knock, followed by Cath's voice. 'Jess? Are you OK? I thought I heard voices.'

'I'm fine. I was talking to PC Page.' Going to the door, I crack it open to see her face, dimly lit by the light from the landing, enough to see her frown.

'Is anything wrong?'

I shake my head. 'No. Everything's fine. It was just something I thought of – to do with earlier.' I break off. 'I think I know where Matt may have been hiding. In Mrs Guthrie's house – across the road. She died recently.' Conveniently. The word shocks me. Could Matt have had a hand in that too?

'God.' Cath looks horrified. 'That's a bit close. As long as you're OK?'

I nod. 'I'm exhausted. I'm going to bed.'

But as I lie in bed, my mind won't rest. As I go over the events of today, I imagine Matt at Mrs Guthrie's upstairs window, hidden in the shadows as he peered from behind the curtains.

I picture his eyes on me as I walked up the lane. The more I think about it, the more certain I am that he'll be wanting his painting back. I envisage his anger when he finds it isn't there.

★

The next morning, I wake early, through the gap in the curtains, peering outside, edgy, constantly on the lookout. For Matt. When I go downstairs, Cath's sitting at Zoe's table, texting on her phone. When she hears me come in, she turns around. 'Did you sleep OK in the end?' Her voice is bright. 'Have you heard anything from the police yet?'

'No.' But I'm sure if there's any news, PC Page will keep me posted.

Cath gets up. 'It's a gorgeous day out there. Shall we go out for breakfast? My shout.'

'I don't know.' She's trying to cheer me up, and I don't want to sound dismissive, but until I know what's happening with my mother, I don't really feel like going anywhere.

'Go on, Jess. It'll do us both good.'

Against my better judgement, I let her sway me. 'I'll just go upstairs and get my stuff.' In my room, I brush my hair, then grab my phone, as Cath's voice comes from her room. 'You ready?'

'Just coming.' I open my door. 'You're right. It's a good idea.' I follow her downstairs. 'Where are we going?'

'There's a place the east side of Hove – a diner. I thought as well as breakfast, some sea air would do us good. I was thinking, that if you haven't heard anything by then, maybe you should call PC Page for an update?'

'Yeah.' With that in mind, I feel a little brighter.

But as we get into her car, I'm frowning, thinking back to a comment she made, a while back. About how she owed my mum. 'What you said before . . . you said you owed Mum. What did you mean by that?'

Cath's quiet for a moment. 'She was always there for me when Oliver was at his worst. I felt it was my turn to do the same for her.'

'Was there any other reason? To do with Matt?' As I mention his name, her hands stiffen on the steering wheel. 'It was just that you said he tried it on with you.'

'There's really not any more to say about it. At the time, I told him where to go. But I've wondered since, that if I'd told your mum at the time, she might have ended their relationship and none of this would have happened. But knowing the way Matt works, he'd have persuaded her to end our friendship, instead. To be honest, I'm embarrassed about the whole thing.'

When my phone rings, I glance at the screen, where a photo of Rik is flashing up. 'Do you mind if I answer it? It's Rik. He's been worried about me.'

'Sure, be my guest.'

'Thanks. I'll be quick.' I pick up my phone. 'Hey Rik, how are you?' I'm silent for a moment, listening. 'Can we catch up later on? I'm in the car at the moment. Cath's taking me for breakfast at a diner along the seafront . . .' I pause. 'OK. I'll let you know.' Blowing a kiss at the phone, I hang up. 'He's going to call me later on.' I pause. 'Do you know when you're going back to Bristol?'

'I haven't decided. I don't want to go while this is still going on. Let's take it as it comes. Hopefully, there'll be some good news before too long. I was thinking maybe later you and I should go back to the house. Finish putting it straight and get rid of anything there to do with Matt.'

'Maybe.' I don't tell her that knowing Matt might be around, even the thought of going there terrifies me. 'Can we see what PC Page says?' As the diner comes into view, Cath pulls over and parks at the side of the road. Getting out, I walk onto the shingle, standing there, looking out across the sea. The sun is low, the sea millpond flat, the breeze cold on my skin as Cath joins me. 'Beautiful, isn't it? The sea is the thing I love most about living in Falmouth.'

'It is lovely.' She's quiet for a moment. 'Shall we get some breakfast?'

Side by side we walk across the shingle towards the diner. Done up like an American beach shack, inside it's light and airy, decorated in a wash of colour and driftwood, with huge windows and a view of the sea. Apart from one or two tables, it's relatively empty. Wandering over to a table in the furthest corner, Cath pulls out a chair for me. 'You have the view.'

The waitress leaves us with menus, but as I peruse mine, my phone buzzes. Glancing at it, PC Page is flashing up on the screen. 'Sorry. I need to take this.' When I answer it, she's brief and to the point.

'It's possible you're right. There's definitely been someone in Mrs Guthrie's house. No-one was there when we went to check, but there's evidence of the sink being used and the sofa being slept on. But no-one's broken in. Whoever's been in there has a key, possibly coming and going when they need to.'

'I'm sure he's going to go back to the house,' I tell her urgently. 'If nothing else, he's going to want the painting.'

'Quite possibly. Jess, to try and flush Matt out, we're issuing a press release, that the police have closed the case, concluding that he's been murdered and washed out to sea. It's presumed his body might never be recovered.'

'When are you doing it?'

'As soon as we can organise it. We'll make sure it goes out

333

on local radio, TV and press. Before it happens, we'll have a plainclothes team monitoring the house. He's certain to be following local news. It's a long shot, but if he thinks we're no longer looking for him, he's free to go back to pick up that painting and whatever else he wants to take – preferably soon, before you're back there. I'm going to have to ask you to stay away from the house again – just for now.'

As she speaks, hope fills me. But when I put the phone down, I'm frowning as I turn to Cath. 'Someone's been in Mrs Guthrie's house. They have a key. The police are issuing a fake press release. They want Matt to believe that the case has been closed and the police are no longer looking for him. It isn't true.' Not telling Cath what PC Page said, about staying away, I stare at her. 'But they're hoping that if he believes it's done and dusted, it might make him a little more reckless. Enough to go back to the house to pick up his painting.'

'My God. I hope it works. When are they doing it?'

'Today.' I pause. 'On local radio, TV and in the press.'

'I ordered you a coffee. I didn't know what else you wanted.'

I shake my head. 'Just the coffee is good.'

'Jess.' From across the table, Cath reaches for my hand. 'You should eat something.'

I shake my head. 'I'm not hungry.' My mind is racing. Matt might go there anyway, before the press release goes out, in which case the police would miss him. Suddenly I'm furious, that they're even taking the chance. 'We have to go there. Now. If we park the car on the main road, then take the back way across the fields into the garden, if he's watching the front, he won't see us.'

Forgetting about breakfast, we hurry back to her car. As she unlocks it, Cath frowns. 'You're sure you want to do this?'

I have a feeling in my bones I can't ignore. 'I have to. What's he going to do? There are two of us. If he's there, we call the police.'

As we drive to Steyning, my certainty grows that my hunch is right and at long last, we're on to him. After parking away from the house, I lead Cath the back way across a sheep field, then over the far end of the wall into the back garden. Making our way towards the house, when we reach the sliding doors, instead of locked, they're cracked open.

Startled, I turn to Cath. 'Someone's in there.'

Her eyes are wide with shock. 'You think it's him?'

Nodding, I tiptoe closer. 'Call the police,' I whisper.

While she gets out her phone, I carefully slide the doors open enough to let me slip through.

Turning, I glance at Cath shaking her head, mouthing at me, '*No, Jess . . . don't go in . . .*'

But I ignore her. Without giving it a second thought, very slowly, without making a sound, I creep through the kitchen, where I hear a noise coming from one of the bedrooms. My heart thudding, I make my way up the stairs. Then in the doorway of my mother's room, I stop.

I watch for a moment, then find my voice. 'Looking for something?'

Across the room, Matt freezes, then turns to me, a look of hatred on his face. I should be terrified, but knowing what he's done, thinking of my mother charged with his murder, I find a strength I didn't know I had. Incensed by his arrogance, that he thinks he can intimidate me, thinking of his twisted mind games, my fear is gone. 'You can't honestly believe you'll get away with this. You're scum, Matt. A despicable human being. You know it and I know it, and soon the whole world will know it.' My voice is trembling, not from fear, but from anger at what he's done to my mother, furious at everything he's done to me; and who knows who else along the way. 'You have no right to fuck up other people's lives.'

He starts to laugh, a cynical, cruel sound. 'You should tell that to your mother and her friend. They didn't care about anyone other than themselves. Two selfish teenagers, wrecking all those lives . . . And all this time, they've got away with it.'

I shake my head. 'You've got this so wrong. My mother is innocent.'

'Keeping their secret all these years? I'd hardly call that innocent.' He laughs again. 'They're both guilty, but quite honestly, I don't care what happens to either of them.'

I watch him feel inside the wardrobe. 'By the way, you won't find anything. The painting's smashed.' I watch rage flicker in his eyes. 'It's outside. I've thrown it away.' It's deliberately inflammatory, but I'm past caring. I want to hurt him as much as he's hurt me.

For a moment he doesn't move. Then he takes a step towards me, sneering. 'Do you know what, sweet little Jess? I'm going to tell you about my brother and after that, I'm going to make sure you can never tell anyone you've seen me. If only you'd stayed away . . .' His eyes narrow. 'But maybe there's a certain justice after Charlie dying, in you also dying far too young. That was all I ever wanted. Justice.'

Knowing he's capable of anything, I'm terrified. Out of the corner of my eye, I glance towards the window, praying the police are on their way. When I look back at him, there's a wildness in his eyes as he goes on.

'He was about your age when he died. It ruined my parents' lives and by default, mine, too. After he died, my poor, weak mother took her own life. She couldn't bear to live with the pain of losing him. She gave no thought to me, her other son, growing up without his mother and his brother.' Words filled with venom as he breaks off, shaking his head. 'Shortly after that, my father sold his business. He'd lost all interest in living. But I haven't told you how Charlie died, have I? Shall I tell you?' I stare at him, horrified, knowing what he's going to say. 'He had a girlfriend who was everything in the world to him. A beautiful, sweet, kind girl called Kimberley. They were going to spend the rest of their lives together. They were the kind of people that you felt better off for knowing. Just being with them, you could feel their love. I don't know what cock and bull story your mother's spun you, but it was her and her stupid friend who killed her. Charlie couldn't come to terms with living without her. So he hung himself. From a tree. Out there. In your garden.' For a moment, his expression is one of extreme sadness. But then he turns to me again. 'I hadn't planned to come here, but then I saw that magazine piece. When I realised who your mother was, after what she did to Charlie and Kimberley, I couldn't let it go. It ate away at me when I read about the cosy little life she'd created for herself, the business she'd built, her lovely daughter. It was too unfair.'

Looking at him, I gasp. 'You even sent the flowers, didn't you? Using your own blood.' I shake my head, feeling sick. 'How could you?'

'I cut a vein. It wasn't difficult. Nothing is if you want it enough.' As his eyes turn away, one of his sleeves slips back, revealing a bandage.

Standing there, I'm shocked into silence as the final pieces fall into place, his story meshing with my mother's as I know he's insane. Hearing a car pull up outside, he glances towards the window.

'You called the fucking police.' As he turns back to look at me, his voice is loaded with venom. 'You'll regret this.' Muttering under his breath, he steps close enough that I can smell his body odour, a menacing look on his face as he threatens me. 'One day, when you're least expecting it, I swear I'll find you, Jess. You'll look around and see me there, and this time, there won't be any police to come to your rescue. You won't be able to get away from me. Think about how it will feel, when at last I catch up with you – because I will. You haven't heard the last of this.'

In that moment, my terror knows new heights. Knowing he's going down, he's left me with something I can never forget. Fear – that if he ever gets out of prison, he's going to look for me; that wherever I go, I'll never be safe. Rooted to the spot, I hear the police coming up the stairs. Then from behind me, comes PC Page's voice.

'Matthew Roche, I am arresting you on suspicion of perverting the course of justice. You do not have to say anything. But, it may harm your defence if you do not mention when questioned something which you later rely on in court. Anything you do say may be given in evidence.'

As she finishes speaking, two more officers walk over to Matt, as she glances towards me. 'Are you OK, Jess?'

I shake my head, watching as they handcuff him, then lead him downstairs, a look of pure malevolence on his face. Then as the police escort him outside and into a car, PC Page turns to me. 'I can't stop now, but I'll call you shortly about your mother.' As she walks away, Cath puts her arms around me.

'I heard what you said to him just now . . . I wanted to applaud. You're strong and brave. I'm so proud of you, Jess. And you were right. He's despicable.'

My legs weak, I sit on the bed, feeling my body start to shake. 'He threatened me, Cath. He said that one day, when I'm least expecting it, he'll find me. He means it.' I look at her, filled with panic. 'He'll do it, in the same way he planned everything with my mother.'

'Jess . . . He won't get away with it. We'll tell the police. They'll add it to their list of charges against him. Come on. I'm taking you back to Zoe's.'

★

An hour later, PC Page calls me, to confirm that my mother's being released and all charges have been dropped. She may be called as a witness at some point, but she's free. When I tell her about the way Matt threatened me, she takes down all the details, trying her best to reassure me.

Then she tells me about a call the police have just received. 'It was from a woman who heard our press release this morning. She'd read about Matt's disappearance in the papers and got in touch because on the night he allegedly disappeared, a man had paid her to book a taxi from Beachy Head to Steyning, offering her £500 if she'd wear some clothes he gave her and book it in the name of Amy. He'd even bought a cheap imitation of your mother's engagement ring. After she got to Steyning, he picked her up and drove her home. He must have got rid of his car later that night. It had bothered the woman that he'd been up to something, but at the time she was desperate for money. But when she recognised Matt's photo, she knew she had to call us.'

Dazed, I think of the irony of the timing. 'It's a pity she didn't come forward sooner.'

'I know. She's a prostitute – apparently he'd found her a week earlier, wandering the streets. He gave her a lift home, to

Kemp Town, when he offered her money just to take a cab ride, as long as she pretended to be your mother. If it's any consolation, it gives us more against Matt. We'll be calling her as a witness.'

There's no mention of Kimberley's murder, from which I take that it's Fiona who's being charged. Taking heart that after all these years, at last there is justice.

Amy

Chapter Thirty-Eight

When I'm taken from my cell to a small room I don't ask, nor am I told, what's happened. Sitting down, I wait for a few minutes, hopeless. Then the door opens and PC Page walks in.

'Amy.' She looks lighter than last time I saw her. 'I have some news.' She sits down opposite me. 'You were right all along. You were set up.'

'Allie?' I breathe the word, incredulous.

'Not by Ms Rose.' Her voice is quiet. 'We've arrested Matt.'

As she speaks, euphoria and confusion swirl around me. '*What*?' I stare at her, unblinking. 'You mean . . .'

'He's very definitely alive. He came back to . . .'

But before she can go on, I interrupt her. 'Does Jess know?'

PC Page nods. 'She does. She was there when he was arrested. He came back to your house to retrieve his painting. Apparently, it was done by his brother. Jess found the door open and while Cath called us, she went upstairs and confronted him. She's very determined, your daughter. He isn't going to be going anywhere very soon.'

'I don't understand.' Dazed, I shake my head. It's too much to take in. '*Why*?'

'After your sister died, you weren't the only one who changed their name,' she says grimly. 'Matthew Roche is Matthew Brooks, the younger brother of Charlie, your sister's boyfriend. After Charlie died, their mother killed herself and their father became a recluse. He died a few years later, when Matthew was eighteen. After his childhood was wrecked overnight, he never got over it. This was about revenge. Did you know Charlie had a brother?'

Still dazed, I try to think back to that time. 'I don't think I did. I only saw Charlie when he came to see Kimberley. I didn't go to his funeral. My parents had sent me away to school by then.'

She looks at me. 'He went to a great deal of trouble to make sure both you and Fiona suffered. He certainly had us fooled, but he slipped up.' She pauses. 'The one thing he hadn't counted on was us finding your grandmother's old notebook. We now know it was Fiona who added the poison to Kimberley's drink and we've charged her. But all charges against you have been dropped. We may well call you as a witness, but you're free to leave here.'

As her words sink in, I can't move. Then very slowly, I feel a weight start to lift.

But she goes on. 'We're looking into the possibility that he might have had something to do with your neighbour's death. There are indications that the fireplace had been blocked off intentionally. Maybe she saw him leave the flowers – or maybe he wanted somewhere safe to hide for a while.'

I stare at her. How many more deaths? Will this ever end?

'Oh – one more thing.' PC Page gets up. 'About that woman who stopped you in Brighton and told you that you were in danger . . . Most people write her off as mad, but one of my colleagues knows her. She's done this to people before – stopped them and told them about their future – and now and then, she's been right. I've no idea what you take from that, but I thought you'd want to know.' Then she adds, 'By the way, I've spoken to Jess. She's on her way here.'

Jess

It's Cath who drives me to Bronzefield. When we get there, I go to reception, but this time no-one goes in. Instead we wait a few minutes, before it's my mother who walks out. She looks lighter, her eyes brighter. As I rush towards her, her arms wrap around me and in that moment, I never want to let go of her. Then as we walk arm in arm towards Cath's car, she glances up at the sky just as the clouds part, the faintest trace of a smile crossing her face. But for the first time in as long as she can remember, she has no secrets to hide. At last, the nightmare is over.

2019

Eeny meeny miny mo, Amy or Fiona, who shall I choose? Does it matter? When whatever one of you did could incriminate both of you.

Then fate took a hand. After reading the magazine piece about Amy the herbalist, something snapped inside me. It took a while to trace where she was. To pick the right time, when Jess would be going away: to build up those social networks, so that when we met, it seemed the most natural thing in the world. Then came the next part, slowly homing in on you, the successful lawyer, knowing it was only a matter of time before that carefully constructed law career would come unpicked, so that when one thread was pulled, all of it would unravel; building you up enough, so that you'd know how it felt when you fell.

Only one of you killed Kimberley, but two of you kept the secret. I didn't care if I hurt both of you. How do I know this? When Kimberley died, Charlie spent his time with her grandmother. United by grief, she told him what she knew. And Charlie told me. Why? We were so close, Charlie and I. He was my brother.

When you want something enough, you'll do anything. Lie.

Cheat. Cut a vein, letting enough blood leak out to fill a small cellophane bag. It isn't difficult to make a bouquet. There's a certain justice about the flowers being dropped, the splashes of blood on skin, over the floor. It will always be there. The tiniest, most invisible microdroplets of me.

The old lady needn't have died. But Mrs Guthrie thought she saw me delivering the flowers in a van. Remained silent when I told her they were a surprise. But was too much of a risk, too easy to deceive about the smoke pouring from her chimney. It didn't take much to block it off when she invited me in.

Trust made everything so easy. Amy's unlocked phone, no password on her laptop. The notebook she left lying about. Stupid, naïve Amy was fair game. My turn for my actions to create ripples. It didn't matter who I brought down first. I knew eventually, I'd get to both of you. It was that secret you kept. All it would take was for one of you to talk, then I knew the other would be unable to remain silent.

But just to be sure, I sent the anonymous letter. Mentioning you, Fiona, just to make sure you didn't escape. But I could just as easily have mentioned Amy. As I've said before, it didn't matter. If there's any justice, the police will convict both of you.

How could either of you think I ever loved you? Ridiculous Amy who let me walk all over her? Let me abuse, control, stonewall her; be vile to her precious daughter. And you, Fiona . . . However smart you think you are, however good at summing people up, you missed one important detail. People like me can't love.

The knife in the workshop with Amy's fingerprints on it, all that blood waiting to be found, even though they'll never find a body, the burned-out car. All of that was me. But this was never about me. This was always for Kimberley and Charlie.

As I said in the message. Kill one man and you are a murderer. But you were guilty collectively of killing not just one person. You ended the lives of several. Back then, you didn't know you had the power to change my life forever. Your actions creating waves, losses multiplying; touching more lives than you ever knew.

Justice remaining unserved. Until now.

Jess

I thought with my mother home, we could carry on with our lives. But when the case of Kimberley's murder goes to court, I'm at her side as she's forced to relive the day her sister died all over again. Only when Fiona is found guilty, then sentenced, is it possible to think about moving on.

Even though Matt's threats towards me are added to the charges against him, fear still hangs over me. I can't shake the unease that one day in the future, when I'm alone somewhere, just as he said, he will find me.

One morning, when I'm tidying the kitchen, under a pile of bills, I find a folded-up piece of paper. Opening it, I start to read.

I promise to hold your hand, to steer you through life's sorrow and darkness, on a path towards justice and hope. I will endeavour to know what's best for you, to protect you from your past, help you build the future you deserve. Then when I can no longer be with you, a part of me will always be with you, watching over you. In the shadows of your heart, on the soft curves of your skin, in the longest forgotten corners of your mind.

Feeling myself shiver, I read it again. 'Mum?' I wave the piece of paper at her. 'I just found this.'

Coming over, she starts as she sees what it is. 'Matt's vows,' she says quietly.

'For your wedding?' When she nods, I go on. 'They're gross. It's like he's pledging to control you.'

Her eyes are sad as she turns to me. 'I suppose for a long time, he was.'

A piece of paper can be burned and that's what we do with it, but it takes more time to rid the house of Matt's reeking presence. To repair the garden to how it was before the police desecrated it. For the story to fade from the press. My mother and I can never go back to who we were, before. But we're stronger. *And we've survived*, I remind her. If we survived this, can't we survive anything?

After repainting the walls and replacing Matt's horrible sofas with comfy second-hand ones, my mother thinks about renting out the house, until the alchemist's curse weaves itself around her again. It's the garden. The irony that the police destroyed it isn't lost on me. We repair the flowerbeds, recover the salvageable plants, but we both know it's never going to be the same.

Then I remember something she said once, about how you're only ever the custodian of a garden. That in the end, it will be handed down to someone else. All the time she's preserved her grandmother's plants, she's been punishing herself. But now that her innocence has been proved, that has to stop.

Kimberley is still here, remembered in the soft fragrance of the rosemary plants, the purity of the white rose. But alongside what remains of the memorial garden, my mother plants forget me nots and honeysuckle, crocus bulbs and yellow tulips, clumps of yarrow, white jasmine that will grow up the back of the house, cascading down around the sliding doors. In the new beds, we plant pink and red rose bushes. Then as a finishing touch, in memory of Charlie, we plant a climbing rose at the base of the apple tree.

By the time she's finished, grief and remembrance are no longer centre stage here. The garden tells a different story now. My mother's story. Already it's on her face, in her eyes as she looks around. No longer a place of sadness, haunting her with guilt, it's a garden that tells a story of love.

Even so, inexplicably, a trace of Matt's presence remains in the house, until one day, as I'm cleaning the kitchen, I find my mother's engagement ring. Picking it up, I study its dull gold and heavy green stone. I never liked it, but now, I imagine it tarnished by Matt's intention, noxious energy radiating from it. Keeping it away from my mother, that night, when she isn't looking, I pull on my trainers and creep outside.

Clutching the ring tightly, I make my way to the furthest part of the garden. For a moment, I stand in the shadows, breathing in the cool air. It's a still night, over the hedge, the bleached stubble field lit by an almost full moon. Still clutching the ring, I step back, then hurl it over the hedge, high into the air, watching it arc into the dark sky, glittering one last time in the moonlight, before disappearing from sight, forever gone.

Acknowledgements

This is my first book to be published by Avon and I'd like to say a huge thank you to my editor, Phoebe Morgan, for her vision for this book, and for not only getting under the skin of it, but pushing me to make it the best I could. It's wonderful both to be working with you and to know my books are in such safe hands.

A massive thank you as always, to my agent, Juliet Mushens, who is everything an author could wish for. I'm incredibly grateful to you for everything you do.

I'd like to thank everyone at Avon and HarperCollins involved in publishing *The Vow*, from the gorgeous cover, through the editing process, to sales, marketing and everything else. Huge gratitude also to Sabah Khan, for all things publicity-related. At the time of writing this, we've a few months to go before publication, but already the publicity wheels are spinning and it really is wonderful to be working with you.

To my family and friends. So much love to Georgie and Tom, and thank you for brainstorming when I get stuck, for being endlessly positive and supportive. You are my world. To

Martin, for helping unravel the glitches when my brain gets tied in knots, and for your endless patience when the pressure is on! To my parents, who first instilled in me a love of books. To my sisters and unwavering supporters – Sarah, Anna and Freddie. To Clare, Lindsay, Katie, Heather and to all my friends, for being more stalwart supporters, coming to book launches, buying my books, spreading the word . . . Thank you to each and every one of you. Your support is awesome!

And lastly, thank you to reviewers, bloggers, booksellers, libraries and to you, my readers. I'm hugely grateful to all of you. Without you, I wouldn't be doing this.